EVERNIGHT

CLAUDIA GRAY

HarperCollins *Children's Books*

First published in hardback in the USA by HarperCollins Inc. in 2008
Published in paperback in the UK by HarperCollins *Children's Books* in 2010
HarperCollins *Children's Books* is a division of HarperCollins*Publishers* Ltd,
77-85 Fulham Palace Road, Hammersmith, London W6 8JB

The HarperCollins website address is
www.harpercollins.co.uk

ISBN 978 0 00 735531 0

Evernight
Copyright © 2008 by Amy Vincent

Printed and bound in England by Clays Ltd, St Ives plc

Typography by Andrea Vandergrift

2

First Edition

Prologue

THE BURNING ARROW THUDDED INTO THE WALL.

Fire. The old, dry wood of the meetinghouse ignited in an instant. Dark, oily smoke filled the air, scratching my lungs and making me choke. Around me, my new friends cried out in shock before grabbing weapons, preparing to fight for their lives.

This is because of me.

Arrow after arrow sliced through the air, stoking the flames higher. Through the haze of ash, I desperately sought Lucas's eyes. I knew he would protect me no matter what, but he was in danger, too. If something happened to Lucas while he was trying to rescue me, I could never forgive myself.

Coughing from the soot-thick air, I grabbed Lucas's hand and ran with him toward the door. But they were ready for us.

Silhouetted against the flames, a dark, forbidding line of figures stood just beyond the edge of the meetinghouse. None of them brandished weapons; they didn't have to in order to make their threat clear. They had come for me. They had come to punish Lucas for breaking their rules. They had come to kill.

This is all happening because of me. If Lucas dies, it will be my fault.

There was nowhere to go, no place to run. We couldn't remain here, not with the blaze around us roaring, already so hot that it stung my skin. Soon the ceiling would collapse and crush us all.

Outside, the vampires waited.

Chapter One

IT WAS THE FIRST DAY OF SCHOOL, WHICH MEANT
it was my last chance to escape.

I didn't have a backpack full of survival gear, a wallet thick
with cash that I could use to buy myself a plane ticket somewhere, or a friend waiting for me down the road in a getaway
car. Basically, I didn't have what most sane people would call
"a plan."

But it didn't matter. There was no way I was going to
remain at Evernight Academy.

The muted morning light was still new in the sky as I
wriggled into my jeans and grabbed a warm black sweater—
this early in the morning, and this high in the hills, even
September felt cold. I knotted my long red hair into a make-
shift bun and stepped into my hiking boots. It felt important
to be very quiet, even though I didn't have to worry about my
parents waking up. They weren't morning people, to say the
least. They'd sleep like the dead until the alarm clock woke

them, and that wouldn't be for another couple of hours.

That would give me a good head start.

Outside my bedroom window, the stone gargoyle glared at me, fangs framing his open grimace. I grabbed my denim jacket and stuck my tongue out at him. "Maybe you like hanging out at the Fortress of the Damned," I muttered. "You're welcome to it."

Before I left, I made my bed. Usually it took a lot of nagging to get me to do that, but I wanted to. I knew I was going to freak my parents out badly enough today, so straightening the covers felt like I was making it up to them a little. Probably they wouldn't see it that way, but I went ahead. As I plumped up the pillows, I had a sudden strange flash of something I'd dreamed the night before, as vivid and immediate as though I were still dreaming:

A flower the color of blood.

Wind howled through the trees all around me, whipping the branches in every direction. The sky overhead churned, thick with roiling clouds. I brushed my windswept hair from my face. I only wanted to look at the flower.

Each rain-beaded petal was vividly red, slender, and blade-like, the way some tropical orchids are. Yet the flower was lush and full, too, and it clung close to the branch like a rose. The flower was the most exotic, mesmerizing thing I'd ever seen. It had to be mine.

Why did that memory make me shiver? It was only a dream. I took a deep breath and focused. It was time to go.

My messenger bag was ready; I'd loaded it up the night before. Just a few things—a book, sunglasses, and a little cash in case I needed to go all the way to Riverton, which was the closest thing to human civilization in the area. That would keep me occupied for the day.

See, I wasn't running away. Not for real, where you make a break and assume a new identity and, I don't know, join the circus or something. No, I was making a statement. Ever since my parents first suggested that we come to Evernight Academy—them as teachers, me as a student—I'd been against it. We'd lived in the same small town my whole life, and I'd attended the same school with the same people since I was five years old. That was just the way I wanted it. There are people who enjoy meeting strangers, who can strike up conversations and make friends quickly, but I'd never been one of those people. Anything but.

It's funny—when people call you "shy," they usually smile. Like it's cute, some funny little habit you'll grow out of when you're older, like the gaps in your grin when your baby teeth fall out. If they knew how it felt—really being shy, not just unsure at first—they wouldn't smile. Not if they knew how the feeling knots up your stomach or makes your palms sweat or robs you of the ability to say anything that makes sense. It's not cute at all.

My parents never smiled when they said it. They were smarter than that, and I always felt like they understood, until they decided that age sixteen was the right time for me to get past it somehow. What better starting place than a boarding school—particularly with them along for the ride?

I could see where they were coming from, sort of. Still, that was theory. The first moment we'd come up the drive at Evernight Academy—and I'd seen this huge, hulking, Gothic stone monstrosity—I'd known that there was no way I could possibly go to school here. Mom and Dad hadn't listened. I would have to make them listen.

On tiptoe, I eased my way through the small faculty apartment my family had shared for the past month. Behind the closed door of my parents' bedroom, I could hear my mother snoring lightly. I shouldered my bag, slowly turned the doorknob, and started downstairs. We lived at the very top of one of Evernight's towers, which sounds cooler than it is. This meant I had to make my way down steps that had been carved out of rock more than two centuries ago, long enough to be worn and uneven. The long spiral staircase had few windows and the lights weren't yet on, making for a dark, difficult trip.

As I reached out for the flower, the hedge rustled. The wind, I thought, but it wasn't the wind. No, the hedge was growing— growing so quickly that I could see it happening. Vines and brambles pushed from the leaves in a tangled snarl. Before I could run, the hedge had almost surrounded me, walling me in behind sticks and leaves and thorns.

The last thing I needed was to start flashing back to my nightmares. I took a deep breath and kept going downstairs until I reached the great hall on the ground floor. It was a majestic space, built to inspire or at least impress: marble-tiled floor, high arched ceiling, and stained glass windows that stretched from floor to rafter, each in a different kaleidoscope pattern—save one, right in the center, which was clear glass. Set-up for the day's events must have been completed the night before, because a podium stood ready for the head-mistress to greet the students who were arriving later today. Nobody else seemed to be awake yet, which meant that there was no one to stop me. A hard tug opened the heavy, carved outside door, and then I was free.

Early morning fog blanketed the world in bluish-gray as I walked across the grounds. When they built Evernight Academy in the 1700s, this country had been wilderness. Even though small towns now dotted the distant countryside, none of them were very close to Evernight; and despite the hillside views and the thick forests, nobody had ever built a house nearby. Who could blame them for not wanting to be anywhere near that place? I glanced behind me at the school's tall stone towers, both of them coiled with the twisted forms of gargoyles, and shivered. Within a few more steps, they began to fade into the fog.

Evernight loomed behind me, the stone walls of its high towers the only barrier the thorns couldn't break. I should have run for the school, but I didn't. Evernight was more dangerous than the thorns, and, besides, I wasn't going to leave the flower behind.

My nightmare was starting to feel more real than reality. Uneasy, I turned from the school and started to jog, fleeing the grounds and vanishing into the forest.

It's all going to be over soon, I told myself as I hurried through the underbrush, fallen pine branches crackling beneath my feet. Even though I was only a few hundred feet from the front door, it felt like much farther; the thick fog made it seem as though I were already deep in the woods. *Mom and Dad will wake up and realize that I'm gone. They'll finally see that I can't take it, that they can't make me do this. They'll come looking for me, and, okay, they'll be mad that I scared them, but they'll understand. They always understand in the end, right? And then we'll leave. We'll get away from Evernight Academy and never, ever come back.*

My heart pounded faster. With every step I took away from Evernight Academy, I felt more afraid, not less. Before, when I'd come up with this scheme, it had seemed like such a good idea. Like it couldn't fail. Now that it was real, and I was alone in the forest running into a wilderness I didn't know, I wasn't so sure. Maybe I was running away for nothing. Maybe they'd drag me back there no matter what.

Thunder rumbled. My heart beat faster. I turned away from Evernight for the last time and looked back at the flower as it trembled upon its branch. A single petal was torn away by the wind. Pushing my hands through the thorns, I felt lashes of pain across my skin, but I kept going, determined.

But when my fingertip touched the flower, it instantly darkened, withering and drying as each petal turned black.

I broke into a run, heading east, trying to put some distance between me and Evernight. My nightmare wouldn't leave me alone: It was that place; it had spooked me, made me scared and hollow. If I got away from there, I'd be okay. Panting, I looked behind me to see how far I'd gone—

And I saw him. A man in the woods, half concealed by the fog, maybe fifty yards from me, wearing a long dark coat. The second I laid eyes on him, he started running after me.

Until that moment, I hadn't known what fear was. Shock jolted through me, cold as ice water, and I found out just how fast I could really run. I didn't scream—there was no point, none, because I'd gone off into the woods so nobody could find me, which was the dumbest thing I'd ever done and looked like it would be the last. I hadn't even brought my cell phone, because there was no service up here. There was no rescue coming. I had to run like hell.

I could hear his footsteps, snapping branches, crunching leaves. He was getting closer. Oh, God, he was fast. How could anybody run that fast?

They taught you how to defend yourself, I thought. *You were supposed to know what to do in a situation like this!* I couldn't remember. I couldn't think. Branches tore at the sleeves of my jacket and snagged the strands of hair that had fallen loose from my bun. I stumbled over a stone, and my teeth sank into my tongue, but I kept running. He was even nearer to me now, too near. I had to go faster. I couldn't go any faster.

"Unh!" I choked as he tackled me, and we fell. The ground slammed into my back, and his weight pressed down on me, his legs tangled up with mine. His hand closed over my mouth, and I pulled my arm free. At my old school, in the self-defense workshop, they always said to go for the eyes, seriously just poke the guy's eyes out. I always thought I could do that if I had to, in order to save myself or someone else, but as terrified as I was I wasn't sure I could stand it. I arched my fingers, trying to screw up my nerve.

At that moment, the guy whispered, "Did you see who was after you?"

For a few seconds, I just stared at him. He lifted his hand from my mouth so I could answer. His body was heavy atop mine, and the world seemed to be spinning. I finally managed to say, "You mean, besides you?"

"Me?" He had no idea what I was talking about. Furtively, he cast a glance behind us, as if on the defensive. "You were running from someone—weren't you?"

"I was just running. There was nobody after me except you."

"You mean, you thought—" The guy jerked back from me that second, so that I was free. "Oh, hell. I'm sorry. I wasn't trying to— Man, I must have scared you to death."

"You were trying to *help*?" I had to say it before I could believe it.

He nodded quickly. His face was still close to mine, too close, blocking out the rest of the world. Nothing seemed to exist except us and the swirling fog. "I know I must've freaked you out, and I'm sorry. I really thought—"

His words weren't helping; I was getting more dizzy, not less. I needed air, quiet, something that I couldn't think of while he was so close to me. I pointed a finger and said something I'd hardly ever said to anyone in my life, definitely never to a stranger and certainly not to the single most terrifying stranger I'd ever met: "You—just—shut up."

He shut up.

With a sigh, I let my head flop back upon the ground. I dug the heels of my hands into my eyes, pressing down so that I saw red. The taste of blood was thick in my mouth, and my heart was still thumping so hard that my ribcage seemed to shake. I could have peed myself, which would have been just about the only way to make this scenario more humiliating than it already was. Instead, I kept taking deep breaths, one after the other, until I felt like I was strong enough to sit up.

When I did, the guy was still there next to me. I managed to ask, "Why did you tackle me?"

"I thought we needed to take cover. To hide from whoever was chasing you, but that turned out to be, uh"—he looked embarrassed—"nobody."

He ducked his head, and I got a good look at him for the first time. There hadn't exactly been time for me to notice anything about him before; when your first impression of somebody is "psycho killer," you don't take time to analyze the details. Now, though, I could see that he wasn't a grown man like I'd assumed. Although he was tall and broad shouldered, he was young, maybe about my age. He had straight, golden-brown hair that fell across his forehead, mussed from the chase. His jaw was strong and angular, and he had a solid, muscular body and amazingly dark green eyes.

But the most remarkable thing of all was what he was wearing beneath his long black coat: battered black boots, black wool trousers, and a dark red V-necked sweater emblazoned with a crest—two ravens embroidered on either side of a silver sword. The crest of Evernight.

"You're a student," I said, "here at the school."

"About to be, anyway." He spoke quietly, as if he were worried about scaring me again. "You?"

I nodded as I shook my tangled hair loose and started to pin it up again. "This is my first year. My parents got jobs as teachers here, so—I'm stuck."

That seemed to strike him as odd, because he frowned at me, and his green eyes were suddenly searching and unsure. In an instant, though, he had recovered and held out his hand. "Lucas Ross."

"Oh. Hey." It felt weird, introducing myself to somebody I'd thought was trying to kill me five minutes before. His hand was broad and cool, and he gripped mine firmly. "I'm Bianca Olivier."

"Your pulse is racing," Lucas murmured. He studied my face intently, and I felt nervous again—but in a much better way. "Okay, if you weren't running from an attacker, why were you running like that? Because that didn't look like a morning jog to me."

I would've lied if I could have thought of any plausible

excuse, but I couldn't. "I got up early to—well, to try and run away."

"Your parents treat you bad? Hurt you?"

"No! Nothing like that." I felt so offended, but I realized that of course that was what Lucas would have to assume. Why else would a totally sane person be running through the woods before the sun was completely up like she was escaping with her life? We'd only just met, so maybe he still counted me as totally sane. I decided not to mention the nightmare flashbacks, because that would probably tip the balance toward crazy. "But I don't want to go to school here. I liked our hometown, and, besides, Evernight Academy is—it's so—"

"Spooky as hell."

"Yeah."

"Where were you going to go? Do you have a job lined up, something like that?"

My cheeks were flushed, and not just from the exertion of the run. "Um, no. I wasn't really running away. Just making a statement. Sort of. I thought if I did this, my parents would finally get how much I don't want to be here, and maybe we could leave."

Lucas blinked for a second, then started to grin. His smile changed all the weird pent-up energy inside me, transforming it from fear into curiosity, even excitement. "Like me with my slingshot."

"What?"

"Back when I was five, I thought my mom was being mean

to me, so I decided to run away. Carried my slingshot with me because I was a big strong man, you see. Could take care of myself. I believe I also took a flashlight and a packet of Oreos."

Despite my embarrassment, I couldn't help smiling. "I think you packed better than I did."

"I swaggered out of the house where we were staying and took myself all the way to . . . the far corner of the backyard. There I made my stand. Stayed out there all day, until it started to rain. I hadn't thought about taking an umbrella."

"The best laid plans." I sighed.

"I know. It's tragic. I came back in, all wet and my stomach aching from eating about twenty Oreos, and my mom—who is a smart lady even if she drives me nuts—well, she acted like nothing had happened." Lucas shrugged. "Which is what your parents are going to do, too. You know that, right?"

"I do now." My throat tightened with disappointment. I'd known the truth all along, really. I'd simply had to do *something*, more to act out my own frustration than to send a message to my parents.

Then Lucas asked a question that astonished me: "Do you want out of here for real?"

"Like—run away? Really run away?"

Lucas nodded, and he looked serious.

He wasn't, though; he couldn't be. No doubt he had asked me that to snap me back to reality. I admitted, "No, I don't. I'll go back. Get ready for school like a good girl."

There was that grin again. "Nobody said anything about being a good girl."

The way he said that made me feel warm and soft inside. "It's just—Evernight Academy—I don't think I'll ever belong there."

"I wouldn't worry about that. Might be a good thing, not belonging there." He looked at me, serious and intent, like he thought he had another idea about where I might belong. Either this guy really liked me, or I was inventing things in my head because I wanted him to like me. I was much too inexperienced to guess which.

Hurriedly, I pushed myself to my feet. As Lucas stood also, I asked, "So what were you doing? When you saw me?"

"Like I said, I thought you were in trouble. There are some rough characters up in these parts. Not everybody has self-control." He brushed a few pine needles from his sweater. "I shouldn't have jumped to conclusions. My instincts got the best of me. Sorry about that."

"It's okay, honestly. I realize you were trying to help. I meant, before you saw me. Orientation doesn't start for another few hours. It's really early. They told students to arrive around ten A.M."

"I've never been very good at playing by the rules."

That was interesting. "So—you're a morning person, getting a jump on the day?"

"Hardly. I haven't gone to bed yet." He had a fantastic grin, and I'd already noticed that he knew how to use it. I didn't mind. "Anyway, my mom couldn't bring me herself. She's away, on business, I guess you'd say. I caught the red-eye train in and thought I'd walk up here first. Get the lie of the land. Rescue any damsels in distress."

When I remembered how fast Lucas had been running after me, and realized that he'd been doing that in an attempt to save my life, the memory changed. The fear was gone, and now it made me smile. "Why did you come to Evernight? I'm stuck here because of my parents, but you could probably have gone someplace else. Someplace better. So, like, anywhere else."

Lucas honestly didn't seem to know how to answer. He pushed branches back as we kept walking through the forest, keeping any of them from scraping my face. Nobody had ever cleared a path for me before. "It's a long story."

"I'm not in a hurry to go back. Besides, we've got a few hours to kill before orientation."

He lowered his head, but kept his eyes fixed on me. There was something undeniably sexy about that move, though I wasn't sure he meant it that way. His eyes were almost exactly the same color as the ivy that grew on the towers at Evernight. "It's also kind of a secret."

"I can keep a secret. I mean, you're going to keep this whole incident secret for me, right? With the running and the freaking out—"

"I'll never tell." After a couple more seconds of consideration, Lucas finally confessed, "An ancestor of mine tried to go to school here almost a hundred and fifty years ago. He washed out, I guess you'd say." Lucas laughed, and it felt like the sunlight had broken through the trees. "So it's up to me to 'restore the family honor.'"

"That's not fair. You shouldn't have to make all your decisions based on what he did or didn't do."

"Not all my decisions. They let me pick out my own socks." I smiled as he tugged up his pants leg to reveal a sliver of argyle sock above his heavy black boot.

"How did your great-grand-whatever wash out?"

Lucas shook his head ruefully. "He got into a duel during his first week."

"A duel? Like, somebody insulted his honor?" I tried to remember what I'd learned about duels from romance novels and movies. All I knew was that Lucas's history was definitely a lot more interesting than mine. "Or was it over a girl?"

"He would've had to move fast, to meet a girl in the first few days of school." Lucas paused, as if he were just realizing that it was the first day of school and he'd already met me. I felt this tug, like something was almost physically pulling me to lean toward him—but then Lucas turned his head and glared at the towers of Evernight, just visible through the pine branches. It was as though the building itself had offended him. "Could've been anything. Back then, they'd duel at the drop of a hat. Family legend has it that the other guy started it, not that it matters. What does matter is that he survived but not without breaking one of the stained glass windows in the great hall."

"Of course. There's one that's just clear glass, and I never understood why."

"Now you do. Evernight's been closed to my family ever since."

"Until now."

"Until now," he agreed. "And I don't mind. I think I can learn a lot here. Doesn't mean I have to like everything about it."

"I'm not sure I like *anything* about it," I confessed. *Except you*, added the voice in my head, which had turned awfully bold all of a sudden.

Lucas seemed to be able to hear that voice. There was something knowing in the way he gazed back at me. With his chiseled features and school uniform, he should've looked like the all-American boy, but he didn't. During the chase, and in the moments afterward when he'd thought we'd be fighting for our lives, I'd glimpsed something a little wild lurking just beneath the surface. He said, "I like the gargoyles, the mountains, and the fresh air. That's it so far."

"You like the gargoyles?"

"I like it when the monsters are smaller than me."

"Never thought of it that way." We had reached the edge of the grounds. The sunlight was bright now, and I sensed that the school was waking up, preparing to receive its students, to swallow them through that arched stone doorway. "I'm dreading this."

"Not too late to run, Bianca," he said lightly.

"I don't want to run. I just don't want to be surrounded by all these strangers. Around people I don't know, I can never talk or act normal or be myself at all—why are you smiling?"

"Seems like you know how to talk to me."

I blinked, astonished at myself. Lucas was right. How was that even possible? I stammered, "With you—I guess—I think you scared me so badly that I got all the fear over with right away."

"Hey, if it works—"

"Yeah." Already I sensed that there was more to it than that. Strangers still terrified me, but he wasn't a stranger. He hadn't been since the first moment I realized that he'd been trying to save my life. I felt as though I'd always known Lucas, as if somehow I'd been waiting years for him to arrive. "I should go back before my parents realize I'm gone."

"Don't let them hassle you."

"They won't."

Lucas didn't seem sure of that, but he nodded as he stepped away from me, edging back into the shadows while I walked into the light. "See you around, then."

I raised one hand in a farewell wave, but Lucas was already gone. He'd disappeared into the forest in an instant.

Chapter Two

STILL SHAKY WITH ADRENALINE, I WALKED BACK up the long spiral staircase until I reached the top apartment in the tower. This time I didn't bother being quiet. I slipped my messenger bag off my shoulder and flopped onto the sofa. A few leaves still clung to my hair, so I picked them out.

"Bianca?" My mother emerged from the bedroom, her hands knotting her bathrobe belt. She smiled drowsily at me. "Did you get up early for a walk, sweetheart?"

"Yeah." I sighed. Not much point in trying to make a dramatic scene anymore.

Dad came out next. He hugged Mom from behind. "I can't believe our little girl is already at Evernight Academy."

"It all happened so fast." She sighed. "The older you get, the faster it goes."

He shook his head. "I know."

I groaned. They talked like this all the time, and we'd made a game of how much it annoyed me. Mom and Dad only smiled wider.

They look too young to be your parents, everybody in my hometown used to say. What they really meant was *too beautiful*. Both things were true.

Her hair was the color of caramel; his was a red so dark that it almost looked black. He was average height but muscular and strong; she was petite in every way. Mom's face was as cool and oval as an antique cameo, while Dad had a square jaw and a nose that looked like he was in a few fights in his youth, but on his face, it worked. Me? I got red hair that could only look red, and skin so pale that it looked more pasty than antique. Everyplace my DNA should have turned right, it swerved left. My parents told me I would grow into my looks, but that's the kind of thing parents say.

"Let's get some breakfast into you," Mom said, heading toward the kitchen. "Or have you already had something?"

"No, not yet." It wouldn't have been a bad idea to eat before my big getaway, I realized; my stomach was growling. If Lucas hadn't stopped me, I'd be wandering around in the woods right now, incredibly hungry and facing a long hike into Riverton. So much for my big escape plans.

The memory of Lucas tackling me, the two of us rolling over into the grass and leaves, flashed through my mind. It had terrified me then, and when I thought of it now I shivered, but it was a completely different kind of feeling.

"Bianca." My father's voice sounded stern, and I looked

up guiltily. Had he somehow guessed what I'd been thinking about? I realized immediately that I was being paranoid, but there was no mistaking how serious he was as he sat beside me. "I know you're not looking forward to this, but Evernight is important for you."

This was the same sort of speech he gave before I had to take cough medicine as a kid. "I really don't want to have this conversation again right now."

"Adrian, leave her alone." Mom handed me a glass before she headed back toward the kitchen, where I could hear something sizzling in a frying pan. "Besides, if we don't hurry, we're going to be late for the pre-orientation faculty meeting."

He looked at the clock and groaned. "Why do they schedule these things so early? It's not as if anyone could want to be down there at this hour."

"I know," she muttered. To them, anytime before noon was too early. Yet they'd worked as schoolteachers my whole life, continuing their long feud with eight A.M.

While I ate breakfast, they got ready, made little jokes that were supposed to cheer me up, and left me alone at the table. That was fine by me. Long after they'd gone downstairs, and the hands of the clock crept closer to orientation time, I remained in my chair. I think I was pretending that, as long as breakfast wasn't over, there was no way I'd have to go meet all those new people.

The fact that Lucas would be down there—a friendly face, a protector—well, it helped a little. But not much.

Finally, when I couldn't put it off any longer, I went into my room and changed into the Evernight uniform. I hated the uniform—I'd never had to wear one before—but the worst part was that returning to my bedroom reminded me once again of the strange nightmare I'd had the night before.

Starched white shirt.

Thorns scratching at my skin, lashing me, telling me to turn back.

Red plaid kilt.

Petals curling up and turning black as though they were burning in the heart of a fire.

Gray sweater with the Evernight crest.

Okay, a good time to stop being hopelessly morbid? Right around now.

Determined to act like a normal teenager for at least the first day of the school year, I stared at my reflection in the mirror. The uniform didn't look terrible on me, but it didn't look great, either. I tugged my hair into a ponytail, picked out a tiny twig I'd missed before, and decided my appearance would have to do.

The gargoyle was still staring, as though he were wondering how anybody could look that dorky. Or maybe he was mocking the total failure of my escape plan. At least I wouldn't have to look at his ugly stone face any longer. I squared my shoulders and left my room—for the last time, really. From now on, it didn't belong to me.

I'd been living on campus with my parents for the past

month, which had given me time to explore virtually the entire school: the great hall and lecture rooms on the first floor, after which it split into two enormous towers. The guys lived in the north tower, along with some of the faculty and a couple of musty filing rooms that seemed to be where permanent records went to die. The girls were in the south tower, along with the rest of the faculty apartments, including my family's. The upper floors of the main building, above the great hall, housed the classrooms and the library. Evernight had been expanded and added to over time, so not every section was in the same style or seemed exactly to fit with the rest. There were passageways that twisted and turned and sometimes led nowhere. From my tower room I looked down on the roof, a patchwork of different arches and shingles and styles. So I'd learned my way around; that was the only way in which I felt prepared for what was to come.

I began down the steps again. No matter how many times I made this trip, I always felt as if I might tumble down the rough, uneven steps, over and over, all the way to the bottom. *Stupid*, I told myself, *worrying about nightmares with dying flowers or about falling down the stairs*. Something a lot scarier than any of that was waiting for me.

I stepped out of the stairwell into the great hall. Early this morning, it had been hushed, cathedral-like. Now it was packed with people, ringing with voices. Despite the din, it seemed as if my footsteps echoed throughout the room; dozens of faces turned toward me at once. Every single person seemed to be staring at the intruder. I might as well have hung a neon sign around my neck that said NEW KID.

The other students clustered together in circles too tight for a newcomer to enter, their eyes dark and quick as they darted over me. It was as though they could see down into the panicked fluttering of my heart. To me, it seemed that they all looked alike—not in any obvious way but in their shared perfection. Every girl's hair shone, whether worn down in a cascade past her shoulders or tied back in a prim, sleek bun. Every guy looked self-assured and strong, with smiles that served as masks. Everybody wore the uniform, with the sweaters and skirts and blazers and trousers in all the acceptable variations: gray, red, plaid, black. The raven crest marked them all, and they wore the symbol as though they owned it. Confidence radiated from them, and superiority, and disdain. I could feel the heat leaching from me as I stood on the outskirts of the room, shifting from foot to foot.

Nobody said hello.

The murmuring welled up again within an instant. Apparently gawky new girls weren't worth more than a few moments of interest. My cheeks were flushed with embarrassment, because obviously I'd already done something wrong, even if I couldn't guess what. Or did they already sense—as I did—that I didn't really belong here?

Where's Lucas? I craned my neck, searching for him in the crowd. Already I felt as though I might be able to face it if Lucas were beside me. Maybe it was crazy to feel like that about a guy I barely knew, but I didn't care. Lucas had to be here, but I couldn't find him. In the middle of all these people, I felt completely alone.

As I edged toward a far corner of the room, I began to realize that a few students were in the same situation as I was—or, at least, they were also new. A guy with sandy hair and a beach-bronze tan was so rumpled that he might have slept in his uniform, but being supercasual didn't win you any points here. He wore a Hawaiian shirt open over his sweater but beneath his blazer, its gaudy cheer almost desperate in Evernight's gloom. A girl had cut her black hair so short that it was more like a boy's, but not in a cute, pixie style; it looked more like she'd haphazardly taken a razor to it. Her uniform hung on her, two sizes too big. The crowds seemed to part around her as if repelled by some force. She might as well have been invisible; even before our first class, she had been branded someone who didn't matter.

How could I be so sure? Because it had just happened to me, too. I was trapped on the edge of the crowd, intimidated by the din, dwarfed by the stone hallway, and as lost as it was possible to be.

"Everyone!"

The voice rang out, instantly shattering the noise into silence. We all turned as one to the far end of the hallway, where Mrs Bethany, the headmistress, had stepped upon the podium.

She was a tall woman, with thick dark hair she wore piled

on top of her head, like someone from the Victorian era. I couldn't begin to guess her age. Her lace-trimmed blouse was gathered at the neck with a golden pin. If you could think of somebody so severe as beautiful, then she was beautiful. I had met her when my parents and I moved into the faculty apartments; she had scared me a little then, but I'd told myself that was because I'd only just met her.

If anything, she was even more imposing now. As I saw her instantly, effortlessly claim command over this roomful of people—the same people who had shut me out by mutual, silent accord before I could even think what to say—I realized for the first time that Mrs Bethany had power. Not just the kind that came with being headmistress but real power, the sort that rises from within.

"Welcome to Evernight." She held out her hands. Her nails were long and translucent. "Some of you have been with us before. Others will have heard about Evernight Academy for years, perhaps from your families, and wondered if you would ever join our school. And we have other new students this year—the result of a change in our admissions policy. We think it's time for our students to meet a wider range of people, from more varied backgrounds, to better prepare them for the world outside the school's walls. Everyone here has much to learn from the other students, and I trust that you will all treat one another with respect."

She might as well have spray-painted, in giant red letters, SOME OF YOU DON'T REALLY BELONG. The "new admissions" policy was no doubt responsible for surfer boy and short-haired girl being here; they weren't intended to be "real" Evernight students at all. They were only supposed to represent a learning experience for the in crowd.

I wasn't part of the new policy. If it weren't for my parents, I wouldn't be here. In other words, I wasn't even "in" enough to be an outcast.

"At Evernight, we do not treat students as children." Mrs Bethany didn't look at any one of us in particular; she seemed to look just over us, a distant kind of gaze that nonetheless took in everything within her field of view. "You have come here to learn how to function as adults in a twenty-first-century world, and that is how you will be expected to behave. That does not mean that Evernight has no rules. Our position in this area requires that we maintain the strictest discipline. We expect much of you."

She didn't say what the repercussions would be for failure, but somehow I thought detention would be only the beginning.

My palms felt sweaty. My cheeks were getting flushed, and I probably stood out like a signal flare. I'd promised myself that I'd be strong and that I wouldn't let the crowd get to me, but so much for promises. The high ceiling and walls of the great hall seemed to be closing in around me. It still felt like I couldn't quite breathe.

My mother somehow got my attention without waving or calling my name, the way moms can. She and Dad were standing at the far end of the row of faculty, waiting to be introduced, and they both gave me hopeful little smiles. They wanted to see me enjoying myself.

It was their hope that got to me. Having to deal with my fear was hard enough without facing their disappointment.

Mrs Bethany concluded, "Classes will begin tomorrow. For today, get settled into your rooms. Meet new classmates. Learn your way around. We will expect you to be ready. We are glad to have you, and we hope that you will make the most of your time at Evernight."

Applause filled the room, and Mrs Bethany acknowledged it by smiling slightly and closing her eyes, a slow, satisfied blink like that of a well-fed cat. Then conversation rose up, even louder than before. There was only one person I wanted to talk to; just as well, since it looked like only one person might possibly be interested in talking to me.

I moved all the way around the room, always right at the edges, keeping my back toward the wall. I searched the crowd hungrily, seeking Lucas's bronze hair, his broad shoulders, those dark green eyes. If I was looking for him, and he was looking for me, we were bound to find each other soon. Despite my fear of large groups, and my tendency to exaggerate them, I knew there were only a couple of hundred students here.

He'll stand out, I told myself. *He's not like these others, cold and snobby and proud.* But I soon realized that wasn't true. Lucas wasn't a snob, but he had the same kind of chiseled good looks, the same toned body, and the same, well, perfection.

He wouldn't stand out much in this beautiful crowd; he would be a natural part of it.

Unlike me.

Slowly the crowd shrank, as the teachers left and the students dispersed. I hung around until I was almost the only one left in the great hall. Surely Lucas would come to find me. He knew how scared I was and felt responsible for scaring me worse. Wouldn't he want to say hello?

But he didn't. Eventually, I had to accept that I'd missed him. That meant there was nothing left for me to do but go meet my roommate.

Slowly I made my way up the stone steps, my new shoes with their hard soles click-clacking too loudly. I wanted to keep climbing all the way to the top, straight back to my parents' faculty apartment. If I did, though, I knew that they'd send me downstairs again immediately. Time enough to get my things and really move out after dinner. For now, the first priority was "getting settled."

I tried to look on the positive side. Maybe my roommate was as freaked-out by school as I was. I remembered the girl with the super-short haircut and hoped it might be her. If I were living with another "outsider," things would probably be easier all around. It would be torture, living with a stranger—actually having somebody I didn't know there all the time, even when I slept—but I hoped the feeling would pass eventually. I didn't dare hope for a friend.

Patrice Deveraux, the form had said. I tried to hang that

name on the girl I remembered, but it didn't quite fit. Still, anything was possible.

I opened the door and realized, heart sinking, that my roommate's name fit her just fine. She wasn't another outsider at all. Instead, she was the total embodiment of the Evernight type.

Patrice's skin was the color of a river at sunrise, the coolest, softest brown, and her curly hair was pulled back into a soft bun, which showed off her pearl earrings and her slim neck. She sat at the dresser, still neatly lining up bottles of nail polish while she looked at me.

"So you're Bianca," she said. No handshake, no hug—just the click of each bottle of polish against the dresser: pale pink, coral, melon, white. "You weren't what I was expecting."

Thanks tons. "You neither."

Patrice cocked her head, studying me, and I wondered if we hated each other already. She lifted one perfectly manicured hand and began ticking off points. "You can borrow my perfume but not my jewelry or clothes." She didn't say anything about borrowing my stuff, but it was pretty obvious she wouldn't ever want to. "I plan to do most of my studying in the library, but if you want to work here, let me know and I'll talk with my friends somewhere else. Help me with the assignments you're good at, and I'll do the same for you. I'm sure we can learn a lot from each other. Sound fair?"

"Definitely."

"All right. We'll get along."

If she'd acted all fake friendly with me right away, I think that would have weirded me out more. As it was, I was sort of reassured that Patrice was so businesslike. "Glad you think so," I said. "I know we're . . . different."

She didn't argue. "Two teachers here are your parents, right?"

"Yeah. I guess word travels fast."

"You'll be fine. They'll take care of you."

I tried to smile at her and hoped she was right. "You've been here at Evernight before?"

"No. First time." Patrice said this as though changing her whole way of living was as simple for her as slipping into a new pair of designer shoes. "It's beautiful, don't you think?"

I left my opinion of the architecture out of it. "You said you had friends here, though."

"Well, of course." Her smile was as delicate as everything else about her, from the peach gloss on her lips to the perfume and nail polish bottles neatly arrayed on the dresser. "Courtney and I met in Switzerland last winter. Vidette was a friend of mine when I was staying in Paris. And Genevieve and I spent a summer together in the Caribbean, once—was it St Thomas? Maybe it was Jamaica. I can't keep these things straight."

My pokey hometown seemed duller than ever. "So you guys all just—run in the same circles."

"More or less." Belatedly, Patrice seemed to realize how awkward I felt. "Eventually they'll be your circles, too."

"I wish I were as sure as you are."

"Oh, you'll see." She dwelled in a world where endless summers in the tropics were everyone's for the taking. I couldn't imagine ever being a part of that. "Do you know anybody here? Besides your parents, I mean."

"Only the people I've met this morning." Meaning Lucas and Patrice, for a grand total of two.

"Plenty of time to make friends." Patrice spoke briskly as she began putting away more of her things: silky scarves the color of ivory, hosiery in shades of taupe or dove gray. Where did she plan to wear things so elegant? Maybe it was unimaginable for Patrice to travel without them. "I hear Evernight is a wonderful place to meet men."

"Meet men?"

"Do you already have someone?"

I wanted to tell her about Lucas, but I couldn't. Whatever had happened between me and Lucas in the forest—it meant something, but my feelings were too new to share. All I said was, "I didn't leave a boyfriend behind in my hometown." I'd known all those guys at my old school since I was a little kid, and I remembered them back when they used to play with Lincoln Logs and mash Play-Doh in my hair. That sort of made it impossible to feel passionate about any of them.

"Boyfriend." Her lips curled upward, as if the word struck her as childish. Patrice wasn't sneering at me, though. I was simply too young and inexperienced for her to take me seriously.

"Patrice? It's Courtney." The girl outside knocked on the

door even while she was opening it, obviously certain she would be welcome. She was even more beautiful than Patrice, with blonde hair that fell almost to her waist and the pouty kind of lips I'd seen only on starlets in TV shows, who could afford stuff like collagen. The same kilt that hung awkwardly at my knees made her legs look a thousand miles long. "Oh, your room is much better than mine. I love it!"

The rooms were all pretty much alike, actually—a bedroom large enough for two people, with white, cast-iron beds and carved wooden dressers on each side. The window looked out upon one of the trees that grew closest to Evernight, but I couldn't think of anything special about it.

Then I realized there was one thing. "We *are* close to the bathrooms," I said.

Courtney and Patrice both stared at me as if I'd done something rude. Were they too refined to acknowledge that we needed bathrooms?

Embarrassed, I kept going. "I've never, um, shared a bathroom before. I mean, I have with my parents, but not with—what, it's like, twelve of us sharing each one? That's going to be crazy in the mornings."

This was their cue to agree and gripe about it. Instead, Courtney kept studying me, curious. I figured her curiosity was only normal, but I wished she would say something. Her narrow-eyed gaze felt threatening, even more so than most strangers' did.

"We're going out in the grounds tonight," she said—to

Patrice, not to me. "To eat. A picnic, you might say."

Meals at Evernight were meant to be taken in the students' rooms. Apparently they explained this as "tradition," the way things were back in ye olden days before anybody had invented the cafeteria. Parents would send care packages to supplement the Spartan grocery allowance delivered each week. This meant I had to learn how to cook using the little microwave my parents had bought me. Patrice obviously didn't worry about such mundane problems. "Sounds like fun. Don't you think so, Bianca?"

Courtney shot her a look; apparently that invitation wasn't meant to be open.

"I'm sorry," I said. "I'm supposed to eat with my parents. Thanks for asking me, though."

Courtney's lush lips could look almost ghoulish when twisted into a smirk. "You still want to hang out with Mommy and Daddy? What, do they feed you with a bottle?"

"*Courtney*," Patrice chastised her, but I could tell that she was amused.

"You've got to see Gwen's room." Courtney began tugging Patrice out the door. "Dark and dreary. She swears it might as well be a dungeon."

They took off together, and whatever fragile connection Patrice and I had created was broken in an instant. Their laughter echoed throughout the hallway. Cheeks burning, I fled my new room, then the dormitory floor, hurrying upward toward my parents' apartment and refuge.

To my surprise, they let me in without a fuss. They didn't even ask why I was early. Instead, Mom gave me a big hug, and Dad said, "Check out our packing job, okay? There are a few things for you to do, but we got you started."

I was so grateful I could've cried. Instead I went to my room, eager for peace and quiet in some safe place.

Only a few pieces of winter clothing still hung in my closet. Everything else had been bundled into Dad's old leather trunk. A quick check of my overnight bag showed makeup, barrettes, shampoo, and the rest all neatly tucked in. Most of my books would stay here; I had too many for the few shelves in our dorm room. But my favorites had been set out for me to box up: *Jane Eyre*, *Wuthering Heights*, my astronomy texts. The bed had been made, and on one pillow was a packet of things for me to hang up on my walls, like postcards friends had sent over the years and some star maps I'd hung on the walls of our old house. But something new had been hung in this room, an affirmation from my parents that this was still my home, too: a small framed print of Klimt's *The Kiss*. I had admired the print in a shop months ago, and apparently they'd bought it as a surprise for me on my first day at the new school.

At first, I was simply grateful for the gift. But then I couldn't quite stop looking at the picture or shake the thought that somehow I'd never really seen it before.

The Kiss was a favorite of mine. From the days when my mother first showed me her books about art, I'd always loved

Klimt. I was in awe of the way he gilded every pane and line, and I liked the prettiness of the pale faces that peeped out from the kaleidoscopic images he created. Now, however, the image had changed for me. I'd never paid as much attention to the way the couple tilted toward each other—the man leaning in from above, as if tugged toward her by some inexorable force. The woman's head fell back in a swoon, giving in to gravity's pull. Her lips were dark against the paleness of her skin, flushed with blood. Most beautiful of all, the picture's shimmering background no longer appeared to be something separate from the man and woman. Now it felt as if it was a rich, warm mist, their love made visible, turning the world around them to gold.

The man's hair was darker than Lucas's, but I was trying to imagine him there nonetheless. My cheeks felt warm—blushing again—but this was a different kind of blush.

I jerked back to the here and now; it felt almost as if I'd fallen asleep and begun to dream. Quickly I smoothed my hair and took a couple of deep breaths. I realized I could hear Glenn Miller's "String of Pearls" on the stereo. Big Band music always meant that Dad was in a good mood.

I couldn't help but smile. At least one of us liked Evernight Academy.

When I finally finished my packing, it was nearly dinnertime. I went into the living room, where music was still playing, to find Mom and Dad dancing together, being a bit silly with it—Dad pursing his lips, mock sexy, and Mom holding the hem of her black skirt in one hand.

Mom spun around in Dad's arms, and he dipped her backward. She tilted her head almost to the floor, smiling, and saw me. "Sweetheart, there you are." She was still upside down as she spoke, but then Dad righted her. "Did you get your packing done?"

"Yeah. Thanks for helping me get started. And thank you for the picture; it's beautiful." They smiled at each other, relieved to have made me happy, at least a little bit.

"Quite a feast tonight." Dad nodded toward the table. "Your mother outdid herself." Mom didn't usually cook big meals; tonight was definitely a special occasion. She'd made all my favorites, more than I could ever eat. I realized that I was starving because I'd gone without lunch, and for the first part of the dinner, Mom and Dad had to speak to each other. My appetite kept my mouth too full to talk.

"Mrs Bethany said they've finally finished refitting the labs," Dad said between sips from his glass. "I hope I have a chance to check them out before the students do. Might have some equipment so modern that I don't know what to do with it."

"This is why I teach history," Mom replied. "The past doesn't change. It just gets longer."

"Will I have you guys for teachers?" I said through a full mouth.

"Swallow your food." The Dad command seemed automatic. "Wait and see tomorrow, like the others."

"Oh. Okay." It wasn't like him to cut me off that way, and I felt taken aback.

"We can't get in the habit of giving you too much extra information," Mom said more gently. "You need to have as much as possible in common with the rest of the students, you know?"

She meant it lightly, but it hit me hard. "Who is it here I'm supposed to have something in common with? The Evernight kids whose families have been coming here for centuries? The outsiders who fit in here even worse than I do? Which group am I supposed to be like?"

Dad sighed. "Bianca, be reasonable. There's no point in arguing about this again."

It was past time to let it go, but I couldn't. "Right, I know. We came here 'for my own good.' How is leaving our home and all my friends good for me? Explain that again, because I never quite got it."

Mom laid her hand over mine. "It's good for you because you've almost never left Arrowwood. Because you rarely even left our neighborhood unless we forced you. And because the handful of friends you made there couldn't possibly sustain you forever."

She made sense, and I knew it.

Dad set his glass down. "You have to learn to adapt to changing circumstances, and you have to become more independent. Those are the most important skills your mother and

I can teach you. You can't always stay our little girl, Bianca, no matter how much we might want you to. This is the best way for us to prepare you for the person you're going to become."

"Stop pretending that this is all about growing up," I said. "It's not, and you know it. This is about what you guys want for me, and you're determined to get your way whether I like it or not."

I stood up and walked away from the table. Instead of slinking back to my room for my sweatshirt, I just grabbed Mom's cardigan from the coat rack and pulled it on over my clothes. Even in early fall, the school grounds were cool after dark.

Mom and Dad didn't ask where I was going. It was an old house rule: anybody on the verge of getting angry had to take a quick walk, a break from the discussion, then come back and say what they really mean. No matter how upset we were, that walk always helped.

As a matter of fact, I created that rule. Made it up when I was nine. So I didn't think my maturity was really the issue.

My uneasiness in the world—the sure, complete belief that I didn't really have a place in it—that wasn't about being a teenager. It was a part of me, and it always had been. Maybe it always would be.

While I walked across the grounds, I cast a glance around, wondering if I might see Lucas in the forest again. It was a stupid idea—why would he spend all his time outside?— but I felt lonely, so I had to look. He wasn't there. Looming behind me, Evernight Academy looked more like a castle than a boarding school. You could imagine princesses locked in cells, princes fighting dragons in the shadows, and evil witches guarding the doors with enchantments. I'd never had less use for fairy tales.

The wind changed direction and brought a flicker of sound—laughter from the west, in the direction of the gazebo in the west yard. No doubt those were the "picnickers." I gathered the cardigan more tightly around me and walked into the woods—not east toward the road, the way I'd run that morning, but instead toward the small lake that lay to the north.

It was too late and too dark to see much, but I liked the wind rustling through the trees, the cool scent of pines, and the owl hooting not so far away. Breathing in and out, I stopped thinking about the picnickers or Evernight or anything else. I could just get lost in the moment.

Then nearby footsteps startled me—*Lucas*, I thought—but it was Dad, his hands in his pockets, strolling toward the same path I stood on. Of course he could find me. "That owl is close. You'd think we would scare him off."

"Probably he smells food. He won't leave if there's a chance of a meal."

As if to prove my point, a heavy, swift flapping of wings shook the branches overhead, and then the owl's dark shape darted to the ground. Terrible squealing revealed that a small mouse or squirrel had just become dinner. The owl swooped away too quickly for us to see. Dad and I only watched. I knew I should admire the owl's hunting skill, but I couldn't help feeling sorry for the mouse.

He said, "If I was harsh in there, I'm sorry. You're a mature young woman, and I shouldn't have suggested otherwise."

"It's okay. I kinda flew off the handle. I know there's no point in arguing about coming here, not anymore."

Dad smiled gently at me. "Bianca, you know that your mother and I didn't ever think we'd be able to have you."

"I know." *Please*, I thought, *not the "miracle baby" speech again.*

"When you came into our lives, we dedicated ourselves to you. Maybe too much. And that's our fault, not yours."

"Dad, no." I loved it when it was just our family together, only the three of us in the world. "Don't talk about it like it's something bad."

"I'm not." He seemed sad, and for the first time I wondered if he didn't really like this either. "But everything changes, sweetheart. The sooner you accept that, the better."

"I know. I'm sorry I'm still letting it get to me." My stomach rumbled, and I wrinkled my nose and asked, hopefully, "Could I reheat my dinner?"

"I have a sneaking suspicion that your mother might have already taken care of that."

She had. For the rest of the evening, we had a good time. I figured I might as well have fun while I could. Tommy Dorsey replaced Glenn Miller, and then Ella Fitzgerald replaced him. We talked and joked about stupid things mostly—movies and TV, all the stuff my parents wouldn't pay any attention to if it weren't for me. Once or twice, though, they tried joking about school.

"You're going to meet some incredible people," Mom promised.

I shook my head, thinking of Courtney. She was already definitely one of the least incredible people I'd ever met. "You can't know that."

"I can and I do."

"What, you can see the future now?" I teased.

"Honey, you've been holding out on me. What else does the soothsayer predict?" Dad asked as he got up to change the records. The man still kept his music collection on vinyl. "This, I want to hear."

Mom played along, putting her fingertips to her temples like a gypsy fortune-teller. "I think Bianca will meet—boys."

Lucas's face flashed in my mind, and my heartbeat quickened within an instant. My parents exchanged looks. Could they hear my pulse pounding all the way across the room? Maybe so.

I tried to make a joke of it. "I hope they're going to be cute."

"Not too cute," Dad interjected, and we all laughed. Mom and Dad really thought it was funny; I was trying to cover the fact that I now had butterflies in my stomach.

It felt weird, not telling them about Lucas. I'd always told them almost everything about my life. Lucas was different, though. Talking about him would break the spell. I wanted him to remain a secret for a while longer. That way, I could keep him for myself.

Already I wanted Lucas to belong only to me.

Chapter Three

"YOU DIDN'T HAVE YOUR UNIFORM TAILORED, did you?" Patrice smoothed her skirt as we prepared for the first day of classes.

Why hadn't I seen it before? Of course all the real Evernight types had sent their uniforms to a tailor—tucked the blouses here and the kilts there so that they were chic and flattering instead of boxy and asexual. Like mine. "No. I didn't think of it."

"You really must remember to do that," Patrice said. "Individual tailoring makes a world of difference. No woman should neglect it." I could already tell that she liked giving advice, showing off how worldly and smart she was. This would have annoyed me more if she hadn't been so obviously right. Sighing, I set back to work, trying to get my hair to lie smooth beneath my headband. Surely I'd see Lucas at some point that day, so I wanted to look my best, or as good as I could look in this stupid uniform.

We picked up our class assignments in an enormous line

in the great hall, slips of paper handed out to us, just the way it would've been done a hundred years ago. The crowds of students were less rowdy than they would have been back at my old school. Everyone here seemed to understand the routine.

Maybe the quiet was only an illusion. My uneasiness seemed to swallow sound, muffling everything, until I wondered if anybody could even hear me if I screamed.

Patrice remained by my side at first, but only because we shared our first class, which was American History, taught by my mother. She was the only parent I would have for a teacher; instead of Dad's biology class, I'd be taking chemistry with a Professor Iwerebon. I felt awkward walking next to Patrice with nothing to say, but I didn't really have any alternative—until I saw Lucas, the sunlight through the frosted glass in the hallways turning his golden-brown hair to bronze. At first I thought he saw Patrice and me, but he kept on walking without breaking his stride.

I began to smile. "I'll catch up with you later, okay?" I said to Patrice, already darting away from her. She shrugged as she looked for other friends to walk with. "Lucas?" I called.

He still didn't seem to hear me. I didn't want to yell after him, so I jogged a couple of steps to catch up. He was headed in the opposite direction from me—not in Mom's class, apparently—but I was willing to run the risk of being late. More loudly, I said, "Lucas!"

He turned his head only enough to glimpse me, then glanced around at the students nearby as though he was worried we would be overheard. "Hey, there."

Where was my protector from the forest? The guy standing in front of me now didn't act like he wanted to take care of me; he acted like he didn't know me. But he didn't know me, did he? We'd talked once in the woods—when he'd tried to save my life, and I'd repaid him by telling him to shut up. Just because I thought that was the start of something didn't mean he did.

In fact, it looked like he definitely didn't. For one second, he turned his head, then gave me a quick wave and a nod— the way you would any random acquaintance. After that, Lucas just kept on walking, until he vanished into the crowd.

There it was—the brush-off. I wondered how I could possibly understand guys even less than I'd thought.

The girls' restroom on that floor was nearby, so I was able to duck into a stall and collect myself instead of bursting into tears. What had I done wrong? Despite how strange our first meeting had been, Lucas and I had ended up having a conversation that was as intimate as any I'd had with my best friends. I didn't know a lot about guys, maybe, but I'd been sure that the connection between us was real. I had been wrong. I was alone at Evernight again, and it felt even worse than before.

Finally, once I was steady, I hurried to Mom's classroom, barely avoiding being tardy. She shot me a look, and I shrugged as I sank into a desk in the back row. Mom quickly snapped out of mother mode into teacher mode.

"So, who here can tell me about the American Revolution?" Mom clasped her hands together, looking expectantly around the room. I slumped down in my seat, even though I knew she wouldn't call on me first. I just wanted to be sure she understood how I felt about it. A guy sitting next to me raised his hand, rescuing the rest of us. Mom smiled a little. "And you are Mr—"

"More. Balthazar More."

The first thing to understand about him is that he looked like a guy who could actually carry off the name "Balthazar" without being mocked for all time. On him, it looked good. He seemed confident about anything my mother might throw at him but not in an annoying way like most of the guys in the room. Just confident.

"Well, Mr More, if you were going to sum up the causes of the American Revolution for me, how would you put it?"

"The tax burdens imposed by the English Parliament were the last straw." He spoke easily, almost lazily. Balthazar was big and broad-shouldered, so much so that he barely fitted into the old-fashioned wooden desk. His posture turned difficulty into grace, as though he'd rather lounge like that than sit up straight any day. "Of course, people were concerned about religious and political freedoms as well."

Mom raised an eyebrow. "So, God and politics are powerful, but as always, money rules the world." Soft laughter echoed around the room. "Fifty years ago, no American high school teacher would have mentioned the taxes. A hundred years ago, and the entire conversation might've been about religion. A hundred and fifty years ago, and the answer would have depended on where you lived. In the North, they'd have taught you about political freedom. In the South, they'd have taught you about economic freedom—which, of course, was impossible without slavery." Patrice made a rude sound. "Of course, in Great Britain, there were those who would have described the United States of America as a bizarre intellectual experiment that was about to go bust."

More laughter now, and I realized that Mom already won over the entire class. Even Balthazar was half smiling at her, in a way that almost made me forget about Lucas.

Not really. But he was nice to look at, with his lazy grin.

"And that, more than anything else, is what I want you to understand about history." Mom pushed up the sleeves of her cardigan as she wrote on the blackboard: *Evolving interpretations*. "People's ideas about the past alter just as much as the present does. The scene in the rearview mirror changes every second. To understand history, it's not enough to know the names and dates and places; a lot of you know all of those already, I'm sure. But you have to understand all the different interpretations that historical events have had over the centuries; that's the only way to get a perspective that stands the test of time. We're going to focus a lot of our energy on that this year."

People leaned forward, opened their notebooks, and looked up at Mom, totally engaged. Then I realized maybe I ought to start taking notes, too. Mom might love me best, but she'd flunk me faster than she would anyone else in her classroom.

The hour flew by, with students asking questions, clearly testing Mom and liking what they found. Their pens scratched out notes faster than I could imagine writing, and more than once, my fingers felt like they would cramp. I hadn't realized how competitive the students would be. No, that's not quite right—it was obvious that they were competitive about clothes, and possessions, and romantic interests. That voracity shivered in the air around them. I just hadn't realized they'd be competitive about schoolwork, too. No matter what it was, at Evernight, every single person wanted to be the best at everything they did.

So, you know, no pressure there.

"Your mother is fantastic," Patrice gushed as she walked through the hallways after class. "She's looking at the big picture, you know? Not only her own little window on the world. So few people have that."

"Yeah. I mean—I'm trying to be like her. Someday."

Just then, Courtney turned the corner. Her blonde hair was pulled up into a tight ponytail that made her eyebrows arch even more disdainfully. Patrice stiffened; apparently her new acceptance of me didn't extend as far as defending me in front of Courtney. I braced myself for Courtney's latest snarky remark. Instead, she sort of smiled at me, and I could tell she thought she was being nicer to me than I deserved. "Party this weekend," she said. "Saturday. By the lake. One hour after curfew."

"Sure." Patrice shrugged just one shoulder, like she couldn't care less about being invited to what was probably the coolest party at Evernight this fall, at least until the Autumn Ball. Or were formal dances not cool? Mom and Dad had made it sound like the biggest event of the year, but their ideas about Evernight were already suspect.

My curiosity about balls and their coolness or lack thereof had kept me from answering Courtney for myself. She glared at me, clearly annoyed I hadn't gushed all over her with thanks. "Well?"

If I'd been gutsier, I'd have told her that she was a snob and a bore and that I had better things to do than go to her party. Instead, I only managed to say, "Um, yeah. Great. That'll be great."

Patrice nudged me as Courtney sauntered, with her blonde ponytail swinging behind her. "See? I told you. People are going to accept you because you're—well, you're their daughter."

How big a loser do you have to be to coast into high school popularity on your parents? Still, I couldn't afford to turn my nose up at any acceptance I won, no matter what the reasons were.

"What kind of party is it going to be, though? I mean, in the grounds? At night?"

"You have been to a party before, right?" Sometimes Patrice didn't sound any nicer than Courtney.

"Of course I have." I was counting my own birthday parties when I was a kid, but Patrice didn't have to know that. "I just was wondering if—there wouldn't be *drinking*, would there?"

Patrice laughed like I'd said something funny. "Oh, Bianca, grow up."

She headed off toward the library, and I got the impression that I wasn't invited to come along. So I walked back to our room alone.

Somehow my parents are cool, I thought. *Does it skip a generation?*

My parents had said that I would soon settle into a pattern, and that when I did, I'd like Evernight more. Well, after the first week, I knew they were only right about the first half.

Classes were okay, mostly. Mom made one reference to me being her daughter, then said, "Neither Bianca nor I will ever mention this fact again. You shouldn't either." Everybody laughed; she had them eating out of the palm of her hand. How did she do that? And why hadn't she taught me how to do it, too?

Other teachers took some getting used to, and I missed the informality and friendliness of my old school. Here, the professors were imposing and powerful, and it was unthinkable not to meet their high expectations. A lifetime spent hiding from the world in the library had prepared me for the work, and I put more time into my studies than ever. The only class that bothered me was English, because that was the one Mrs Bethany taught. Something about her—just the way she held herself or how she cocked her head before someone answered a question in class—well, she was intimidating.

Still, academics weren't going to be a problem. That much I'd already figured out. My social life was a different story.

Courtney and the other Evernight types had decided that I wasn't somebody to despise; my well-liked parents had won me the right to be safely ignored, but that was all. Meanwhile, the "new admissions" kids regarded me with suspicion. I roomed with Patrice, and apparently that was reason enough to assume that I wasn't going to side against her and her friends. The cliques had formed within a day, and I was caught exactly in the middle.

The only other "outcast" I'd reached out to at all was Raquel Vargas, the girl with the short haircut. One morning we'd griped about the amount of trigonometry homework we had, but that was almost it for social contact. Raquel, I sensed, didn't make friends easily; she seemed lonely but withdrawn into herself. Not that different from me, really, but somehow even more miserable.

The other students made sure of that.

"Same black sweater, same black pants," Courtney sing-songed one day as she sauntered along, passing near Raquel. "Same stupid bracelet, too. And I bet we see them again tomorrow."

Raquel shot back, "Not everybody can afford to buy every version of the uniform, you know."

"No, I guess not," said Erich, a guy who hung out with

Courtney a lot. He had black hair and a thin, pointed face. "Only the people who actually belong here."

Courtney and all her friends laughed. Raquel's cheeks flushed dark, but she simply stalked away from them as the laughter got even louder. As she walked past me, our eyes met. I tried to show, without words, that I felt bad for her, but that only seemed to make her angrier. Apparently Raquel didn't have much use for pity.

I sensed that, if we'd met somewhere else, Raquel and I might have found we had a lot in common. But as bad as I felt for her, I wasn't sure I needed to spend time with anybody more depressed than I was.

I thought that I wouldn't have been half as depressed, despite everything, if I'd been able to understand what had happened between me and Lucas.

We were in Professor Iwerebon's chemistry class together, but sat at opposite ends of the room. Every moment I wasn't trying to interpret the teacher's thick Nigerian accent, I was surreptitiously watching Lucas. He didn't meet my eyes before or after class, and he never spoke to me. The weirdest thing about this was that Lucas wasn't remotely shy about speaking up to anybody else. He was quick to cut down anybody he thought was being pretentious, snobby, or hurtful—in short, virtually anybody who was the "Evernight type," at any time at all.

For instance, on the grounds one day, two guys started laughing when a girl—*not* the Evernight type—dropped her backpack, then half stumbled over it. Lucas, strolling right behind them, said, "That's ironic."

"What?" Erich was one of the guys laughing. "That this school lets in total losers now?" The girl who had dropped her bag blushed.

"Even if that were true, it wouldn't be irony," Lucas pointed out. "Irony is the contrast between what's said and what happens."

Erich made a face. "What are you talking about?"

"You laughed at her for stumbling right before you fell flat on your face."

I couldn't see exactly how Lucas tripped Erich, but I knew that he'd done it even before Erich went sprawling into the grass. A few people laughed, but most of Courtney's friends glared at Lucas, like he'd done something wrong by standing up for that girl.

"See, that's irony," Lucas said as kept walking.

If I'd had the chance, I would've told Lucas that I thought he'd done the right thing, and I wouldn't have cared if Erich and Courtney and those guys were watching. I didn't get the chance, though. Lucas moved past me as if I'd become invisible.

Erich hated Lucas. Courtney hated Lucas. Patrice hated Lucas. So far as I could tell, virtually everyone at Evernight Academy hated Lucas, except the goofy surfer-type guy I'd noticed on the first day—and me. Okay, Lucas *was* kind of a troublemaker, but I thought he was brave and honest, which were qualities more people at the school could stand to share.

Apparently, though, I would have to admire Lucas from a distance. For now, I was still alone.

"Aren't you ready yet?" Patrice crouched upon our windowsill. The night outlined her slender body, graceful even as she prepared to make the leap to the nearest tree branch. "The monitors will be back soon."

Evernight was policed by hall monitors every night. My parents were the only teachers I hadn't yet seen lurking in a hallway, waiting to pounce upon any rule breakers. This was good reason to get out while we could, but I kept trying to fix my appearance in the mirror.

"Fix" was the operative word. Patrice looked effortlessly chic in slim slacks and a pale pink sweater that made her skin glow. Me, on the other hand—I was trying to make jeans and a black T-shirt look good. Without much success, I might add.

"Bianca, come on." Patrice's patience had run out. "I'm going now. Come with me or don't."

"I'm coming." What did it matter how I looked, anyway? I was only going to this party because I hadn't had the guts to refuse.

Patrice leaped to the tree branch, then to the ground, her landing as controlled as a gymnast descending from the uneven parallel bars. I managed to follow her, bark scraping my palms. The fear of discovery made me acutely aware of the noises around us: laughter from somebody's room inside, the first fall leaves rustling on the ground, the hooting of another owl on the hunt.

The night air was cool enough to make me shiver as we ran across the grounds into the woods. Patrice could get through the underbrush without making a sound, a talent I envied. Maybe someday I'd be that coordinated, but it was hard to imagine.

At last we saw the firelight. They'd built a bonfire by the edge of the lake, small enough to avoid attracting attention but big enough to give warmth and cast eerie, flickering light. The students were huddled together, here or there, leaning in to talk in whispers or laugh. I wondered if this was the laughter I'd heard the night of the picnic. Superficially, they looked like any other group of teenagers, hanging out—but there was an energy in the air that heightened my senses, added tension to everyone's movements and cruelty to most of the smiles. I remembered what I'd thought when I'd met Lucas in the woods during our frightening first encounter; sometimes, when you looked at certain people, you could glimpse something a little bit wild beneath the surface. I felt that wildness here.

Music from somebody's radio played, trancelike and smooth. I didn't know the singer; the lyrics weren't in English. Patrice seemed to vanish into a circle of her friends right away, which left me standing alone, wondering what to do with my hands.

Pockets? No, that looks stupid. Hands on hips? What, like I'm angry about something? No. Okay, even thinking about this is lame.

"Hello there," Balthazar said. I hadn't seen him coming up behind me. He wore a black suede blazer and held a bottle in one hand. The firelight painted his face in warm light; he had curly hair, a strong jaw, and a heavy brow. He looked like a tough guy, a bruiser, somebody who would be quicker with a punch than a joke. But his eyes made him approachable and even sexy, because there was intelligence there and humor, too. There was no cruelty in his smile. "Want a beer? There's still some left."

"That's okay." He had to know I was blushing, even in the dark. "I'm, uh, not legal."

Not legal? Like anyone here cared about that. I should've just painted GEEK on my forehead and saved everybody time.

Balthazar smiled, but not like he was laughing at me. "You know, children used to drink wine at the dinner table with their parents. And doctors used to advise women whose babies didn't nurse well to feed them a little beer as extra food."

"That was then, this is now."

"Fair enough." He didn't press me, and I realized that he wasn't drunk in the slightest. I began to relax. Balthazar had a way of putting people at ease, despite his size and his obvious strength. "I've been meaning to say hello to you since the first day."

"Really?" I hope I didn't squeak.

"I warn you now, I'm up to no good." Balthazar must have gotten a good look at the expression on my face, because he laughed, a deep, rumbling sound. "Your mother said she'd taught you before, so I wanted a few hints on how to read her. I need to know my teacher's secrets, right?"

I decided that Mom wouldn't mind my telling him. "You want to watch for her bouncing on her heels."

"Bouncing?"

"Yeah. That usually means she's excited about something, interested in it, you know? And if she's interested in it, she thinks you should be, too."

"Which means it's going to show up on a test."

"You got it."

He laughed again; he had a dimple in his chin that made him seem almost playful. I almost felt disloyal to Lucas, noticing how handsome Balthazar looked, but it was impossible not to. After the way Lucas had ignored me this past week, I wasn't sure he had a right to my loyalty. Besides, it felt good, having a gorgeous guy paying attention to me.

Balthazar stepped a little closer. "I'm going to be glad we met. I can tell."

I grinned back at him, and for a whole three seconds it looked like the party was going to be fun. That's when Courtney showed up. She was wearing a black skirt cut really high, and a white blouse open really low in the front. She wasn't very curvy, but she made up for it by not wearing a bra, which was now very obvious. "Balthazar. I'm so glad we get to catch up."

"We're caught up," Balthazar seemed even less happy to see her than I was. She didn't get the picture, or she ignored it.

"Seems like ages since we've hung out. Too long. We last saw each other in London, right?"

"St Petersburg," he corrected her. He could rattle off the city's name like throwing away a paper cup. Apparently he was bold and worldly enough to cross the oceans without a second thought.

Courtney's hands smoothed down the front of his blazer, the movement of her fingers outlining his powerful physique. I envied her then—not her starlet looks or her continental travels, but her daring. If I'd been half as brave with Lucas in the woods, been able touch him or use his "good girl" comment as a way to flirt, maybe he wouldn't act like we were strangers now. Courtney's voice sliced through my fantasizing. "You're not really doing anything here, are you, Balthazar?"

"I was talking to Bianca."

Courtney glanced over her shoulder at me; her long blonde hair hung loose to her waist, and it rippled as she tossed her head. "Do you have something interesting to share, Bianca?"

"I—" *What was I supposed to say?* Anything would've been better than what I did say, which was, "Um, no."

"Then you don't mind if we take a few moments, do you?" She started towing Balthazar off without waiting for an answer. He shot me a look, and I knew that if I spoke even one word, he would stop. But I just stood there helplessly and watched them go.

A couple of people giggled. I glanced to one side and saw Erich, and despite the shifting shadows of the firelight, I was pretty sure he was pointing at me.

I slunk away from the fire, meaning only to be someplace out of the way until I could grab Patrice or somebody else who might pass for friendly. But every single step I took away from the others felt good, and before I knew it, I was leaving.

If we hadn't sneaked out after curfew, I would've run straight through the door and up to my room. I remembered my law-breaker status in time, though, and stopped myself. Instead I headed westward to the gazebo on the lawn to pull myself together, then plan my re-entry.

As I made my way up the steps, I saw someone standing there. At first, though, I didn't recognize who it could be— whoever it was held binoculars in front of his face. When the moonlight highlighted his bronze hair, I knew. "Lucas?"

"Hey there, Bianca." It took a few seconds for him to lower the binoculars and grin at me. "Nice night for a party."

I stared at the binoculars. "What are you doing?"

"What's it look like I'm doing? I'm spying on the party." He was almost as abrupt as he had been in the hallway—until he got a good look at my face. I must've still looked miserable, because he asked, more gently, "You okay?"

"I'm fine. I'm a loser, but I'm fine."

Lucas laughed. "I saw you cut out of there in a hurry. Anybody giving you trouble?"

"No. Not really. But the whole thing felt—threatening, I guess. You know how I am with strangers."

"Good for you. That's not your scene."

"No kidding." I stared at the binoculars. Only somebody with excellent night vision would be able to use them to see anything, though I guessed the bonfire's light helped. "Why are you spying on the party?"

"Looking to see if anybody gets drunk or careless, or wanders off on his own."

"What, are you Mrs Bethany's hall monitor now?"

"Hardly." Lucas set the binoculars down. He was dressed to blend into the shadows—black trousers and a long-sleeved T-shirt that outlined his muscular arms and chest. He was wirier than Balthazar but more cut, too. There was something almost aggressively masculine about him. "Just wondering what the hell those guys do when they're not bullying, preening, or sucking up. Seems like they wouldn't have much time left over for anything else." He cast me an appraising glance. "You seem to like them well enough."

"What?"

He shrugged. "You're always hanging out with that crowd."

"I'm not! Patrice is my roommate, so I have to spend time with her, and her friends come by all the time, but I can't really avoid them. I mean, a couple of them are okay, but most of them scare me to death."

"None of them are okay. You can trust me on that."

I thought I could've made an argument on Balthazar's behalf, but I didn't want to talk about Balthazar right now. I also realized that Lucas had put me on the defensive, and he didn't have the right to do that. "Wait, that's why you've been so cold to me? Why you act like we don't know each other?"

"If that crew had gotten their claws into you—a sweet girl like you—I didn't want to have to watch. Not if I couldn't do anything about it." The depth of feeling in his voice startled me. We were still a few feet away from each other, but it seemed as though I'd never been closer to anyone. "When I saw you run out of there, I realized you still had a chance."

"Trust me, I'm not part of that group," I said. "I think they only asked me to the party to laugh at me. I only went because I—well, I have to know *somebody* here. You were the only friend I had, and I thought I'd lost you."

Lucas linked his hands around some of the gazebo's scroll-work, and I did the same, so that we were side by side. We were both entwined with the scrollwork now, like the ivy. "I hurt your feelings, didn't I?"

In a small voice, I admitted, "You kind of did. I mean— I know we only talked once—"

"But it meant something to you." Our eyes met for only an instant. "It meant something to me, too. I just didn't realize— Well, I thought it was only me."

Lucas hadn't realized I liked him back? I was never, ever going to understand men. "I came up to talk to you on the first day of classes."

"Yeah, and just before that, you were walking and talking with Patrice Deveraux, who is about as in as they get here. Her kind and my kind—let's face it, we don't mix." His face looked unpleasant for a moment. "You told me you hardly ever spoke to strangers, so I figured you guys must be pretty friendly."

"She's my roommate. I kind of have to be able to talk to her to get through the day."

"Okay, I got it wrong. Sorry."

There was more to it than that, I sensed. But Lucas seemed

to genuinely regret having jumped to conclusions, which was enough for me. My protector had always been watching out for me, even if I hadn't known. Realizing that gave me a warm feeling, as if a long coat had been thrown over my shoulders to keep me cozy and dry.

The silence between us stretched out, but it wasn't awkward. Sometimes there are people you can be quiet with, and you never feel the need to fill the gap with meaningless chitchat. I'd only become that close to a couple of people in my hometown, and I'd always thought it took years. Lucas and I were already there.

I remembered Courtney's daring and decided I could be at least half as bold as she was. Though I'd never been good at making conversation, I'd give it a try. "Do you not get along with your roommate?"

"Vic?" Lucas smiled a little. "He's pretty good, as roommates go. Oblivious, mostly. Goofy. But he's an okay guy."

The word *goofy* made me think I knew who this was. "Vic is the guy who wears Hawaiian shirts under his blazer sometimes, right?"

"That's the one."

"We haven't talked, but he seems like fun."

"He is. Maybe we can all hang out sometime."

My heart pounding, I ventured, "That would be nice, but . . . I'd rather spend time with you." Our eyes met, and I felt like I'd crossed some line. Was that a bad thing or a good one?

"We could—but—" Why was Lucas hesitating? "Bianca, I hope we're friends. I like you. But it's not a smart idea for you to spend a lot of time with me. You've seen that I'm not exactly the most popular guy on campus. I'm not here to make pals."

"Are you here to make enemies? The way you and Erich fight, sometimes it seems like it."

"Would you rather I was friendly with Erich?"

Erich was a class-A jerk, and we both knew it. "No, of course not. You're just kind of, well, confrontational. I mean, do you really hate all these guys so much? I don't like them, but you—it's like you can't even stand the sight of them."

"I trust my instincts."

I couldn't really argue with that. "They're people you don't want on your bad side, not if you can help it."

"Bianca, if you and I—if we—"

If we what? I could think of so many answers to that question, and I liked most of them. Our eyes met, locking so that it seemed impossible to look away. Lucas's intensity was almost overpowering even when it wasn't focused on me, and when it was—like now, as he studied every feature of my face, weighed all his words to me before he spoke them aloud—he could take my breath away.

Finally Lucas finished, "I couldn't stand it if they took it out on you. And eventually they would."

He was protecting me? That would have been endearing, if it hadn't been crazy. "You know, I don't think I have any social cred for you to damage."

"Don't be so sure."

"Don't be so stubborn."

We were quiet together for a while. Moonlight filtered

down between the leaves of ivy, and Lucas was close enough that I could recognize his scent—something that reminded me of cedar and pine, like the woods that surrounded us, as if he were somehow a part of this dark place.

"I've kinda messed things up, haven't I?" Lucas sounded almost as bashful as I felt. "I'm not used to this."

I raised one eyebrow. "Talking to girls?" Looking the way Lucas did, I doubted that.

However, there was no mistaking his sincerity when he nodded. The devilish glint had faded from his eyes. "I've spent a lot of years moving around. Traveling from place to place. Anybody I cared about—it seemed like they were gone too soon. I guess I learned to keep people at a distance."

"You made me feel like I'd been stupid to trust you."

"Don't feel that way. This is my problem. I'd hate for it to be yours."

My whole life had been spent in a small town, and I'd always thought that made me worse at meeting strangers. But now that Lucas said it, I could see that a peripatetic existence might have the same effect: isolate you, turn your thoughts inward, so that reaching out to others was the hardest thing in the world.

So perhaps his anger was a lot like my shyness. It was a sign that we were each lonely. Maybe we didn't have to stay lonely too much longer.

Quietly, I said, "Aren't you tired of running and hiding? I know I am."

"I don't run and hide," Lucas retorted. Then he was silent

for a second, considering. "Well, damn."

"I could be wrong."

"You're not." Lucas watched me for a while longer, and just when I was starting to feel like I'd been too open, he said, "I shouldn't do this."

"This?" My heart began to thump a little faster.

Lucas just shook his head and grinned. The devilish look was back. "When it gets complicated later on, don't say I didn't warn you."

"Maybe I'm the complicated one."

He smiled even more broadly. "I can see it's going to take us a while to settle this." I loved it when he smiled at me that way, and I hoped we'd hang out at the gazebo for hours. But at that moment, Lucas cocked his head. "Do you hear that?"

"What?" But then I did hear it: the faraway sound of the school's front door opening repeatedly and footsteps on the front walk. "They're coming out to bust the party!"

"Sucks to be Courtney," Lucas said. "And it gives us a chance to get back inside."

We ran across the grounds, listening to the sounds of the party being broken up, and gave each other big smiles as we sailed through the front door, home free.

"See you soon," Lucas whispered as he let my arm go and headed toward his hall. And as I ran back to my own room and my own bed, that one word kept ringing in my ears: *soon.*

Chapter Four

I REACHED MY ROOM JUST IN TIME TO JUMP under the covers before Patrice walked in, accompanied by Mrs Bethany. Pale light from the hallway outlined the head-mistress, so that all I could see was her silhouette.

"You know why we have rules here, Patrice." Her voice was soft, but there was no mistaking that she was serious. It was more than a little intimidating, and I wasn't even the one she was scolding. "You should understand that those rules need to be obeyed. We can't go running across the countryside at night. People would talk. Students would lose control. The result could be tragedy. Am I clear?"

Patrice nodded, and then the door swung shut. I sat up in bed and whispered, "Was it awful?"

"No, just a mess," Patrice grumbled as she started strip-ping off her clothes. We'd been changing in the same room together for more than a week now, but I was still kind of embarrassed by it. She wasn't. Even as she yanked off her shirt, she was staring at me. "You're still dressed!"

"Um, yeah."

"I thought you left the party early."

"I did. But I—I couldn't get back into the school right away. They were patrolling. Then they realized where you guys were and took off. I only got in here about three minutes before you did."

Patrice shrugged as she reached for her nightshirt. I did my best to get changed without turning away from my corner. The conversation was over, and I'd successfully lied to my roommate for the first time.

Maybe I should've told Patrice why I was late. Most girls would probably be bubbling over to tell everyone all about the gorgeous guy they'd just made a connection with. But I liked the secret. That made it more special, somehow, the fact that only I knew. *Lucas likes me, and I like him back. I think maybe, soon, we're going to be together.*

That last thought was probably taking it a little far, I decided as I slid beneath the blankets again. All the same, I couldn't help myself. My mind was racing too fast for me to sleep, and I smiled against my pillowcase.

He's mine.

"Heard there was quite a party last night," Dad said, as he placed a hamburger and fries in front of me at my family's table.

"Mmm-hmmm," I answered through a mouthful of fries. Then I caught myself and mumbled, "I mean, that's what I heard, too."

Mom and Dad traded looks, and I got the impression that

they were more amused than ticked off. That was a relief.

This was the first of what would be our weekly Sunday dinners. Every second I could be back with my family in the faculty apartment instead of surrounded by Evernight kids was good with me. Even though they were trying to act all casual about it, I could tell that my parents had missed me almost as much as I'd missed them. Duke Ellington was on the stereo, and despite the parental interrogation, everything was again right with the world.

"Things didn't get out of hand, did they?" Mom had apparently decided to ignore the fact that I'd denied being there. "From what I heard, it was mostly beer and music."

"Not that I know of." It wasn't really a denial; I mean, I did only attend the party for about fifteen minutes.

Dad shook his head and said to Mom, "It doesn't matter if it was just beer. The rules have to be obeyed, Celia. I don't worry about Bianca, but some of the others—"

"I'm not against rules. But it's natural for the older students to rebel against them occasionally. Better to have a few minor slipups from time to time than some major incident." Mom turned her attention back to me. "What's your favorite class so far?"

"Yours, of course." I gave her a look, asking if she really thought I was silly enough to answer any other way, and she laughed.

"Besides mine." Mom put her chin in her hand, ignoring the entire elbows-on-the-table rule. "English, maybe? You've always loved that most."

"Not with Mrs Bethany."

This didn't earn me any sympathy. "Listen to her." Dad was stern, and he set his glass down on the old oak table too hard, with a thunk. "She's someone that you need to take seriously."

I thought: *Stupid, she's their* boss. *What would happen if word got around that their kid was bad-mouthing the head-mistress? Think about somebody beside yourself for a change.*

"I'll try harder," I promised.

"I know you will." Mom covered my hand with her own.

On Monday, I went into English class determined to make a fresh start. We had recently started mythology and folklore, both subjects I'd always enjoyed. Surely if I could prove myself to Mrs Bethany in any area, it would be that.

Well, apparently I couldn't prove myself to Mrs Bethany.

"I expect that relatively few of you will have read our next assignment," she said, as a stack of paperbacks made its way around the room. Mrs Bethany always smelled slightly of lavender—feminine, yet sharp. "However, I imagine that virtually all of you have heard of it."

The paperbacks reached my desk, and I took a copy of Bram Stoker's *Dracula*. From the next row of desks, I heard Raquel mutter, "Vampires?"

As soon as she'd said it, a weird sort of electricity seemed to crackle through the room. Mrs Bethany pounced. "Do you have a problem with the assignment, Miss Vargas?"

Her eyes glittered as she fixed her birdlike gaze on Raquel, who looked like she would have gladly bitten off her tongue to have kept from saying anything. Already her one uniform sweater had begun to pill and look worn around the elbows. "No, ma'am."

"It sounded as though you did. Please, Miss Vargas, enlighten us." Mrs Bethany folded her arms in front of her chest, amused by whatever joke she was playing. Her fingernails were thick and strangely grooved. "If Norse sagas about giant monsters strike you as worthy of your notice, why not novels about vampires?"

Whatever Raquel said would be wrong. She'd try to answer, and Mrs Bethany would shoot her down no matter what, and we could go on like that for most of the class. That was the way Mrs Bethany had amused herself during every class period so far, finding someone to torment, usually for the amusement of the students whose powerful families she obviously preferred. The smart thing to do would've been for me to shut up and let Raquel be Mrs Bethany's whipping boy for the day, but I couldn't stand watching it.

Tentatively, I raised my hand. Mrs Bethany barely glanced at me. "Yes, Miss Olivier?"

"*Dracula*'s not a very good book, though, is it?" Everyone stared at me, shocked that somebody else had contradicted Mrs Bethany. "It has such flowery language, and all those letters within letters."

"I see that someone disapproves of the epistolary form that so many distinguished authors employed during the eighteenth and nineteenth centuries." The click-click of Mrs Bethany's shoes on the tile floor seemed unnaturally loud as she walked toward me, Raquel forgotten. The scent of lavender grew stronger. "Do you find it antiquated? Out of date?"

Why did I ever raise my hand? "It just isn't a very fast-moving book. That's all."

"Speed is, of course, the standard by which all literature is to be judged." A few snickers around the room made me squirm in my seat. "Perhaps you want your classmates to wonder why anyone would ever study this?"

"We're studying folklore," Courtney interjected. She wasn't rescuing me, just showing off. I wondered if that was to put me down or get Balthazar to look at her. For days she'd been making sure her kilt showed off her legs to their best advantage every time she sat down, but so far he seemed unmoved. "One common element in folklore around the world is the vampire."

Mrs Bethany simply nodded at Courtney. "In modern Western culture no vampire myth is more famous than that of Dracula. Where better to begin?"

I surprised everyone, including myself, by saying, "*The Turn of the Screw.*"

"I beg your pardon?" Mrs Bethany raised her eyebrows. Nobody in the room seemed to understand what I was getting at—except Balthazar, who was obviously biting his lip to keep from laughing.

"*The Turn of the Screw*. The Henry James novella about ghosts, at least maybe about ghosts." I wasn't going to start the old debate about whether or not the main character was insane. I'd always found ghosts really scary, but they were easier to face in fiction than Mrs Bethany was in the flesh. "Ghosts are even more universal in folklore than vampires. And Henry James is a better writer than Bram Stoker."

"When you are designing the class, Miss Olivier, you may begin with ghosts." My teacher's voice could have cut glass. I had to suppress a shiver as she stood over me, more stone-faced than any gargoyle. "Here, we will begin by studying vampires. We will learn how differently vampires have been perceived by different cultures over the ages, from the distant past until today. If you find it dull, take heart. We'll get to ghosts soon enough even for you."

After that, I knew to shut up and stay quiet.

In the hallway after class, tremulous with that strange weakness that always follows humiliation, I walked slowly through the throng of students. It seemed as if everyone was laughing with a friend except me. Raquel and I might have consoled each other, but she had already skulked away.

Then I heard someone say, "Another Henry James reader."

I turned to see Balthazar, who had fallen into step at my side. Maybe he was there to offer support; maybe he was just trying to avoid Courtney. Either way, I was grateful to see a friendly face. "Well, I've read *The Turn of the Screw* and *Daisy Miller*. That's about it."

"Try *Portrait of a Lady* sometime. I think you would like that one."

"Really? Why?" I assumed that Balthazar would say something about how good the book was, but he surprised me.

"It's about a woman who wants to define herself, instead of letting other people define her." He navigated easily through the crowd without ever taking his eyes from me. The only other guy who had ever looked at me so intently was Lucas. "I had a hunch that you might respond to that."

"You might be right," I said. "I'll check it out of the library. And—thanks. For the recommendation." *And*, I thought, *for thinking of me that way*.

"You're welcome." Balthazar grinned, showing off the dimple in his chin again, but then we both heard Courtney's laugh, not far away. He gave me a mock-scared look that made me laugh. "Gotta run."

"Hurry!" I whispered as he dodged down the nearest hallway. Although Balthazar's encouragement had helped, I still felt wrung out after Mrs Bethany's interrogation. I decided to take a quick walk on the grounds for some fresh air and quiet before I ate. Maybe I could have a few precious minutes alone.

Unfortunately, I was far from the only one with the same idea. Several students were milling around outside, playing music and talking. I noticed a group of girls sitting in the shade, none of them apparently headed back to their rooms for lunch. Probably they were dieting for the Autumn Ball, I decided as I watched them whispering together in the shadows cast by one of the old elm trees.

There was only one person in the grounds I wanted to see. I recognized him from the first day, and Lucas's description. "Vic?" I called.

Vic grinned at me. "Yo!"

You'd have thought we were old friends, instead of speaking for the first time. His floppy, sandy-brown hair stuck out from the sides of the Phillies cap he wore, and he carried an iPod emblazoned with a skin swirled with orange and green. As he loped to my side and tugged out his earbuds, I said, "Hey. Have you seen Lucas?"

"That guy, he's *crazy*." In Vic's world, *crazy* seemed to be a compliment. "He cut out of study hall, and I was, like, what are you doing? And he was all, just cover for me, right? So I did, until now, but you're not gonna nark on him. You're cool."

Since Vic and I had never even spoken before, how could he know I was cool? Then I wondered if Lucas told him, and that made me smile. "Do you know where he is?"

"If a teacher asks me, I don't know anything. Since it's you, I think it might have to do with the carriage house."

The carriage house to the north, near the lake, had been where they'd kept the horses and buggies back in the old days. Now it had been remade into Evernight Academy's administrative offices and Mrs Bethany's residence. What would Lucas be doing there?

"I think I'll take a stroll over that way," I suggested. "Just going for a walk. Not doing anything in particular."

"Ohhhh, riiiiiiiight," Vic said, nodding his head, like I'd actually said something really sly. "You got it."

He's not the sharpest knife in the drawer, I decided as I casually wandered in the general direction of the carriage house. Despite that, Vic seemed like a nice guy. Not the Evernight type at all, thank God. Nobody noticed me as I slipped farther away from the rest of the students. I guessed that was the one good thing about being beneath attention: you could get away with a lot more.

There was no forest here to shelter me, just softly rolling grounds, thick with clover, and a few trees at regular intervals, probably planted long ago to provide shade. In the underbrush I saw a small dead squirrel, a shriveled scrap of its former self. The wind ruffled its tail forlornly. I wrinkled my nose and tried to ignore it, concentrating instead on my search. I walked slower and more quietly, hoping to hear Lucas.

The carriage house was long and white, only one storey high. No point in having a second floor if you're building for horses, I guess. More tall trees surrounded it, shadowing everything so deeply that it was almost dark, and only a few wavering ribbons of sunlight touched the ground. Tiptoeing toward the back, I leaned around the corner and saw Lucas dropping out of Mrs Bethany's window. He landed easily and carefully shut the window behind him.

Then he turned and saw me. For a long second, we simply stared at each other. It felt like he was the one who had caught me doing something wrong, rather than the other way around.

"Hey," I blurted out.

Instead of offering an excuse for his behavior, Lucas smiled. "Hey. Why aren't you at lunch?"

As he strolled to my side, I realized that he was going to pretend nothing was wrong, that I hadn't seen anything out of the ordinary. Or was I the one who had done that by saying hello instead of asking him what he'd been up to? "I guess I'm not that hungry."

"Not like you to avoid the subject."

"The subject of lunch?"

"I was thinking more how you're not asking me why I broke into Mrs Bethany's office."

I breathed out a sigh of relief, and we both started to laugh. "Okay, if you're willing to tell me, it must not be anything too bad."

"My mom keeps saying that she'll only sign the consent form for me to go into Riverton on our free Saturdays if I have straight A's at midterm. But I had a hunch she'd already signed it, and I don't feel so good about chemistry, so I decided to check. See if the consent form was in my file. Like I told you before, I'm not good at playing by the rules."

"Of course." Even if it was wrong of him to do it, it wasn't *too* wrong, was it? Trusting Lucas came easily to me. "So, did you find it?"

"Yep." Lucas's self-satisfaction was obviously overdone to

make me smile, which it did. "Even if I get a B, I'm in the clear."

"What's so important about the free weekends? I spent some time in town over the summer, before you guys got here. Trust me, there's not a lot to see."

We walked in the shade, carefully weaving our way closer to Evernight, making our way around the side so that we could merge into the other students without being observed. Both of us were pretty good at being sneaky. "Just thought that might be a good place for us to spend some time together. Away from Evernight. What do you think?"

Given our conversation at the gazebo, I shouldn't have felt so surprised or bowled over. But I did, and it was simultaneously scary and kind of wonderful. "Yeah. I mean, I'd like that."

"Me, too."

After that, neither of us spoke for a little while. I wished that he would take my hand, but I wasn't quite brave enough to take his yet. Feverishly, I tried to think of something entertaining in Riverton, a town that was larger than Arrowwood and yet even more boring. There was a movie theater, at least, one that showed classic films before the regular late shows, sometimes. "Do you like old movies?" I ventured.

Lucas's eyes lit up. "I love movies— —old, new, whatever. John Ford to Quentin Tarantino, it's all good."

Relieved, I smiled back at him. Maybe everything really was about to be fine.

* * *

Later that week, the seasons shifted overnight. The cold awakened me first thing in the morning, and I could feel the change down in my bones.

I pulled the blankets more tightly around me, but that didn't do much good. Fall had laced the windowpanes with frost. I'd need to pull down the heavy comforter from the top shelf of my closet later; from now on, it would be harder to stay warm.

The light was still soft and pink, and I knew it was just past dawn. Groaning, I sat up and resigned myself to being awake. I could've fetched the comforter and tried to snatch a few more hours of sleep, but I needed to get in some work on my English paper on *Dracula* or face yet more of the wrath of Mrs Bethany. So I slipped into my robe and tiptoed past Patrice, who slept soundly, as if the cold couldn't penetrate the thin sheet over her.

Evernight's bathrooms had been built in an earlier era, one in which students were probably so grateful to have an indoor toilet that they weren't picky about things like plumbing. Too few stalls, no conveniences like electrical outlets or even mirrors, and separate faucets for hot and cold water in the tiny sinks—I'd hated them from the start. At least by now I had learned to scoop a handful of icy water in my palm before letting the steaming-hot water pour into that. This way, I could wash my face without scalding my fingers. The tile floor was so chilly against my bare feet that I made a mental note to wear socks to bed until spring.

As soon as I turned off the faucets, I heard something

else—crying, soft and quiet. I patted my face dry with my washcloth as I walked toward the sound. "Hello? Is somebody there?"

The sniffling stopped. Just when I thought I was intruding, Raquel's face peeked out of one of the stalls. She wore pajamas and the tan-leather braided bracelet that she always seemed to have on. Her eyes were red. "Bianca?" she whispered.

"Yeah. Are you okay?"

She shook her head and wiped at her cheeks. "I'm freaking out. I can't sleep."

"It got cold all of a sudden, didn't it?" I felt stupid even saying that. I knew as well as Raquel did that she wasn't sobbing in the bathroom at dawn because the weather was frosty.

"I have to tell you something." Raquel's hand closed over my wrist, her grip stronger than I would've thought. Her face was pale, her nose reddened from crying. "I need you to tell me if you think I'm going insane."

This is a weird question to be asked, no matter who's asking, no matter when or where or how. Carefully, I asked, "Do *you* think you're going insane?"

"Maybe?" Raquel laughed unevenly, and that reassured me. If she could see the funny side of this, then probably she was basically okay.

I glanced around behind us, but the bathroom was empty. At that hour, we were sure to have the place to ourselves for quite a while. "Are you having bad dreams or something?"

"Vampires. Black capes, fangs, the works." She tried to

laugh. "You wouldn't think anybody out of kindergarten could still be scared of vampires, but in my dreams— Bianca, they're terrible."

"I had a nightmare about a dying flower the night before classes started," I said. I wanted to distract her from her own nightmares; maybe sharing mine would help, even if I did feel sort of stupid talking about it out loud. "An orchid or a lily or something, wilting in the middle of a storm. It scared me so badly I couldn't shake it from my mind the whole next day."

"I can't get them out of my head, though. These dead hands, grabbing at me—"

"You're only thinking about that because of the *Dracula* assignment," I said. "We'll be done with Bram Stoker in another week. You'll see."

"I know that; I'm not stupid. But the nightmares will just change into something else. I don't ever feel safe. It's like there's this person—this presence—someone, *something* that's getting too close. Something terrible." Raquel leaned closer and whispered, "Don't you ever feel like there's something at this school that's . . . evil?"

"Courtney, sometimes." I tried to turn it into a joke.

"Not that kind of evil. Real evil." Her voice shook. "Do you believe in real evil?"

Nobody had ever asked me that, but I knew the answer. "Yeah. I do."

Raquel swallowed so hard I could hear it, and we stared at

each other for a few moments, unsure what to say next. I knew that I ought to keep reassuring her, but the intensity of her fear forced me to listen.

"I always feel like I'm being watched here," she said. "Always. Even when I'm alone. I know it sounds crazy, but it's real. Sometimes I feel like my nightmares last even after I wake up. Late at night I hear things—scrapes and thumps on the roof. When I look out the window, I swear sometimes I see a shadow running into the forest. And the squirrels— you've seen them, right? How they're dying?"

"A couple." Maybe it was the autumn chill in the drafty old bathroom making me shiver, but maybe it was Raquel's fear.

"Do you ever feel safe here? Ever?"

I stammered, "I don't feel safe, but I don't think it's anything weird." Then again, *weird* meant different things to different people. "It's just this school. This place. The gargoyles and the stone and the cold—and the attitudes—it makes me feel so out of place. Alone. And scared."

"Evernight sucks the life out of you." Raquel laughed weakly. "Listen to me. Life sucking. Still with the vampires."

"You just need some rest," I said firmly, sounding too much like my mother. "Some rest, and something different to read."

"Rest sounds good. Do you think the school nurse would give out sleeping pills?"

"I'm not sure there is a school nurse." When Raquel's nose wrinkled in consternation, I suggested, "You could probably grab something over the counter at the drugstore when we go into Riverton."

"I guess. It's a good idea, anyway." She paused, then gave me a watery smile. "Thanks for listening to me. I know that I sound nuts."

I shook my head. "Not at all. Like I said, Evernight just gets to people."

"The drugstore," Raquel said quietly as she gathered her things to go back to her room. "Sleeping pills. That way, I'll sleep through it."

"Sleep through what?"

"The sounds on the roof." Her face was grave now, that of someone older than her years. "Because somebody *is* up there at night. I can hear it. That part isn't a nightmare, Bianca. It's real."

For a long time after she had gone back to bed, I stood alone in the bathroom, still shivering.

Chapter Five

NORMALLY, YOU'D THINK THE GIRL GOING OUT on her first date ever would have dibs on the mirror. But when the Friday night of the Riverton trip came, Patrice was so busy looking at herself that I might as well have been dressing in the dark. She kept studying her face and figure in the full-length mirror, squinting and turning, unable to find whatever she was searching for, whether imperfections or beauty. "You look fine," I said. "Eat something, will you? You're practically invisible."

"The Autumn Ball isn't even a month away. I want to look my best."

"What good is going to the Autumn Ball if you can't enjoy it?"

"I'll enjoy it even more this way." Patrice smiled at me. She had a way of being both patronizing and completely sincere. "Someday you'll understand."

I didn't like it when she talked down to me like that, but

she was in my good books. For my date, Patrice had let me borrow a soft, ivory-colored sweater she owned, acting as if this was the biggest favor anyone had ever done for anyone. Maybe she was right. In that sweater, my figure—well, you could tell that I had one, something the dowdy Evernight plaids and blazers never revealed.

"None of you guys are going?" I asked as I tried pulling my hair back into a high ponytail. I didn't have to explain who "you guys" meant.

"Erich's throwing another party by the lake." Patrice shrugged. She still wore her pink satin robe, and her hair was covered with a lacy scarf. Probably the party wouldn't start until after midnight, not if she hadn't even started getting ready. "Most of the teachers will be in town chaperoning. That makes it a prime night here."

"I don't admit that Evernight Academy has prime nights."

"It's not as though they keep us in a cage, Bianca. Also, that hairstyle is not working for you."

I sighed. "I know. I can see for myself."

"Hold still." Patrice came up behind me, shook out the uneven braids I'd painstakingly woven, and ruffled her fingers through the strands. Then she gathered my hair back in a soft knot just at the nape of my neck. A few tendrils slipped loose to frame my face—messy but beautiful, just the way I always wanted my hair to look. Watching this transformation in the mirror, I thought it looked almost as if my hair had been fixed by magic.

"How did you do that?"

"You learn over time." She smiled, prouder of her handiwork than of me. "Your hair's a wonderful color, you know. When it falls over the ivory of this sweater, you get to show it off more. See?"

When did this shade of red become a "wonderful color" for hair? I smiled at my reflection, thinking that as long as Lucas and I were going out, any miracle was possible.

"Beautiful," Patrice said, and this time, somehow, I realized that she meant it. The compliment was still impersonal—I thought that the idea of beauty meant more to her than I did. But she wouldn't say I looked beautiful if she didn't think so.

Bashful and delighted, I stared at my reflection a little while longer. If Patrice could see something beautiful in me, then maybe Lucas could, too.

"You look great!" Lucas called.

I nodded at him, trying to maintain eye contact as we each pushed through the students squeezing into the bus that would take us into town. Evernight Academy didn't have anything as ordinary as a normal yellow school bus; this was a small luxury shuttle, the kind of thing a swanky hotel might operate, which had probably been rented for the occasion. I'd been shoved on in the first wave, and Lucas was still struggling to get near the door. At least I could see his smile through the window.

"Dee-luxe." Vic laughed, flopping down into the seat

next to me. He was wearing a fedora that looked like something from the 1940s, and he actually was pretty cute—but he still wasn't who I wanted to ride with. My face must have fallen, because he nudged my shoulder. "No worries. I'm just keeping the seat warm for Lucas."

"Thanks."

If it hadn't been for Vic, I wouldn't have gotten to sit with Lucas at all. People couldn't get onto that bus fast enough, and it seemed like about two dozen students—in fact, virtually all the kids who weren't the "Evernight type"—were determined to get into Riverton. Given how boring Riverton was, probably they just wanted to get away from school, and anyplace else would do. I knew how they felt.

Vic gallantly surrendered his seat when Lucas finally made his way to my side, but I wouldn't say the date started then. We were completely surrounded by other students, all of whom were laughing, talking, and shouting, relieved to be off the claustrophobic school grounds at last. Raquel was a few rows away, talking animatedly to her roommate; I must have put her fears at ease, at least for now. A few people cast curious glances in my direction that weren't exactly friendly. Apparently I was still suspected of being part of the in crowd, which was so wrong it was funny. Vic knelt on the seat in front of us, determined to tell us all about the amp he was going to buy at a music store that was open late in town.

"What are you going to do with an amp?" I shouted over the din as we bounced along the road to town. "They're not going to let you play electric guitar in your room."

Vic shrugged, a grin still splashed across his face. "It's enough just to look at it, man! To know I have something so excellent. Gonna make me smile every day."

"You never stop smiling. You smile in your sleep." Despite the teasing way Lucas said this, I could tell that, down deep, he liked Vic.

"Only way to live, you know?"

Vic was the exact opposite of the Evernight type, and I decided I liked him, too. "So what are you going to do while we're at the movies?"

"Explore. Wander. Feel the earth beneath my feet." Vic waggled his eyebrows. "Maybe meet some hotties in town."

"Better buy the amp later, then," Lucas pointed out. "It's going to cut into your action if you have to lug that thing around with you." Vic nodded seriously, and I hid my smile behind my hand.

So Lucas and I weren't really alone together until we were walking along Riverton's main street, just a block from the theater. We both brightened when we saw what was on the marquee.

"*Suspicion*," he said. "Directed by Alfred Hitchcock. He's a genius."

"Starring Cary Grant." When Lucas gave me a look, I added, "You have your priorities, I have mine."

Several other students milled around in the lobby. This probably had less to do with a sudden revival in Cary Grant's popularity than it did with the fact that Riverton didn't offer much in the way of amusement. We were genuinely looking forward to it, though—at least, until we saw who the chaperones for the theater were.

"Believe me," Mom said, "we're as appalled as you are."

"We thought for sure you'd get something to eat." Dad had his arm around her shoulders, as though this were their date, not ours. We were all standing in front of the posterboard in the lobby, Joan Fontaine staring out at us in alarm, as though she were facing my dilemma instead of her own. "That's the reason we decided to take positions here. Somebody else is covering the diner."

Encouragingly, Mom added, "Not too late for pancakes. We won't be offended."

"It's okay." It was so not okay to spend my first date with my parents, but what was I supposed to say? "Turns out Lucas loves old movies, so—we're good, right?"

"Right." Lucas didn't look like we were good. Somehow he looked even more freaked-out than I felt.

"Unless you like pancakes," I said.

"No. I mean, yes, I like pancakes, but I like old movies more." He lifted his chin, and it was almost as though he were challenging my parents to intimidate him. "We'll stay."

My parents, instead of becoming intimidating, grinned.

I'd told them last Sunday at dinner that Lucas and I were going into Riverton together. I didn't really spell it out any more than that, for fear of paralyzing them with shock, but they definitely got the gist. To my surprise and relief, they hadn't interrogated me; in fact, they'd glanced at each other first, weighing their own reactions even before mine. It was probably strange to have your "miracle baby" become old enough to go out with someone. Dad mentioned calmly that Lucas seemed like a good guy, then asked me if I wanted more macaroni and cheese.

In short, whatever crazy overprotective reaction Lucas was expecting didn't materialize. Mom said only, "In case you're trying to avoid us—and I would guess that you are—we're headed to the balcony, because that's where most of the students are going to go."

Dad nodded. "Balconies are powerful temptations, and they exert a strong gravitational pull on fountain drinks in the hands of teenagers. I've seen it happen."

Straight-faced, Lucas said, "I think I remember that from junior high science."

My parents laughed. I basked in the warm rush of relief. They liked Lucas, and maybe someday soon they'd invite him to Sunday dinner. Already I could see Lucas beside me all the time, all the places in my life where he would fit.

Lucas didn't look as certain—his eyes were wary as he led me into the theater—but I figured that was pretty much the standard guy response to parents.

We chose seats beneath the balcony, where Mom and Dad would have no chance of seeing us. Lucas and I sat close to each other, our bodies sort of angled together, and my shoulder and knee brushed against his.

"Never done this," he said.

"Been to an old-style movie house?" I glanced appreciatively at the gilded scrollwork that decorated the walls and balcony, and the dark red velvet curtain. "They really are beautiful."

"That's not what I meant." For all his aggressiveness, Lucas could seem almost bashful at times; that only happened when he talked to me. "I never got to just—go out with a girl before."

"This is your first date, too?"

"'Date'—people still use that word?" I would've felt embarrassed if he hadn't playfully nudged my elbow with his. "I just mean, I never got to be with anybody like this. Hang out without any pressure or knowing that I'd have to move on in another week or two."

"You make it sound like you never felt at home anywhere."

"Not until now."

I shot him a skeptical look. "Evernight feels like *home*? Give me a break."

Lucas's slow grin crept across his face. "I didn't mean Evernight."

At that moment, the houselights dimmed, and thank goodness. Otherwise I probably would've said something stupid instead of reveling in the moment.

Suspicion was one of the Cary Grant movies I hadn't seen before. This woman, Joan Fontaine, married Cary even though he was sort of reckless and spent too much money. She did this because he's Cary freakin' Grant, which makes him worth losing a few bucks. Lucas wasn't convinced by this reasoning. "You don't think it's weird that he's researching poisons?" he whispered. "Who researches poisons as a hobby? At least admit that's a weird hobby."

"No man who looks like that can be a murderer," I insisted.

"Has anybody ever suggested that you might be too quick to trust people?"

"Shut up." I elbowed Lucas in the side, which jostled a few kernels of popcorn from our bag.

I enjoyed the movie, but I enjoyed being close to Lucas even more. It was amazing how much we could communicate without saying anything—a sidelong glance of amusement or the easy way our hands brushed against each other and he twined his fingers with mine. The pad of his thumb traced small circles in my palm, and that alone was enough to make my heart race. What would it be like to be held by him?

In the end, I was proved right. Cary turned out to have been researching the poisons so he could commit suicide and save poor Joan Fontaine from his many debts. She insisted they would work it out, and they drove off together. Lucas shook his head as the last shot faded. "That ending is fake, you know. Hitchcock meant for him to be guilty. The studio made him redeem Cary Grant in the end so audiences would like it."

"The ending isn't fake if it's the ending." I insisted. The

lights came up for the brief intermission before the late show began. "Let's go someplace else, okay? We've got a while before the bus."

Lucas glanced upward, and I could tell he wouldn't mind getting farther from the parental chaperones. "Come on."

We made our way along Riverton's small main street, where it seemed like every single open store or restaurant was crowded with refugees from Evernight Academy. Lucas and I silently passed each of them, searching for what we really wanted—a place to be alone. The idea that Lucas wanted some privacy for us made me feel both thrilled and a little bit intimidated. The night was cool, and the autumn leaves were rustling as we went down the sidewalk, stealing glances at each other as we made small talk.

At last, once we'd walked beyond the bus station that marked the end of the main street, we found an old pizza place just past the corner that looked like it hadn't been redecorated since about 1961. Instead of ordering a whole pie, we just grabbed some plain cheese slices and sodas and slid into a booth. We faced each other across a table with a red-and-white checked cloth and a Chianti bottle thickly covered with candle wax. A jukebox in the corner was playing some Elton John song from before we were born.

"I like places like this," Lucas said. "They feel real. Not like some corporate focus group designed every inch of it."

"Me, too." I would've told Lucas that I liked eating eggplant on the moon, if he liked it, too. At the moment, though,

I was telling the truth. "You can relax and be yourself here."

"Be myself." Lucas's smile was sort of faraway, like he had a private joke. "That ought to be easier than it is."

I knew what he meant.

We were all but alone in the pizza parlor; the only other occupied table had about four guys who seemed to have come from a construction site, with plaster dust clinging to their T-shirts and a couple of empty pitchers testifying to the beer they'd already drunk. They were laughing loudly at their own jokes, but I didn't mind. That gave me an excuse to lean across the table and be a little closer to Lucas.

"So, Cary Grant," Lucas began, shaking red pepper flakes onto his slice. "That's pretty much your dream guy, huh?"

"He's sort of the king of dream guys, isn't he? I've had a crush on him ever since I first saw *Holiday* when I was about five or six."

You would think Lucas the movie buff would agree with that, but he didn't. "Most girls in high school would be crushed out on movie stars who, you know, are making movies now. Or somebody on TV."

I took a bite of pizza and had a very awkward cheese-strand situation to deal with for a second. Once I finally had a mouthful, I mumbled, "I like a whole lot of actors, but who doesn't love Cary Grant the most?"

"Even though I totally agree that this fact is tragic, let's face it: A lot of people our age haven't even heard of Cary Grant."

"Criminal." I tried to imagine what Mrs Bethany's face

would look like if I suggested a Cinema History elective. "My parents always introduced me to the movies and books that they loved back before I was born."

"Cary Grant was big in the 1940s, Bianca. He was making movies seventy years ago."

"And his movies have been on TV ever since. It's easy to catch up on old movies if you just try."

Lucas hesitated, and I felt a tug of dread, a swift, urgent need to change the subject to something else, anything else. I was one second too late, because Lucas said, "You said your parents brought you to Evernight so you could meet more people, get a bigger view of the world. But it seems to me like they've spent a whole lot of time making sure your world stays as small as possible."

"Excuse me?"

"Forget I said it." He sighed heavily as he dropped his pizza crust onto his plate. "I shouldn't have brought this up now. This should be fun."

Probably I should have let it go. The last thing I wanted to do on my first night out with Lucas was argue. But I couldn't. "No, I want to understand. What do you even know about my parents?"

"I know that they packed you off to Evernight, which is basically the last place on earth the twenty-first century hasn't reached. No cell phones; no wireless; cable Internet service only in a computer lab that has, like, four machines; no televisions; almost no contact with the outside world—"

"It's a boarding school! It's supposed to be separate from

the rest of the world!"

"They want *you* separate from the rest of the world. So they've taught you to love the things they love, not what girls your age are supposed to love."

"I make up my own mind about what I like and what I don't." I could feel my cheeks flushing hot with anger. Usually when I got this mad, I ended up bursting into tears, but I was determined not to. "Besides, you're the Hitchcock fan. You like old movies, too. Does that mean your parents run your life?"

He leaned across the table, and his dark green eyes were intense, holding me fast. I'd wanted him to look at me like this all night, but this wasn't the way I'd wanted it to happen. "You tried to run away from your family once. You brush it off like some stupid stunt you were trying to pull."

"That's all it was."

"I think you were onto something. I think you were right to feel weird about Evernight. And I think you ought to listen to that voice inside yourself and stop listening so much to your parents."

Lucas couldn't be saying these things. If my parents ever heard him talking like this— No, I couldn't even think about that. "Just because Evernight sucks doesn't mean my parents are bad parents, and you have a lot of nerve criticizing them when you hardly know them. You don't know anything about my family, and I don't understand why you care."

"Because—" He stopped, as if startled by his own words.

Slowly, almost disbelieving, he said, "I care because I care about you."

Oh, why did he have to say that now? Like this? I shook my head. "You're not making any sense."

"Hey." One of the construction workers had just punched up some tacky eighties metal on the jukebox. Now he was strolling toward us, off balance. "You givin' that little girl trouble?"

"We're okay," I said hastily. This was not the time to discover that chivalry wasn't dead. "Honestly, it's okay."

Lucas acted like he hadn't even heard me. He glared at the guy and snapped, "This isn't any of your business."

That was like dropping a match into a pool of gasoline. The construction worker swaggered closer, and his friends all stood up. "You go treating your girlfriend like that in public and damn straight it's my business."

"He wasn't giving me trouble!" I was still angry with Lucas, but the situation was clearly getting out of control. "It's great that you guys are, uh, looking out for women—seriously, it is—but there's no problem here."

"Stay out of this," Lucas said, his voice low. There was a note in it I'd never heard before, an almost unnatural intensity. A shiver went up my spine. "She's not your concern."

"You think you own her or somethin'? So you can treat her however you want? You remind me of the pig my sister married." The construction worker looked angrier than ever. "You think I won't give you what I gave him, you're dreamin', kid."

In desperation I looked around for a waiter or the store owner. My parents. Raquel. Basically, I was hoping for somebody, anybody, who might put a stop to this before the drunk construction guys beat Lucas to a pulp—because they were huge and there were four of them and by now they were all clearly spoiling for a fight.

I never imagined that Lucas would strike first.

He moved too fast for me to see. There was a blur of motion, and then the construction worker was sprawling backward into his friends. Lucas's arm was extended, his fist clenched, and it took a moment to sink in: *Oh, my God, he just hit somebody.*

"What the hell?" One of the other workers came at Lucas, who dodged him so quickly that it was like he was there, and then he wasn't. Instead he was at an angle, able to shove his opponent away so hard that I thought he'd fall down.

"Hey!" A man in his forties, wearing a sauce-stained apron, walked into the dining area. I didn't care if he was the owner, the chef, or Papa John—I'd never been so glad to see anybody in my life. "What's going on here?"

"There's no trouble!" Okay, I was lying, but it didn't matter. I slid out of the booth and started backing toward the door. "We're going. It's over."

The construction workers and Lucas kept staring at each other, like they wanted nothing more than to kick the fight into high gear, but mercifully Lucas followed me. As the door swung shut behind us, I could hear the owner muttering something about kids from that damn school.

As soon as we were in the street, Lucas turned to me. "Are you okay?"

"No thanks to you!" I started walking quickly back toward the main street. "What's gotten into you? You started a fight with that guy for no reason!"

"He started it!"

"No, he started the *argument*. You started the fight."

"I was protecting you."

"He thought he was, too. Maybe he was drunk and gross about it, but he didn't mean any harm."

"You don't understand how dangerous a place the world really is, Bianca."

Every other time Lucas had talked like that—as if he were so much older than I, and he wanted to teach me and shelter me—it had made me feel all warm and happy inside. Now it made me angrier. "You act like you know everything, and then you behave like an idiot and start a fight with four guys! And I saw how you fight, too. You've done this before."

Lucas had been walking alongside me, but his steps slowed, like he was shocked. I realized that what had really shocked him was that I'd figured it out. I was right. Lucas had been in fights like this before now, and more than once.

"Bianca—"

"Save it." I held up my hand, and we walked in silence back to the rental bus, which already was surrounded by students milling around, most of them with shopping bags or sodas in hand.

Lucas swung into the seat beside me, like he was still hoping we'd talk, but I folded my arms across my chest and stared at the window. Vic bounced into the seat in front of us and crowed, "Yo, guys, what's up?" Then he got a look at our faces. "Hey, looks like it might be a good time for me to tell one of my long rambling stories that goes nowhere."

"Great plan," Lucas said shortly.

True to his word, Vic went on and on about surfboards and bands and weird dreams he'd had once upon a time, and he didn't stop talking until we were back at school. That saved me from having to talk to Lucas; and, for his part, Lucas didn't say anything at all.

Chapter Six

AFTER THE TRIP TO RIVERTON, I FELT LIKE A fool who had thrown Lucas away for nothing.

Those construction workers had been drinking. Plus, there were four of them and only one of him. Maybe Lucas had needed to show them he meant business to avoid getting beaten to a pulp. If he'd done the only thing he could, what right did I have to judge him?

"No way," Raquel said when I confided in her the next day, walking across the grounds. The leaves had finished changing color, so that the hills in the distance were no longer green but crimson and gold. "If a guy gets violent, you get out. Period. Be thankful you saw his temper in action before you were the one he was angry at."

Her vehemence startled me. "You sound like you know what you're talking about."

"What, you never watched a Lifetime Original Movie?" Raquel didn't meet my eyes, just fiddled with the braided leather bracelet on her wrist. "Everybody knows that. Men who hit are bad men."

"I know he overreacted. But there's no way Lucas could ever hurt me."

Raquel shrugged and pulled her school blazer more tightly around her, as if she felt a chill, though it wasn't that cold out. For the first time, I wondered how much of her quiet demeanor and boyish appearance were a means of hiding herself from attention she didn't want. "Nobody ever thinks that something bad can happen until it happens. Besides, he kept telling you how much everybody here sucked and how you shouldn't be friends with your roommate or just about anybody else, right?"

"Well . . . yeah, but—"

"But nothing. Lucas was trying to isolate you from everyone else so he'd have more power over you." Raquel shook her head. "You're better off without him."

I knew she was wrong about Lucas, but I also knew that I hadn't come close to figuring him out.

Why had Lucas started criticizing my parents? The only time he'd ever seen us all together was at the movie theater, and they'd been friendly and welcoming. He'd claimed that it was about my halfhearted attempt to run away on the first day of school, but I didn't know if I entirely believed that. If he had a problem with Mom and Dad, he'd obviously dreamed it up for some bizarre paranoid reason that I was better off not having to deal with.

Explanations invented themselves in my head. Perhaps he'd had some girlfriend before me—probably chic and sophisticated, a girl who had traveled all around the world—and her parents had been snobbish and unfair. They'd shut Lucas out, maybe had forbidden him to ever see their daughter again, and so now he was scarred and distrustful.

This imagined story did me absolutely no good whatsoever. First of all, it made me feel sorry for Lucas, like I understood why he'd behaved so strangely, when really I didn't. Also, I felt insecure compared to this theoretical sophisticated previous girlfriend—and how sad is it if you feel threatened by a person who doesn't even exist?

I don't think I'd realized just how important Lucas had become to me until then—until we were separated and I had real reasons for staying away from him. Chemistry class, the only one we shared, was an hour of torture every day; I could almost feel him near me, the way you can feel a fire's presence in a cold room. Yet I never spoke to him, and he never spoke to me, respecting the silence I had demanded and maintained. I didn't see how he could be in more pain than I was. Logic said I was better off walking away, but logic didn't matter to me. I missed Lucas all the time, and it seemed like the more I told myself to leave him alone, the more I longed to be with him.

Did he feel the same way? I couldn't be sure. All I knew for certain was that he was wrong about my parents.

"How are you feeling, Bianca?" Mom asked softly as we cleared away my dishes from our Sunday dinner.

I hadn't slept well, hadn't eaten much, and mostly just wanted to pull a blanket over my head for the next two years or so. But for virtually the first time in my life, I didn't want to confide in them. They were Lucas's teachers; it wouldn't be fair to Lucas to tell them about his suspicions. Besides, talking about the fact that Lucas and I were apparently over before we'd even started would have made the loss more real. "I'm fine."

Mom and Dad exchanged glances. They could tell I was lying, but they weren't going to press me. "Tell you what," Dad said, heading toward the record player. "Don't go back downstairs just yet."

"Really?" Normally, the Sunday dinner rules dictated that I return to the dorms for studying not long after dinner had ended.

"It's a clear night, and I thought you might want to get in some telescope time. Besides, I was about to put Frank Sinatra on. I know how you love Ol' Blue Eyes."

"'Fly Me to the Moon,'" I requested, and within a few seconds, Frank was singing it to us all. I showed them both the Andromeda galaxy, directing them to look up from Pegasus, then go northeast until they saw it, the soft fuzzy glow of a billion stars far away. After that, I spent a long time combing through the cosmos, each familiar star like a long-lost friend.

* * *

The next day, on my way to history class, I glimpsed Lucas in the hallway at the very same moment he spotted me. Sunlight from the stained glass windows painted him the colors of autumn, and it seemed to me that he had never been more handsome.

When our gazes met, though, the moment lost all its beauty. Lucas looked hurt, as bewildered and lost as I'd been feeling ever since the argument in the restaurant—and for a terrible second I felt guilty, because I knew that I'd hurt him. I could see guilt in his eyes, too. Then he clenched his jaw and turned from me, shoulders slightly hunched. Within seconds, he was lost in the crowd of uniforms, one more invisible person at Evernight.

Maybe he was telling himself, once again, that it was best to keep his distance from people. I remembered how he had acted when we were together—so much happier and looser, more free—and I hated the idea that I might have forced him to shut himself off from the world again.

"Lucas's totally dragging ass around the dorm room," Vic informed me later that day when we ran into each other on the stairwell. For once, Vic was dressed normally—at least, from the ankles up, because the red Chucks he had on his feet were definitely not part of the uniform. "He's kind of a moody guy anyway, but this is beyond moody. This is supermoody. Megamoody. X-treme moodiness." He made an *X* with his arms to spell out the last.

"Did he send you here to plead his case?" I tried to make

it sound light. I don't think I did very well; my voice was so ragged that anybody could tell I'd been crying earlier that day—even someone as oblivious as Vic.

"He didn't send me. He's not like that." Vic shrugged. "Just wondering about the source of the drama."

"There's no drama."

"There's totally drama, and you're not going to tell me about it, but, hey, that's okay. Because it's not my business."

I felt so disappointed. I would have been angry if Lucas had sent Vic to argue on his behalf, but it was depressing to realize that Lucas was going to let me go without a fight. "Okay."

Vic nudged my elbow with his. "You and me are still friends, right? You guys get joint custody in the divorce. Generous visitation rights."

"Divorce?" Despite myself, I laughed. Only Vic could call the aftermath of a bad first date a divorce. We hadn't exactly been friends beforehand, so "still" was an exaggeration, but it would've been mean to point that out. Besides, I liked Vic. "We're still friends."

"Excellent. The weirdos have to stick together around here."

"Are you calling me a weirdo?"

"Highest honor I can bestow." He held out his hands as we walked through the corridors, taking it all in with one gesture: the high ceilings, the dark, scrolling woodwork that framed every hall and door, the shaded light that filtered through old windows and streaked long, irregular shadows on the floor. "This place is the capital of weird. So what's weird here is what's normal anywhere else. That's how I look at it, anyway."

I sighed. "You know, I think you've got a point."

He was definitely right about needing as many friends as I could get in a place like Evernight Academy. It wasn't as if I'd ever liked it here, but my brief time with Lucas had taught me how it felt not to be so desperately alone. Now that he was gone, my isolation stood out in sharper relief. Realizing how much better it could have been only made it harder to bear how unfriendly and intimidating this place actually was.

The change in seasons didn't help. The school's Gothic architecture had been softened slightly by the lush ivy and the sloping green lawn. The narrow windows and strangely tinted light hadn't been able to fully mask the brightness of the late-summer sun. Now, however, dusk came earlier, making Evernight seem more isolated than ever before. As the temperature cooled, a lasting chill crept into the classrooms and dormitories, and sometimes it seemed that the featherings of frost on the windowpanes were etching themselves permanently into the glass. Even the beautiful autumn leaves rustled in the wind, a lonely, shivery sort of sound. They'd already started falling, leaving the first few branches bare, like naked claws scrabbling at the gray-clouded sky.

I wondered if perhaps the founders of the school had created an Autumn Ball to cheer the students up at such a melancholy time of year.

"I don't think so," Balthazar said. We were at the same table in the library; he'd first invited me to study with him a couple of days after the ill-fated Riverton trip. At my old school, I hadn't studied with anyone, because "studying" usually turned into "talking and goofing off," and then the assignments stretched out even longer. I preferred to get my homework over and done with. But Balthazar turned out to feel the same way, and we'd spent a lot of time together in the two weeks since, working side by side, hardly saying a word for hours. The conversation didn't start until we were packing up our books. "I suspect the school's founders loved autumn. It brings out Evernight's true nature, I think."

"That's why they'd need cheering up."

He grinned and slung his leather satchel over one shoulder. "This is not the most terrible school on the face of the earth, Bianca." Balthazar was teasing me, but I could tell that he was genuinely concerned. "I wish you were having more fun here."

"That makes two of us," I said, glancing at the corner where I'd seen Lucas reading a few minutes before. He was still there, lamplight making his bronze hair shine, but he didn't so much as turn his eyes in our direction.

"You could like it if you gave it a fair chance." Balthazar held the library door for me as we went out. "You ought to explore a little more. Try harder to get to know people."

I shot him a look. "Like Courtney?"

"Correction: Try harder to get to know the *right* people." When Balthazar said "the right people," he didn't mean the richest or the most popular; he meant the ones that might be worth getting to know. Thus far, the only member of the in crowd who seemed remotely worth knowing was Balthazar himself, so I thought I wasn't doing too badly on that score.

"I don't think Evernight is right for everybody," I confessed. "I'm positive it's not right for me. I know it serves a purpose, but I'll be glad when I graduate."

"I will, too, but not for the same reason." Balthazar walked slowly by my side, carefully measuring his long stride so that I wouldn't fall behind. Sometimes it hit me how big he was—tall and broad, powerfully built—and a weird little tingle would start in my belly. "Evernight always makes me feel like I can understand the whole world. Like I can master it. Every new subject I study, every innovation I learn about— it's like I can't wait to get out there and try everything for myself."

His enthusiasm wasn't enough to make me like the school, but it did make me smile for what felt like the first time in ages. "Well, at least one of us is happy."

"I hope we'll both be happy before too long," Balthazar said softly. His dark eyes were studying me intently, and that warm tingly feeling started again.

We'd reached the archway that led to the girls' dormitory wing, and he stopped right at the boundary. I could imagine him in the nineteenth century, all courtly manners, and a smile tugged at my lips as I envisioned him bowing from the waist.

Balthazar looked like he might be about to say something,

but at that moment Patrice walked up, apparently done with her own schoolwork. "Oh, Bianca, there you are." Easily, she took my arm as if we were best friends. "You must explain our latest assignment in Modern Technology to me. I can't make any sense of it."

"Um—okay." As I was being towed down the hallway, I looked back at Balthazar and waved. He looked more amused than disappointed. I muttered to Patrice, "We were talking."

"I realize that," she whispered. "This way he'll keep wishing he'd gotten a chance to talk to you more. That means he'll return to you more quickly."

"Really?"

"In my experience, it works rather well. Besides, I really do need you to explain."

This wasn't the first time I'd had to shepherd Patrice through that particular course, or the first time I'd wondered why I bothered signing up for it at all. "Not a problem." I sighed.

Patrice giggled, and for a moment she was almost girlish. "Balthazar's the most attractive man here, if you ask me. Not precisely my type, but those shoulders? Those dark eyes? You've done rather well for yourself."

"We're just friends," I protested as we returned to our room.

"Just friends. Hmmm." Patrice's eyes sparkled with amusement. "I wonder if Courtney would agree."

I held up my hands, trying to cut this conversation off

before it got even more uncomfortable than it already was. "Don't tell Courtney about this, okay? I don't need the hassle."

She arched one eyebrow. "Don't tell her about what? I thought you said there was nothing to tell."

"If you want help with your homework, you're going to drop the subject. Now."

Slightly offended, Patrice shrugged. "Suit yourself. If I were you, I'd be excited about attracting the attention of a guy like Balthazar. But, by all means, let's talk about homework instead."

Honestly, I *was* a little proud that Balthazar liked me. I wasn't convinced that he wanted to be anything more than a friend, but he definitely flirted with me sometimes. After the mess with Lucas, it felt good to be flirted with—as if I really were beautiful and fascinating instead of the shy, awkward girl in the corner.

Balthazar was kind, smart, and he had a sly sense of humor. Everyone liked him, probably because he seemed to like most people in return. Even Raquel, who detested virtually all the in crowd, said hello to him in the hallway, and he always said hello back. He wasn't snobbish or cold. And he really was devastatingly good-looking.

He was everything a girl could ask for, basically. But he wasn't Lucas.

Back at my old school, the teachers always decorated for Halloween. Orange plastic pumpkins were set in the windows, waiting to be filled with Tootsie Rolls and Butterfingers, and construction paper witches flew across every wall. Last year, the principal hung candy-corn lights around her office door, which also had a sign that said, in green shaky letters, *Boo!* I always thought it was cheesy and fake, and it never occurred to me that I might someday miss it.

Nobody hung decorations at Evernight.

"Maybe they think the gargoyles are scary enough," Raquel suggested over our lunch in her dorm room.

I remembered the one outside my bedroom window and tried to imagine him draped in candy-corn lights. "Yeah, I see what you mean. If your school actually is a dank, scary dungeon from hell, Halloween decorations are sort of beside the point."

"Too bad we don't run a haunted house. You know, for little kids from Riverton? We could dress up, make it really scary. Play devils and demons for a weekend. Some of these jerks wouldn't have to act that much. We could raise money for the school."

"I don't think Evernight Academy needs more money."

"Good point," she admitted. "But we could raise money for charity, maybe. Like a help hotline or suicide prevention or something. I don't think many of these people care about charity, but they'd probably do it just for their college applications. None of these rich bitches even talk about college, probably because they're all legacies at Harvard or Yale or something, but still, they've got to apply. So they might go for the idea, right?"

The images flickered in my mind: cobwebs on the staircases, students laughing maniacally and the sound echoing throughout the great hall, and innocent little kids, wide-eyed with terror as Courtney or Vidette waved long black fingernails above their heads. "We're too late, though—Halloween's only two weeks away. Maybe next year."

"If I come back here next year, please shoot me." Raquel groaned, flopping backward onto her bed. "My parents say I should stick it out, because I got a scholarship to come here and otherwise it's just my old public school, with the metal detectors and no honors program. But I hate this. I hate it."

My stomach rumbled. The tuna salad and crackers Raquel and I had shared wasn't nearly enough to satisfy my hunger; I'd need to eat again in my room. I didn't want her to realize that, though. "It's got to get better."

"Do you really believe that?"

"No." We both looked at each other, expressions bleak, and then burst out laughing.

As our laughter died down, I realized that I could hear shouting—not close by but farther down the hall. Raquel lived not far from the central archway that connected the girls' dorms to the classroom areas; to me, it sounded like the noise was coming from there. "Hey, do you hear—"

"Yeah." Raquel pushed herself up on her elbows, listening. "I think it's a fight."

"A fight?"

"Trust somebody who used to go to the meanest public school in Boston. I know a fight when I hear one."

"Come on." I grabbed my book bag and started out the door, but Raquel grabbed at the sleeve of my sweater.

"What are you doing? We don't want to get in the middle of anything." Her eyes were wide. "Don't ask for trouble."

She made sense, but I couldn't listen. If there was a fight, I had to make sure—absolutely sure—that Lucas wasn't mixed up in it. "Stay here if you want. I'm going."

Raquel let me leave.

I hurried toward the sounds of yelling and even screaming. That was Courtney's voice, savage with glee, shouting, "Take him out!"

"Guys, yo, guys!" Those were Vic's words echoing in the corridor. "Knock it off!"

Heart sinking, I turned the corner just in time to see Erich punch Lucas in the face.

Lucas went sprawling backward, falling on his ass in front of the whole school. The Evernight types started laughing, and Courtney even applauded. Lucas's lips were smeared with blood, stark against his pale skin. When he realized that he was looking up at me, he shut his eyes tightly. Maybe the embarrassment hurt more than the blow.

"Don't insult me again," Erich commanded. He held up his hands, studying them as if satisfied with his handiwork. His knuckles were smeared with Lucas's dark blood. "Or next time, I'll shut you up permanently."

Lucas sat up, staring at Erich intently. A weird silence fell over the crowd, as if everything had become a lot more serious— as if the fight weren't over but had only begun. It wasn't dread I sensed, though; it was anticipation. Eagerness. The desire for punishment. "Next time this is going to turn out a whole lot different."

"Yeah, I guess so," Erich jeered. "Next time, it's *really* going to hurt." He stalked away, the conquering hero in the eyes of Courtney and the others who followed him. Everyone else sort of hurried away before any teachers could arrive. Only Vic and I stayed.

Vic knelt by Lucas's side. "You look like crap, by the way."

"Thanks for breaking it to me gently." Lucas took a deep breath, then groaned. Vic helped steady him and offered a wadded-up tissue for the blood trickling from Lucas's nose.

I didn't know what to say. All I could think was how terrible Lucas looked. Erich had clearly gotten the better of him. Ever since the incident in the pizza parlor, I'd been thinking of Lucas as a much rougher guy, somebody who got into fights all the time for the hell of it. Well, now he'd just gotten into another fight. Did that prove I'd been correct? Or did the fact that he'd gotten the stuffing knocked out of him prove that Lucas wasn't such a tough guy after all?

Finally I asked, "Are you all right?"

"Sure, fine." Lucas didn't look up. "You only need one or two molars, really. The rest are spares."

"You lost teeth?" Vic blanched.

"One of them is kind of loose, but I think it's sticking around." Lucas paused, then said to me, "I told you it would be like this eventually."

He had told me that, someday, he would be a pariah at Evernight. Sure enough, the day had arrived. But why was he pretending that he had left me alone for my own good? I was the one who had walked away from him.

"As long as you're okay," I said. I left him again, while he was still sprawled on the floor. Maybe this time he would notice which one of us was doing the walking.

Confusion and sadness settled over me, making my shoulders sag and my throat tighten. I bit my lip, hard enough for me to taste blood. It braced me up, but I still couldn't go back to Raquel's dorm room; I wasn't ready to deal with her questions. So I headed up to the library to hide out for the next half hour or so until political science. Surely I could find something to read, maybe some books on astronomy or even just a fashion magazine. If I hid behind a book for a while, maybe I'd feel better.

As I walked toward the door, it swung open to reveal Balthazar. He cast a comic glance down the hallway. "Is the coast clear?"

"What?"

"I assumed you were hiding out from the battle royale between Lucas and Erich."

"The battle's over." I sighed. "Erich won."

"Sorry to hear that."

"You are? I thought most kids here didn't like Lucas."

"He's definitely a troublemaker," Balthazar said. "But so is Erich, and Erich's got other people here on his side. I guess I have a soft spot for the underdog in any fight."

I leaned against the wall. Already I felt exhausted, as if it were midnight instead of early afternoon. "Sometimes it feels so tense here that I'm surprised the whole place doesn't shatter like glass."

"So relax. Don't study for a while," Balthazar coaxed.

"I'm not here to study. I'm just going to hang out, I guess."

"Hang out—in the library. Okay. You know what?" He leaned slightly closer to me. "You need to get out more."

I was too miserable to laugh, but I did smile. "That's an understatement."

"Then let me make a suggestion." Balthazar hesitated just long enough to let me understand what he was about to do, then folded his hand around mine. "Come with me to the Autumn Ball."

Despite all Patrice's hints and jokes, I hadn't ever dreamed that Balthazar would ask me. He was the handsomest guy in the school, and he could've invited anyone. Even though we got along and were friends—and even though I wasn't immune to his considerable charm—I'd never envisioned this moment.

And I'd never thought that my first impulse would be to tell him no.

That was stupid, though. The only reason I wanted to refuse Balthazar's invitation was because I was still hoping for someone else to ask me, and that someone wasn't ever going to ask, because I'd pushed him away for good.

Balthazar looked down at me tenderly, his brown eyes hopeful. I could only say, "I'd love to."

"Great." That smile of his deepened the dimple in his chin. "We'll have fun."

"Thanks for asking me."

He shook his head, as if disbelieving. "I'm the lucky one here. Trust me on that."

I smiled up at him, because that was one of the nicest things anybody had ever said to me. Totally not true, given that the most popular guy in school was taking the class geek to the big dance—we all know who the lucky one is in that scenario—but really nice.

My smile was a lie, though. I hated myself for looking up into Balthazar's handsome face and wishing that he was Lucas, but I did.

Chapter Seven

THE FIRST PACKAGES ARRIVED AT HALLOWEEN'S mail call. Long cardboard boxes, some of them bearing the elegantly scripted labels of expensive retailers, a few from addresses in New York and Paris. Patrice's came from Milan.

"Lilac." Tissue paper rustled as she lifted her gown for the Autumn Ball. Patrice held the pale silk up to her body, supposedly letting me see what it would look like on but really almost hugging it. "Don't you think it's a lovely color? I know it's not in vogue right now, but I adore it."

"It's going to look wonderful on you." Already I could tell that the shade would flatter Patrice's complexion. "You must have gone to a hundred big parties like this."

Patrice pretended to be modest. "Oh, they all blur together after a while. Will this be your first dance?"

"We had a couple at my old school," I said, not mentioning that these were held in the school gym, with music provided by the A/V geek who mostly played his extremely lame mashups. Patrice wouldn't understand that at all, much less the fact that I spent each one of those dances standing awkwardly against the wall or hiding in the girls' bathroom.

"Well, you're in for a treat. They don't give balls like this any longer. It's magic, Bianca, it really is." Her face lit up with anticipation, and I wished I could share her excitement.

The two weeks between Balthazar's invitation and the ball itself were confusing for me, because my emotions kept tugging me in a thousand different directions at once. I could look at dresses in a catalog with my mother, happily picking out favorites, and within the next hour be so lonely for Lucas that it felt like I could hardly breathe. Balthazar smiled at me to give me strength during one of Mrs Bethany's in-class grillings, and I thought about what a great guy he was. Then I drowned in waves of guilt, because I felt like I was leading Balthazar on. It wasn't like he had dropped to his knees and promised to love me forever, but I knew he wanted me to feel more for him than I did.

At night, I lay in bed and imagined Balthazar kissing me or holding my face in his hands. The images were meaningless; I might as well have been remembering a scene from a movie. Then, as I became sleepier and my thoughts wandered, my fantasies changed. The dark eyes gazing at me became forest green, and it was Lucas with me, his mouth on mine. I'd never been kissed, but as I lay beneath my blanket, twisting restlessly, I could imagine it so clearly. My body seemed to know more than I did. My heart raced, and my cheeks flushed with heat, and sometimes I hardly slept at all. The fantasies of Lucas were better than any dreams.

I told myself that I wouldn't keep going on like this. I was going to the Autumn Ball with the handsomest guy in the whole school. It was the one really wonderful thing that had happened to me so far at Evernight Academy, and I wanted to enjoy it. No matter how many times I repeated that in my mind, though, I never believed the dance could really make me happy.

That changed when I put on my dress the night of the dance.

"I took it in a little at the waist." Mom wore a tape measure around her neck and a few straight pins stuck into the cuffs of her shirt. She knew how to sew—really sew, any kind of clothing you can think of—and had altered the catalog-bought dress for me. (She wouldn't alter my uniforms for me, though, explaining that she only had so much time in the day. This turned into a suggestion that I learn how to sew myself, but no way. Mom didn't believe in sewing machines, and I couldn't see me spending my free Sunday afternoons learning how to use a thimble.) "I lowered the neckline some, too."

"You want me to flash the guys?" We both laughed. It was kind of ridiculous for me to act modest while I was standing in front of her in panties and a strapless bra. "This plus more makeup than I've ever worn before—Dad's not going to be happy with you."

"I think your father will manage to endure, especially once he sees how gorgeous you're going to look."

I stepped into the midnight-blue dress, which rustled softly as Mom helped me pull it up. She zipped up the side, and at first I thought she'd taken it in too much—but then she hooked the clasp, and I realized that I could still breathe. The bodice was molded perfectly to me, until it melted into the full skirt. "Wow," I whispered, spreading the soft, filmy fabric with my hands, marveling at how good it felt to touch. "I want to see."

Before I could move to the mirror, my mother stopped me. "Wait. Not until I do your hair."

"I just want to look at the dress! Not my hair."

"Trust me. You'll be so happy if you wait to get the full effect." She beamed. "Besides, I'm really enjoying this."

I couldn't exactly say no to the woman who had spent the last week altering my dress. So I sat on the edge of the bed and let her start brushing and braiding.

"Balthazar's a terrific guy," she said. "Seems that way to me, at least."

"Yeah. Definitely."

"Hmm. That sounded less than enthusiastic."

"It isn't. At least, I don't mean it to be." My protests sounded weak, even to me. "I just don't know him very well yet. That's all."

"You study together all the time. I'd say you know him well enough for a first date." Mom's deft fingers wove a slender braid at my temple. "Is this about Lucas, maybe? Whatever happened with you two?"

He tried to turn me against you and then started beating up on construction workers in town, Mom. So naturally he's the one I want to be with. Maybe you and Dad would like to go chase Lucas with flaming torches now? "Nothing really. We're not right for each other. That's all."

"You still care about him, though." She spoke so gently, and I wished I could just turn around and hug her. "If it helps any, you and Balthazar obviously have more in common. He's someone you could be serious about. But I'm getting ahead of myself. You're sixteen, and you don't need to think about being serious. You need to have fun at this dance."

"I will. Just wearing this dress is sort of amazing."

"It needs something else." Mom stood in front of me, studying her handiwork with her hands on her hips. Then her face lit up. "Eureka!"

"Mom, what are you doing?" To my dismay, my mother was walking over to my telescope, scissors in hand, and snipping off the ends of my strings of paper origami stars. "Mom! I love those!"

"We'll fix them later." She held two small strands now, the ones with only the tiniest stars on the end. Their silvery paint sparkled as she put them in my hands. "Hang onto those for a second, will you?"

"You're nuts," I said, the moment I realized what she was doing.

"Tell me that again after you see it." After Mom slid the last bobby pin in place, she wheeled me around to face the mirror. "Look."

At first I couldn't believe that the girl in the reflection

was me. The midnight-blue dress made my pale skin look as creamy and perfect as silk. My makeup wasn't all that different from what I usually wore, but my mother's experienced hands had shaded everything more softly. My dark-red hair was pulled back from my forehead in several small braids of varying widths, then flowed down my neck—the way women might have worn their hair in the Middle Ages. Instead of a wreath of flowers like they wore in old pictures, I wore silver stars in my hair, small enough to look like jeweled clips. They glinted as I turned my head from side to side, studying myself from every angle. "Oh, Mom. How did you do this?"

Tears were welling in my mother's eyes. She was such a sap, in the best way. "I had a beautiful daughter, that's how."

She always told me I was pretty, but this was the first time I'd ever thought Mom might be telling the truth. I wasn't some magazine-cover knockout like Courtney or Patrice—but this was beauty, too.

When we went into the living room, my father looked about as shocked as I felt. He and Mom hugged each other, and she whispered, "We did good, huh?"

"We definitely did."

They kissed each other like I wasn't there. I cleared my throat. "Uh, guys? I thought teenagers were the ones who were supposed to make out on prom night."

"Sorry, honey." Dad put one hand on my shoulder; his hand felt cool to me, as if I were glowing with warmth. "You're absolutely stunning. I hope Balthazar knows what a lucky guy he is."

"He'd better," I said, and they laughed.

I could tell that Mom and Dad wanted to go downstairs with me, but to my relief, they didn't. That would have been taking chaperoning a little too far. Besides, I liked having a few moments to myself as I went, the skirt of my dress lifted in one hand and fluttering as I made my way down the steps. It gave me a chance to convince myself that all of this was real and not some dream.

Below me I could hear laughter and talk and soft strains of music; the dance had already begun, and I was running late. With luck, Patrice would be right about keeping guys waiting.

The second I reached the bottom of the stone steps and walked into the candlelit great hall, Balthazar turned, as if he'd somehow sensed I was coming. Just one glance at his eyes, at the way he was staring at me, made me realize Patrice had definitely been right. "Bianca," he said, stepping closer. "You look amazing."

"So do you." Balthazar was wearing a tuxedo, classic, the way Cary Grant dressed back in the 1940s. As handsome as he was, though, I couldn't help glimpsing the great hall behind him and sighing, "Oh, wow."

The hall was hung with bowers of ivy and illuminated with tall white candles that had been set in front of old, hand-hammered plates of brass, so that they reflected even more light. On a small stand in the corner sat the band, not a bunch of rock'n'rollers in blue jeans and T-shirts but classical musicians in tuxes even more formal than Balthazar's, playing a waltz. Dozens of couples danced, in a perfect pattern, like a scene from a picture two centuries old. A few of the new students stood against the wall, guys in suits meant to be campy or cool, girls in short dresses with sequins; they all seemed to be aware that they'd misjudged the occasion.

"I just realized I should have asked you this before— Can you waltz?" Balthazar offered me his arm.

I took it as I said, "Yes. Well, mostly. My parents taught me all the old dances, but I've never done them with anyone else. Or anyplace but at home."

"First time for everything." He led me further into the great hall, so that the candlelight shone more brightly all around us. "Let's begin."

Balthazar swung us into the dance as if he'd rehearsed it; he knew exactly where we belonged and exactly how to move. Any doubts I had about my waltzing ability vanished immediately. I remembered the steps well enough, and Balthazar was a wonderful lead, his broad hand against the small of my back guiding me expertly. Nearby I saw Patrice smile at me approvingly, before she was whisked away in the next move of the dance.

After that, the dance stretched into one long, happy blur. Balthazar never got tired of dancing, and neither did I. Energy flowed through me like electricity, and I felt as if I could've danced for days without slowing down. Patrice's smiles and Courtney's disbelieving stare told me that I looked beautiful, and more than that—I felt beautiful.

I'd never realized just how wonderful that kind of dancing was before. Not only did I know the steps but everyone else did also. Each couple was a part of the dance, everyone moving in time, all the women extending their arms at just the right angle, just the right time. Our long, full skirts all twirled with us, creating colorful swirling rows ahead of the guys' black shoes, everyone's steps precisely on the beat. It wasn't confining—it was liberating, the freedom from confusion or doubt. Every move flowed from the one before it. Maybe this was what it was like to dance in the ballet. We were all moving together to create something beautiful, even magical.

For the first time since I'd arrived at Evernight Academy, I knew exactly what to do. I knew how to move, how to smile. I felt comfortable with Balthazar and basked in the warmth of his admiration. I fitted in.

I'd never seen how I could be a part of the world of Evernight, but the path stretched before me then, broad and deep and welcoming—

"If that crew had gotten their claws into you—a sweet girl like you—I didn't want to have to watch."

Lucas's voice echoed in my mind, so clear that he might as well have whispered into my ear. I stumbled, and the rhythm of the dance was lost to me in an instant. Balthazar quickly steered me off the dance floor with his arm across my shoulders. "Are you all right?"

"I'm fine," I lied. "I just—it's so warm. I think I'm getting overheated."

"Let's get some fresh air."

As Balthazar guided me through the dancers, I realized what I'd nearly done. I had been proud to be a part of Evernight—a place where the strong preyed upon the weak, where the beautiful looked down on the ordinary and where snobbery was more important than friendliness. Just because they'd stopped picking on me for one night, I was ready to forget what bastards most of them were.

Only remembering Lucas had brought me to my senses.

We stepped out onto the grounds. No chaperones lurked outside. Apparently Mrs Bethany and the other teachers expected the late-fall chill to keep most students indoors, and when the cold air hit my bare shoulders and back, I could see why. Before I could start shivering, Balthazar took off his tuxedo and wrapped it around my shoulders. "Better?"

"Yeah. I just need a second."

He leaned closer, clearly concerned. Balthazar was such a gentleman, such a good and decent person. I wished he'd asked someone else to the dance, a girl who would appreciate him. He said only, "Let's walk for a while."

"Walk?"

"Unless you'd prefer to return to the dance—"

"No!" If I went back in there, maybe the spell would fall

over me again and cloud my mind. I needed my head clear until I could understand what I'd nearly done. "I mean, no, not yet. Let's go."

The stars were brilliant overhead. It was a cloudless night, perfect for stargazing. I wished I could retreat back to the room at the top of the turret and look through my telescope at stars far away instead of all the confusion that surrounded me here. Behind us, the music and laughter of the dance slowly faded as we walked deeper into the woods.

At last, Balthazar said, "Okay, who is he?"

"Who?"

"The guy you're crazy about." Balthazar's smile was sad.

"What?" I was so embarrassed, both for my sake and his, that I tried to bluff my way out of it. "I'm not seeing anybody else."

"Give me some credit, Bianca. I've had enough experience to tell when a woman is thinking about another man."

"I'm sorry," I whispered, abashed. "I didn't mean to hurt you."

"I can take it." He put both his hands on my shoulders. "We're friends, right? That means I want you to be happy. I'd rather you were happy with me—"

"Balthazar—"

"—but I know it's not always that simple."

I shook my head. "No. It's not. Because you're the most amazing guy, and you ought to be the one I'm thinking about."

"There's no 'ought to' when it comes to love. Trust me on

this." His shirt was brilliant white in the moonlight. Somehow Balthazar had never looked as handsome as he did when he was letting me go. "Is it that guy Vic? I see you talking to him sometimes."

"Vic?" I had to laugh. "No. He's great, but we're just friends."

"Then who?"

At first I was reluctant to tell him. Then I realized that I wanted to, because we really had become close friends after the past few weeks of spending time together. He always had time to listen, and he took my opinions seriously, even though I was younger and so much more sheltered than he was. Now Balthazar's perspective meant something to me, too. "Lucas Ross."

"The underdog wins a round." Balthazar didn't seem very pleased. Then again, why would he be pleased when I told him about some other guy I liked more? "I can see what you see in him."

"You can?"

"Sure. He's a good-looking guy, I guess."

"That's not it." I wanted him to know what I truly meant. "It's not like I haven't noticed that Lucas's attractive. But he's the only person who understands what it's like for me."

"I could understand. Or I could try." Balthazar glanced downward, and I realized that, as cool as he was playing it, this conversation was tough for him. "No more pleading. I promise."

As gently as I could, I said, "You belong here, Balthazar. That's why you can't understand what it's like for the rest of us who don't."

"You could belong here if you wanted to."

"I don't."

He raised one eyebrow. "Then you'll have some problems down the line."

"That's not what I mean." Balthazar was trying to speak about the future, years and years away, and I didn't want to think about that when things were confusing enough already. "I'm talking about high school. You've been around and seen the world. I don't think you can realize how—how big this place is for me. How frightening it feels. If I let myself, I could fall into the trap of letting Evernight decide who and what I am. That's not what I want. Lucas feels the same way."

Balthazar considered that for a few seconds. Finally he nodded. I didn't think I'd convinced him, but he'd heard me. "Lucas's not a bad person," he admitted. "Not as far as I know him, anyway. I've seen him stand up for students who were being picked on, and the things he talks about in class—he's smart."

I smiled. After weeks of doubting Lucas, it felt good to hear someone saying nice things about him.

Balthazar wasn't done. "But he has a hot temper. You saw his fight with Erich, so you know that." I felt guiltily grateful that Balthazar knew nothing about what had happened in the Riverton pizza parlor. "He's defensive, too.

I can see how Evernight might make somebody like him defensive, but that doesn't change that he's sometimes—"

"Volatile," I finished. "Yes, I've seen it. I don't know if we'll ever get together, because of that. But you deserve to know what I'm feeling."

"All I'm saying is, watch yourself. If he hurts you, get out fast." He gave me a crooked smile. "Then maybe I can catch you on the rebound."

I put one hand on his arm. "I should be so lucky."

Balthazar kissed my forehead. He smelled like pipe smoke and leather, and I halfway wished I'd waited to say all this until after I'd gotten to really kiss him at least once. "Ready to go inside?" he asked.

"A few more minutes. I like it out here. Besides, you can see the stars tonight."

"That's right. You love astronomy." He put his hands in his trouser pockets and walked alongside me as we continued into the woods, peering up at the constellations that winked through the leaf-bare branches overhead. "That's Orion, isn't it?"

"Yes. The Hunter." I lifted one hand to outline the legs, the belt, the arm stretching upward to deliver a blow. "See the really bright star in his shoulder? That's Betelgeuse."

"Which one is it?" Probably Balthazar didn't really care much about astronomy, but I thought he was relieved to have something to talk about besides his romantic disappointment. I knew how he felt.

"Here, lean down." As he bent beside me, I guided one of

his arms upward, so that his own finger pointed to the star. "Do you see it now?"

Balthazar smiled. "I think so. Isn't there a nebula in Orion?"

"Yeah, halfway down. I'll show you."

A voice behind us said, "Bianca?"

We both whirled around. I'd recognized the voice immediately but hadn't believed my own ears. Maybe hope was misleading me. But there in the darkness stood Lucas in his uniform. He was glaring—not at me, not even at us together, but at Balthazar.

I whispered, "Lucas, what are you doing here?"

"Making sure you're okay."

Balthazar didn't like that. He straightened up. "Bianca is completely safe."

"It's late. It's dark. You've got her out here alone."

"She walked out here of her own free will." Then Balthazar took a deep breath, obviously working to calm himself. "If you'd rather be Bianca's escort, maybe that would be best."

Lucas was clearly taken aback. He'd expected a fight, not resignation.

"I'll come in with you," I told Balthazar. Regardless of what we'd just talked about, or how I felt, he was my date. I owed him that.

But Balthazar shook his head. "That's okay. I don't feel like dancing anymore."

Confused and embarrassed, I slipped off the tuxedo,

bracing myself against the cool air, and said, "Thanks. For everything."

"If you need me, let me know." As he shrugged his jacket back on, Balthazar shot Lucas a look, then walked back toward the school alone.

As soon as Balthazar had left us, I muttered, "That was completely unnecessary."

"He was leaning over you. Looming."

"I was showing him the stars!" I hugged myself, trying to stay warm. "Did you think he was about to kiss me?"

"No."

"Liar," I retorted.

Lucas groaned. "Okay, I was trying to keep him away from you. I couldn't just watch that guy put the moves on you and not do something about it." Then he took off his school blazer and offered it to me. It wasn't as elegant a gesture as it had been from Balthazar—but then, from Balthazar it had been simple good manners, the kind of behavior that was part of being a gentleman. Lucas, I thought, was desperate to do anything to show that he could take care of me, at least a little.

I took the jacket from him and slipped into it. The lining was still warm from his body. "Thank you."

"Shame to cover up the dress." He looked me up and down, a smile tugging at one corner of his mouth.

"Don't flirt with me." Part of me wanted to hear Lucas flirting all night, but I knew that we had to have this conversation, now. "Talk to me."

"Okay. We'll talk."

After that, of course, neither of us knew exactly what to say. Mostly to stall for time, I kept walking, Lucas by my side. We heard a rustling in the leaves far away, but then we heard giggling. Apparently other couples were sneaking out into the woods tonight. From the sound of things, they were having more fun than we were.

I finally realized I'd have to speak first. "You shouldn't have said that about my parents."

"I was out of line." Lucas sighed. "They care about you. Anybody can see that."

"Then why were you being so weird about them?"

He considered that, clearly unsure how to answer. "We haven't talked much about my mom."

I blinked. "No. I guess we haven't."

"She's kind of intense." Lucas stared at his feet as we walked across a thick, soft carpet of brown pine needles. Nearby an apple tree was surrounded by fallen fruit that nobody had picked, each apple now brown and soft. Their sweet scent gentled the air. "She tries to run my whole life for me, and she comes pretty close."

"I have a lot of trouble imagining anybody bossing you around."

"That's because you haven't met Mom."

"She'll change as you get older," I suggested. "I know my parents used to be a lot more protective than they are."

"She's not like your parents." Lucas laughed, and the

sound was strange for some reason I couldn't define. "Mom sees the world in black and white. You have to be strong to make it, she says. As far as she's concerned, the world only has two kinds of people in it: predators and prey."

"That sounds—hard core."

"Hard core is a good term for her. She has very definite ideas about who I should be and what I should do. I might not agree with her all the time, but, you know—she's still my mom. What she says has an effect on me." He sighed heavily. "That's probably not much of an explanation, but it has a lot to do with how I behaved in Riverton."

The more I thought about what Lucas was saying, the more I realized how much it explained. Lucas had assumed that my parents were trying to run my life because his mother always tried to run his. "I get it. I really do."

"It's cold." Lucas took my hand. My heart fluttered faster. "Come on. Let's get back to the school."

We walked together toward Evernight, stepping out of the woods onto the grounds, where we could see the brilliant lights in the great hall and the silhouettes of dancing couples. I imagined the way this night might have gone if Lucas and I had never argued and he'd been my date to the Autumn Ball. It was almost too perfect to think about. "I don't want to go inside yet."

"It's cold."

"Your jacket is keeping me warm."

"Yeah, but it isn't keeping *me* warm." He grinned at me.

Lucas always seemed older than me, except when he smiled.

"Wait just a little," I pleaded, tugging him toward the gazebo where we'd met. "We'll keep each other warm."

"Well, when you put it that way—"

We sat down in the gazebo, stars above clouded by the thick ivy, and Lucas put his arms around me. I lay my head against his shoulder. Just like that, all the doubt and confusion I'd felt for the past few weeks was gone. I'd been happy during the ball itself, but only because I'd forgotten myself in the whirl. This was different. I knew where I was—who I was—and I was completely at peace. Although I remembered all the reasons I'd doubted Lucas, when we were as close as this, I could trust him completely. I wasn't afraid of anything in the world. It was safe to let go. Closing my eyes, I nuzzled my face into the curve of his neck. Lucas shivered, and I didn't think it was because of the cold.

"You know I'm only looking out for you, right?" he whispered. I could feel his lips brushing against my forehead. "I want to keep you safe."

"I don't need you to protect me from danger, Lucas." I slipped my arms around his waist and hugged him tightly. "I need you to protect me from being lonely. Don't fight for me. Be with me. That's what I need."

He laughed, a strange, sad sound. "You need somebody to look out for you. Make sure everything's okay. I want to be that guy."

I lifted my face to his. We were so close that my eyelashes

brushed his chin, and I could feel the warmth of body heat in the small space between our mouths. It took all my courage to say, "Lucas, all I need is you."

Lucas touched my cheek, then brushed his lips against mine. That first touch stole my breath, but I already knew that I wasn't afraid any longer. I was with Lucas, and nothing could ever hurt me.

I kissed him, and my dreams had told me the truth—I did know how to kiss Lucas. How to touch him. The knowledge had been inside me all the time, waiting for the spark that would make it catch fire and come alive. Lucas crushed me so hard against his chest that I could hardly breathe. We kissed deep and slow, hard and soft, a thousand different ways. All of it was right.

His blazer fell from my shoulders, exposing my arms and back to the cool night air. His hands slid upward to cover me, and I could feel his palms upon my shoulder blades and his fingertips on my spine. The feel of his skin against mine was so good—better than I'd guessed it could be—and my head fell backward as I sighed in delight. Lucas kissed my mouth, my cheek, my ear, my throat.

"Bianca." His whisper was soft against my skin. Lucas's lips were brushing against the hollow of my throat. "We should stop."

"I don't want to stop."

"Out here—we shouldn't get—carried away—"

"You don't have to stop." I kissed his hair and his forehead.

All I could think about was that he belonged to me now, me and no one else.

When our lips met again, the kiss was different—charged, almost desperate. Lucas and I were breathing faster, not able to speak. Nothing in the world existed except him and the thrumming deep inside me, the one that insisted he was *mine, mine, mine.*

His fingers brushed the slim strap of my dress, until it slipped down my shoulder, exposing the very top curve of my breast. Lucas traced the line from my ear to my shoulder with his thumb. I wanted him to go further, to touch me in every way I needed to be touched. My mind was clouded, almost like I couldn't think at all; there was only my body and what it demanded from me. I knew what I had to do, even if I couldn't imagine it yet. I knew.

Stop, I told myself. But Lucas and I were past stopping. I needed him, all of him, now.

I took his face in my hands and pressed my lips softly to his mouth, his chin, and his neck. I could see his pulse throbbing just beneath the skin, and then the hunger was too much to hold back.

I bit into Lucas's throat, hard. I heard him gasp in pain and shock, but in that moment the blood rushed over my tongue. The thick metallic taste of it spread through me like fire, hot and uncontrollable and dangerous and beautiful. I swallowed, and the feel of Lucas's blood in my throat was sweeter than anything else I'd ever known.

Lucas tried to push away from me, but he was already weak. As he began to slump backward, I caught him in my arms so that I could keep drinking deeply. I felt as though I were drawing his soul into me along with his blood. We had never been closer than this.

Mine, I thought. *Mine.*

Then Lucas went completely limp. He'd passed out. That realization crashed into me like a wave of cold water, shocking me out of the trance.

I gasped and let Lucas go. He fell bonelessly to the floor of the gazebo with a thud. The wide gash my teeth had left in his throat was dark and wet in the moonlight, glistening like spilled ink. A small stream of blood trickled across the wood and pooled around a small silver star that had fallen from my hair.

"Help," I choked out. It was hardly more than a whisper. My lips were still sticky and hot with Lucas's blood. "Somebody, please. Help!"

I stumbled down the gazebo steps, desperate to find someone, anyone. My parents would be furious—Mrs Bethany would be a thousand times worse—but somebody had to help Lucas. "Is anyone out there?"

"What is wrong with you?" Courtney stepped out of the woods, clearly annoyed. Her lacy white dress was rumpled, and I could see her date standing behind her; apparently I'd interrupted a hook-up session. "Wait—on your mouth—is that blood?"

"Lucas." I was too deep in shock to even try to explain. "Please. Help Lucas."

Courtney tossed her long blonde hair and stepped up into the gazebo to see Lucas lying there, his throat ripped open. She breathed, "Oh, my God." Then she turned back to me with a smug smile. "About time you grew up and became a vampire like the rest of us."

Chapter Eight

"DID I KILL LUCAS? IS HE OKAY?" I SOBBED. I couldn't stop crying. My mother's arm was around my shoulder; I blindly let her lead me away from the gazebo. My father had run ahead with Lucas's unconscious body in his arms. Some of the teachers were nearby, making sure none of the other students realized there was a disturbance. "Mom, what did I do?"

"Lucas's alive." Her voice had never sounded gentler. "He'll make it."

"Are you sure?"

"Pretty sure." We went up the stone steps, and I nearly stumbled over each one. My entire body was shaking so hard that I could barely walk. Mom stroked my hair, which had tumbled loose from its braids and hung limply around my face. "Honey, go up to our rooms, okay? Wash your face. Calm down."

I shook my head. "I want to be with Lucas."

"He won't even know you're there."

"Mom. *Please.*"

She started to refuse, but then I saw her realize that there was no point in arguing. "Come on."

My father had taken Lucas to the carriage house. When I first walked in, I wondered why there was an apartment in the carriage house, paneled with black-stained wood and hung with sepia-tinted photographs in old oval frames. Then I remembered that this was where Mrs Bethany lived. I was too shaken up even to be afraid of her. When I tried to push into the bedroom to see Lucas, Mom shook her head. "Wash your face with some cold water. Take a few deep breaths. Pull yourself together, honey. Then we'll talk." Smiling unevenly, she added, "Everything's all right. You'll see."

My clammy, trembling hands fumbled with the glass doorknob to the bathroom. As soon as I glimpsed my face in the mirror, I realized why my mother had kept telling me to wash my face. My lips were stained with Lucas's blood. A few drops had been smeared across my cheeks. Instantly I turned on the taps, desperate to clean away the evidence of what I'd done—but as the cool water began flowing over my fingers, I found myself looking at the bloodstains more closely. My lips were so red, and they were still swollen from our kisses.

Slowly, I traced the outline of my lips with the tip of my tongue. I could taste Lucas's blood, and it was as if he were as close to me in that moment as he had been in my arms.

So this is what it means, I thought. All my life, my parents had told me that someday blood would be more than blood, more than just something from the butcher's shop they gave me with my dinner. I had never been able to comprehend what they meant. Now I understood. In some ways, it really was just like my first kiss with Lucas; my body had known what I needed and wanted long before my mind could even guess.

Then I thought about Lucas, leaning back for my kiss and trusting me completely. Guilt made me start crying again, and then I splashed water on my face and the back of my neck. It took several minutes of deep breaths before I could walk out of the bathroom again.

Mrs Bethany's bed was a carved black monstrosity, with spiral columns that supported the canopy overhead. It was obviously centuries old. Unconscious in the center of the bed, Lucas was as pale as the bandage covering his throat, but he was breathing.

"He's all right," I whispered.

"You didn't drink enough blood to hurt him." My father looked at me for the first time since he'd run to the gazebo. I'd been afraid of seeing condemnation—or, given what I'd been doing when the urge to bite hit, embarrassment—but Dad was calm, even kind. "You have to make an effort to drink more than a pint or so at a time."

"Then why did Lucas pass out?"

"The bite does that to them," Mom said. By "them" she meant humans. Normally she made an effort not to draw a distinction, because she liked to say that people were people no matter what, but the dividing line between us had never been clearer. "It's like they're—hypnotized, maybe, or under a spell. They'll fight hard at first, but soon they slip into this trance."

"Good thing, too, because that means he won't remember a thing tomorrow." Dad held Lucas's wrist in his hand, checking the pulse. "We'll invent a story to tell him about the wound, something simple about an accident. That old gazebo has a couple of loose crossbars—maybe one of them could've fallen. Whacked him on the head."

"I don't like lying to Lucas."

Mom shook her head. "Honey, you've always understood that there are things that the people around us don't need to know."

"Lucas's not most people."

What I knew, and they didn't, was that Lucas was suspicious of Evernight Academy already. Of course he didn't know the truth about this place—if he had, he'd never have walked through the front door—but he understood that something was up, that there was more to this school than met the eye. I could be proud of Lucas's sharp instincts at the same time I recognized that they made everything a lot more difficult.

But how could I even think of telling him the truth? *Sorry I almost killed you last night?* I nodded slowly, accepting what I had to do. Lucas couldn't know how badly I'd failed him. He'd never forgive me—if he even believed me when I started talking about vampires. He might as easily think I'd gone insane.

"Okay," I conceded. "We have to lie. I understand."

"If only I understood," Mrs Bethany said crisply. She walked through the bedroom doorway, hands clasped in front of her. Instead of her usual lacy blouses and dark skirts, she wore a deep purple ball gown and black satin gloves that came up to her elbows. Black pearl earrings shimmered as she shook her head. "When we invited human students to join us here at Evernight, we knew there could be security troubles. We've lectured all our older students, monitored the hallways, kept the groups as separate as possible—and with good results, I thought. I would never have expected an outburst from *you*, Miss Olivier."

My parents both rose to their feet. At first I thought they were showing Mrs Bethany respect as their boss—they'd always deferred to her and taught me to do the same. But then my father stepped forward to defend me. "You know that Bianca isn't like the rest of us. This is the first time she's ever tasted living blood. She didn't realize how it could affect her."

Mrs Bethany's lips turned slightly upward in a prim, unpleasant smile. "Bianca is, of course, a special case. So few vampires are born, rather than made. Do you know, you're only the third one I've met since 1812?"

My parents had told me that only a handful of vampire babies were conceived every century; they'd been together for almost 350 years before Mom stunned them both by getting pregnant with me. I always thought they'd been exaggerating a little to make me feel unique. Now I realized it was the absolute truth.

Mrs Bethany wasn't done. "I would think that being raised by vampires—with a knowledge of our nature and our needs—wouldn't that be an advantage? A reason for more self-control, rather than less?"

"I'm sorry." I couldn't let my parents take the blame for this, not when it was my fault alone. "Dad and Mom always told me how it would happen someday. That I'd feel this need to bite. I still didn't understand, not really. Not until it happened to me."

She nodded, considering this. Her dark eyes flicked over to Lucas once, as if he were litter we'd left in her room. "He'll live? No permanent harm done, then. We'll assign Bianca's punishment tomorrow."

Mom shot me an apologetic glance. "Bianca has sworn to us she wouldn't do anything like this again."

"If word should get around the school that someone has bitten one of the new students and suffered no consequences, there will be other incidents." Mrs Bethany gathered her skirt in one hand. "Some of them might not end as well. It is vital that no more human students are so much as touched, as we cannot afford even a whisper of suspicion. Such a transgression must not go unpunished."

For the first time ever, Mrs Bethany and I were in complete agreement. I felt terrible for having hurt Lucas, and a few evenings of hall-cleaning duty were the least I deserved. But I saw one difficulty right away. "I can't have detention. Or be forced to clean up or anything like that."

Her eyebrows arched even higher. "Are you above such menial tasks?"

"If I'm being punished in some obvious way, Lucas will ask why. We don't want him to ask any questions. Right?"

I'd made my point. Mrs Bethany nodded once, but I could tell she was displeased that I'd bested her. "Then you will write a ten-page paper on—let us say—the use of the epistolary form in novels of the eighteenth and nineteenth centuries. Due in two weeks."

It was a measure of how depressed and freaked-out I already was that this assignment couldn't make me feel any worse.

Mrs Bethany stepped closer to me, the full skirts of her gown rustling like birds' wings. The fragrance of lavender curled around me like smoke. It was difficult for me to meet her eyes; I felt so exposed, so ashamed. "For more than two centuries, Evernight Academy has served as a sanctuary for our kind. Those of us who appear young enough to be students can come here to learn about how the world has changed, so that they can re-enter society and move freely without arousing suspicion. This is a place of learning. A place of safety. It can remain so only if the humans beyond our walls—and now, within our walls—have safety as well. If our students lose control and take human life, Evernight would soon come under suspicion. This sanctuary would fall.

Two centuries of tradition would end. I have safeguarded this school almost all that time, Miss Olivier. I do not intend to see the balance upset by you or by anyone. Am I quite clear?"

"Yes, ma'am," I whispered. "I'm so sorry. It won't happen again."

"You say that now." She glanced at Lucas, coolly curious. "We'll see what happens when Mr Ross wakes." Then she swept out to return to the ball.

It was strange to think that, just a few hundred feet away, people were still waltzing.

"I'll stay with Lucas," Dad said. "Celia, you take Bianca back to the school."

"I can't go back to my dorm room now. I want to be here when Lucas wakes up," I pleaded.

Mom shook her head. "It's better for you both if you're not. Your presence might remind him of what really happened, and Lucas needs to forget. I tell you what—come up to your old room. Just for tonight. Nobody will mind."

My snug turret room at the top of the tower had never sounded more welcoming. I even wanted to see the gargoyle again. "That sounds great. Thank you both so much, for everything." Tears welled in my eyes again. "You saved me and Lucas tonight."

"Don't be so melodramatic." Dad's smile softened his words. "Lucas would've lived no matter what. And you would've bitten somebody eventually. I wish you'd waited awhile, but I guess our little girl had to grow up sometime."

"Adrian?" My mother took Dad's hand and started pulling

him from the room. "We should talk about that thing."

"Thing? What thing?"

"The thing that's in the hallway."

"Oh." My dad got it about the same time I did. Mom had found an excuse to give me a moment alone with Lucas.

As soon as they'd gone, I sat on the edge of the bed by Lucas's side. He was still handsome, despite his pale skin and the dark circles beneath his eyes. His bronze hair looked almost brown next to his pallor, and when I lay my hand on his forehead, he was cool to the touch.

"I'm so sorry I hurt you." A hot tear trickled down my cheek. Poor Lucas, always trying to protect me from danger. He'd never guessed that I was the dangerous one.

Later that night, I stared at my beautiful dress, now stained with blood. Mom had hung it on the hook on my bedroom door. "I thought the dance was going to be so perfect," I whispered.

"I wish it could've been, honey." She sat beside my bed, stroking my hair, the way she used to when I was small. "Everything will be better in the morning. You'll see."

"You're sure Lucas won't be a vampire when he wakes up?"

"I'm sure. Lucas didn't lose nearly enough blood to put his life in danger. And this is the first time you've bitten him—right?"

"Right." I sniffled.

"Only people who have been bitten multiple times become vampires, and even then only when the last bite is fatal. And like we told you, killing someone by drinking their blood is actually pretty hard work. No matter what, you have to die to become a vampire, and Lucas's not going to die."

"I'm a vampire, and I never died."

"That's different, honey. You know that. You were born special." Mom touched my chin, turning my head so that we faced each other. Behind her I could see the gargoyle grinning at us, like an eavesdropper. "*You* won't become a true vampire until you kill someone. When you do that, you'll die too— but only for a little while. It'll be just like taking a nap."

My parents had told me all of this, of course, a thousand times at least, just like they told me to brush my teeth before bed or to get a full name and phone number if somebody called while they were out. Most vampires never killed anyone, they said, and even though I couldn't imagine hurting anyone, they insisted there were ways to do it that would be okay. We'd been over and over my eventual transformation: I could go to a hospital or nursing home, find someone really old or near death, and do it that way. They'd always told me it would be that simple—ending someone's suffering, maybe even giving them the chance to live forever as a vampire, too, if we planned ahead and made sure I would have more than one opportunity to drink. The explanation was nice and neat, the way they liked me to leave my room.

What had happened between Lucas and me had proved that reality wasn't as tidy as my parents' explanations.

"I don't have to become a vampire before I'm ready," I said. That was another thing they'd told me countless times, and I expected my mother to agree automatically.

Instead she was quiet for a few moments. "We'll see, Bianca. We'll see."

"What do you mean?"

"You've tasted the blood of a living person. Basically, you've turned over the hourglass—your body will begin reacting like a vampire now, sometimes." I must have looked terrified, because she squeezed my hand. "Don't worry. It's not like you have to change this week or even this year, probably. But your need to do the things we do will be stronger now, and get stronger all the time. Besides all that, you care about Lucas. The two of you will be very—well, drawn together now. When your body is changing as fast as your heart, it's a powerful combination." Mom leaned her head against the wall, and I wondered if she was remembering the mid-1600s, when she was alive and Dad was a handsome, mysterious stranger. "Try not to get in over your head."

"I'll be strong," I promised.

"I know you'll try, honey. That's all we can ask."

What did she mean by that? I didn't know, and I should've asked. But I couldn't. The future was rushing toward me too quickly, and I felt as tired as if I'd been awake for days. I closed my eyes tightly as I pressed my face into my pillow and longed for the forgetfulness of sleep.

Even before I opened my eyes the next morning, I could tell the difference.

Every sense was sharper. I could feel almost every thread

in the sheets against my skin, and I heard not only my parents talking in the front room but sounds from several floors below us—Professor Iwerebon yelling at someone who was trying to sneak in after a night of partying, footsteps on the stone floors, a leaky faucet somewhere. If I'd tried, I might have been able to count the leaves rustling in the tree outside. When I opened my eyes, the daylight was almost blinding.

At first I thought my parents must have been wrong. I'd become a true vampire overnight, and that meant that Lucas was—

No. My heart was still beating. While I lived, Lucas lived. I couldn't die and complete my transformation into a vampire until I had taken a life.

But if that was the case, what was happening to me?

During breakfast, Dad explained. "You're feeling the first hints of what it's going to be like when you change. You drank blood from a human being; now you know how it affects you. It gets even more powerful later."

"I hate it." I was squinting against the light in our kitchen. Even the oatmeal Mom had given me tasted overpoweringly strong; it was like I could sense the root and the stalk and the dirt of where the oats had come from. My morning glass of blood, on the other hand, had never been blander. I'd always thought it tasted good, but now I realized it was a pale imitation of what I was supposed to be drinking. "How do you take this?"

"It's not always as vivid as it feels at first. For you, today, it will probably wear off in another hour or two." Mom patted my shoulder. She had her glass of blood in her other hand, apparently satisfied with it. "As for later—well, you get used to the reactions after a while. Good thing, too. Otherwise none of us would ever get any sleep."

My head was already pounding from the stimulation. I'd never had more than a half a beer in my life, but I suspected this was a lot like a hangover. "I'd rather not get used to it, thanks."

"Bianca." Dad's voice was sharp with the anger he hadn't shown last night. Even Mom looked surprised. "Never let me hear you talk like that again."

"Dad—I just meant—"

"You have a destiny, Bianca. You were born to be a vampire. You've never questioned that before, and I don't intend for you to start now. Am I clear?" He grabbed his glass and stalked out of the room.

"Clear," I said feebly to the space where he'd been.

By the time I went downstairs in jeans and my pale-yellow hoodie, my senses were already going back to normal. In some ways, I felt relieved. The brightness and din had nearly overwhelmed me, and at least I didn't have to hear Courtney bitching about her hair anymore. Yet I felt a kind of loss, too. What had been my normal world now felt strangely quiet and far away.

All that really mattered was that I felt better and could visit Lucas. After what had happened, I knew he couldn't possibly be up and around, but at least I could visit him in Mrs Bethany's apartment. He'd be so horrified, waking up there, and who knew what story Mrs Bethany had told him?

Even thinking about that made my body tense up, as if anticipating a blow. Mom swore that Lucas wouldn't remember, but how could that be true? I hadn't thought about it at the time, but I realized that my bite had to have hurt like hell. He would have been shocked and angry and probably frightened, too. I knew I should hope that he'd forgotten it all, but then I would wonder if he'd forgotten our kisses, too. Regardless, it was time to face what I'd done.

I set out across the grounds, ignoring the few students playing rugby on the far corner of the lawn, though I saw some of them glancing in my direction and heard some vaguely dirty laughter. Courtney had been talking, no doubt; probably every vampire in the school knew what I'd done. Ashamed and angry, I hurried toward the carriage house— and stopped mid-step as I saw Lucas walking toward me. He recognized me and raised one hand, almost bashful.

I wanted to run away. Lucas deserved better than that, so I would have to overcome my shame. Forcing myself to go toward him, I called, "Lucas? Are you okay?"

"Yeah." The leaves crunched under his feet as we finally met. "Jesus, what happened?"

My mouth felt dry. "Didn't they tell you?"

"They told me, but—a crossbar hit me in the head? Seriously?" His cheeks were flushed with embarrassment, and he almost seemed angry—at the gazebo or gravity or something. I'd seen Lucas lose his cool before, but I'd never seen him like this. "Gashed my neck open on the stupid cast-iron railing—that has got to be about the lamest— I'm just hacked off something had to get in the way while I was kissing you for the first time."

Somebody bolder would've kissed Lucas again right then. I just gaped at him. He looked fine, basically. Lucas was still pale, and a thick white bandage covered the side of his neck, but otherwise it could have been any other day. In the distance, I could see that a few people were watching us curiously. I tried to ignore the fact that we had an audience.

"I thought—I mean, I guess—" Before I could get any more incoherent, I quickly said, "At first I thought you fainted. Sometimes I have that effect on guys. It's too intense. They can't take it."

Lucas laughed. The sound was sort of hollow, but he was laughing. It was really okay; he really didn't know a thing. Relieved, I put my arms around him and hugged him tight. Lucas held me, too, and for a few moments we stood there, wrapped in each other, and I could pretend nothing had gone wrong at all.

His hair gleamed like bronze in the sunlight, and I breathed in the scent of him, so much like the woods that surrounded us. It felt so good, the knowledge that he was mine—I could hold him like this, out in the open, because we belonged to each other now. And every second we touched, the memories became stronger: kissing him, feeling his hands on my back, the salty softness of his skin between my teeth and hot blood gushing into my mouth.

Mine.

Now I knew what my mother had meant. Biting a human wasn't as simple as taking a sip from a glass. When I drank Lucas's blood, he became a part of me—and I became a part of him. We were bound now, in ways I couldn't control and Lucas could never understand.

Did that make the way he held me less real? I closed my eyes tightly and hoped it didn't. It was too late to do anything else.

"Bianca?" he murmured into my hair.

"Yeah?"

"Last night—I just fell into the railing like that? Mrs Bethany told me how it went down, but it seems to me— Well, I don't remember any of it. But you do? You remember?"

His old suspicions about Evernight must've been kicking in again. The obvious thing to do was say yes. I couldn't bring myself to do it; it was one lie too many. "Kind of. I mean, it was all really confusing, and I—I guess I panicked. It's all kind of a blur, if you want to know the truth."

That was the worst dodge imaginable, but to my astonishment, Lucas seemed to believe it. He relaxed in my arms and nodded, like he understood everything now. "I'll never let you down again. I promise."

"You never let me down, Lucas. You never could." Guilt crushed me, and I clung to him more tightly. "I won't let you down either."

I'll keep you safe from every danger, I swore. *Even from myself.*

Chapter Nine

AFTER THAT, IT SEEMED AS IF I LIVED IN TWO worlds at once. In one of them, Lucas and I were finally together. That felt like the place I'd always wanted to be my whole life. In the other, I was a liar who didn't deserve to be with Lucas or anyone.

"It just seems weird to me." Lucas's whisper was pitched low, so that it wouldn't carry through the library.

"What seems weird?"

Lucas glanced around before he answered me, to make sure nobody would overhear. He needn't have worried. We sat in one of the far archways, one lined with hand-bound books a couple of centuries old—one of the most private corners of the school. "That neither of us really remembers that night."

"You got hurt." When in doubt, I stuck to the story that Mrs Bethany had come up with. Lucas didn't wholly buy it yet, but in time he would. He had to. Everything depended on that. "Lots of times, people forget what happened just before they got hurt. It makes sense, doesn't it? That iron scroll-work is sharp."

"I've kissed girls before . . ." His words trailed off as he saw the look on my face. "Nobody like you. Nobody even close to you."

I ducked my head to hide my embarrassed smile.

Lucas continued, "Anyway, it doesn't make me pass out. Not ever. You are a seriously great kisser—trust me on that—but not even you could make me black out."

"That's not why you passed out," I suggested, pretending that I really wanted to go back to reading the gardening book I'd found; the only reason I'd picked it up in the first place was some lingering curiosity about what the flower was that I'd glimpsed in my dream months before. "You passed out because this huge iron bar whacked you in the head. Hello."

"That doesn't explain why *you* don't remember."

"You know I have some problems with anxiety, right? I freak out sometimes. When we first met, I was in the middle of a huge freak-out. Huge! There are parts of my great escape that I don't remember very well either. When you got hit in the head, I probably freaked out again. I mean, you could've been killed." That part, at least, was close to the truth. "No wonder I was scared."

"There's no bump on my head. Just a bruise, like I fell or something."

"We put an ice pack on it. We took care of you."

Unconvinced, Lucas said, "Still doesn't make sense."

"I don't know why you're still thinking about this." Even saying that made me a liar again, and worse than before. Sticking to the story was something that I had to do for Lucas's own protection, because if Mrs Bethany ever realized that he knew something was up, she might—might—oh, I didn't know what she might do, but I suspected it wouldn't be good. But telling Lucas that he was wrong to have doubts, that the good and sensible questions he had about Evernight and his memory lapse that night were just foolishness—that was worse. That was asking Lucas to doubt himself, and I didn't want to do that. I now knew how bad it felt, doubting yourself. "Please, Lucas, let it go."

Lucas slowly nodded. "We'll talk about it some other time."

When he dropped the subject and stopped worrying about the night of the Autumn Ball, our time together was wonderful. Almost perfect. We studied together in the library or in my mother's classroom, sometimes with Vic or Raquel along. We ate lunch together on the grounds, sandwiches wrapped in brown bags and stuffed into our coat pockets. I daydreamed about him during class, rousing myself from my happy stupor only as often as I had to in order to keep from flunking out. On the days when we had chemistry together, we walked to and from Iwerebon's room, side by side. Other days, he found me as soon as classes were over, as if he'd been thinking about me even more than I'd been thinking about him.

"Face it," Lucas whispered to me one Sunday afternoon

when I'd invited him up to my parents' apartment. (They had tactfully greeted us, then let us hang out in my room for the rest of the day.) We lay together on the floor, not touching but close beside each other, staring up at the Klimt print. "I don't know anything about art."

"You don't have to know anything about it. You just have to look at it and say what you feel."

"I'm not so great at saying what I feel."

"Yeah, I noticed. Just give it a try, okay?"

"Well, okay." He thought about it long and hard, staring up at *The Kiss* all the while. "I guess—I guess I like the way he's holding her face in his hands. Like she's the one thing in the world that makes him happy, that really belongs to him."

"Do you really see that in the painting? To me he looks— strong, I guess." The man in *The Kiss* certainly looked in control of the situation to me; the swooning woman seemed to like it that way, at least for the moment.

Lucas turned to me, and I let my head loll to one side so that we were face-to-face. The way that he looked at me— intent, serious, filled with longing—made me hold my breath. He said only, "Trust me. I know I got that one right."

We kissed each other, and then Dad picked the perfect moment to call us for our dinner. Parental timing is uncanny. They made the most of dinner, even eating food and acting like they enjoyed it.

Being close to Lucas meant that I had less time to be with my other friends, though I wished it didn't. Balthazar was still as kind as ever, always greeting me in the hallway and nodding to Lucas, as though Lucas were his pal and not someone who had nearly tackled him the night of the Autumn Ball. But his eyes were sad, and I knew that I'd hurt Balthazar by not giving him a chance.

Raquel was lonely, too. Even though we invited her along for study nights sometimes, she and I never shared lunch anymore. She hadn't made any other friends that I knew of. Lucas and I had a half-baked idea of setting her up with Vic, but the two of them simply didn't click. They hung out together with us and had fun, but that was that.

I apologized to her once for spending less time with her, but she blew it off. "You're in love. That makes you actually kind of boring to people who aren't in love. You know, the sane ones."

"I'm not boring," I protested. "At least not more than I was before."

Raquel responded by clasping her hands together and looking up at the library ceiling with her eyes slightly unfocused. "Did you know that Lucas likes sunshine? He does! Flowers and bunny rabbits, too. Now let me tell you all about the fascinating laces in Lucas's fascinating shoes."

"Shut *up*." I swatted her shoulder, and she laughed. Still, I felt the odd distance between us. "I don't mean to leave you alone."

"You don't. We're cool." Raquel opened her biology textbook, obviously ready to drop the subject.

Carefully, I said, "You seem okay with Lucas."

She shrugged and didn't look up from her book. "Sure. Shouldn't I be?"

"Just—some of the stuff we talked about before—it's not a problem. Really." Raquel had been so sure that Lucas might attack me, never realizing that it was the other way around. "I want you to see him for who he is."

"A fabulous, wonderful guy who loves sunshine and barfs roses." Raquel was joking but not quite joking. When she met my eyes at last, she sighed. "He seems okay."

I knew I wouldn't get any further with her that day, so I changed the subject.

While my best friend at Evernight wasn't thrilled that I was with Lucas, a lot of my worst enemies thought it was a great idea. They were actually *glad* I'd bitten him.

"I knew you'd get with the program eventually," Courtney said to me in Modern Technology, the one class no human students had been enrolled in. "You're a born vampire. That's, like, super-rare and powerful and stuff. There was no way you could stay an enormous loser forever."

"Wow, thanks, Courtney," I said flatly. "Can we talk about something else?"

"Don't see why you're all weird about it." Erich gave me a smarmy grin while he fiddled with the day's assignment, an iPod. "I mean, I figure any guy as greasy as Lucas Ross has an aftertaste, but hey, fresh blood is fresh blood."

"We should all get to snack sometimes," Gwen insisted.

"Hello, this school now comes complete with a walking buffet, and nobody gets to take a bite?" A few people mumbled agreement.

"Everyone pay attention," demanded Mr Yee, our teacher. Like all other teachers at Evernight, he was an extremely powerful vampire—one who had remained part of the world for a very long time and yet retained his edge. Mr Yee wasn't especially old; he'd told us that he'd died in the 1880s. But his strength and authority radiated from him almost as powerfully as they did from Mrs Bethany. That was why each of the students, even those centuries older than him, gave him respect. At his command, we all fell silent. "You've had a few minutes with the iPods now. Your first questions?"

Patrice raised her hand first. "You said that most electronic devices can establish wireless connections now. But it doesn't seem like this one does."

"Very good, Patrice." When Mr Yee praised her, Patrice shot me a grateful smile. I'd talked her through the whole idea of wireless communications a few times. "This limitation is one of the few design flaws of the iPod. Subsequent models are likely to incorporate some form of wireless connection, and, of course, there's also the iPhone—which we'll cover next week."

"If the information inside the iPod actually re-creates the song," Balthazar said thoughtfully, "then the sound quality would depend completely on what kind of speakers or headphones you used. Right?"

"Mostly, yes. There are superior recording formats, but

any casual listener and even some pros wouldn't be able to tell the difference, as long as the iPod was hooked up to a superior audio system. Anyone else?" Mr Yee looked around the room and then sighed. "Yes, Ranulf?"

"What spirits animate this box?"

"We've been over this." Putting his hands on Ranulf's desk, Mr Yee slowly said, "No spirits animate any of the machines we've studied in class. Or will study, moving forward. In fact, no spirits animate any machines at all. Is that finally clear?"

Ranulf nodded slowly but didn't look convinced. He wore his brown hair in a pudding-bowl haircut and had an open, guileless face. After a moment, he ventured, "What about the spirits of the metal from which this box is made?"

Mr Yee slumped, as if defeated. "Is there anyone from the medieval period who might be able to help Ranulf with the transition here?" Genevieve nodded and went to his side.

"God, it's not that hard—it's just, like, a turbo Walkman or something." Courtney shot Ranulf a skeptical glare. She was one of the few at Evernight who never seemed to have lost touch with the modern world; as far as I could tell, Courtney had mostly come here to socialize. Worse luck for the rest of us. I sighed and went back to creating a new playlist with my favorite songs for Lucas. Modern Technology really was too easy for me.

Weirdly, the place where it was hardest to forget the trouble lurking just beneath the surface was English class. Our folklore studies were behind us, and now we were making a review of the classics and digging into Jane Austen, one of my favorites. I thought there was no way I could go wrong there. Mrs Bethany's class was like some mirror universe for literature, someplace where everything got turned on its head, including me. Even books I'd read before and knew inside out became strange in her classroom, as if they'd been translated into some rough, guttural foreign language. But *Pride and Prejudice*—that would be different. Or so I thought.

"Charlotte Lucas is desperate." I'd actually raised my hand, *volunteering* to get called on. Why did I ever think that was a good idea? "In that day and age, if women didn't get married, they were, well, nobody. They could never have money or homes of their own. If they didn't want to be a burden on their parents for forever, they had to marry." I couldn't believe I needed to tell *her* that.

"Interesting," Mrs Bethany said. "Interesting" was her synonym for "wrong." I started to sweat. She walked in a slow circle around the room, and the afternoon sunlight glinted on the gold brooch at the throat of her frilly lace blouse. I could see the grooves in her long, thick nails. "Tell me, was Jane Austen married?"

"No."

"She was proposed to, once. Her family was quite clear on that point in their various memoirs. A man of means offered his hand in marriage to Jane Austen, but she refused him. Did she have to get married, Miss Olivier?"

"Well, no, but she was a writer. Her books would've made—"

"Less money than you might think." Mrs Bethany was pleased I'd walked into her trap. Only now did I see that the folklore section of our reading had been to teach the vampires how twenty-first-century society thought about the supernatural, and that the classics were ways of studying how attitudes were different between their histories and now. "The Austen family was not especially wealthy. Whereas the Lucases—were they poor?"

"No," Courtney piped up. Since she was no longer bothering to put me down, I figured she was doing it to get Balthazar to look at her. Since the ball, she'd renewed her efforts to win him over, but as far as I could tell, he was still unmoved. Courtney continued, "The father is Sir William Lucas, the only member of the gentry in town. They're wealthy enough that Charlotte doesn't have to marry anybody, not if she doesn't really want to."

"Do you think she really wants to marry Mr Collins?" I retorted. "He's a pompous idiot."

Courtney shrugged. "She wants to be married, and he's a means to an end."

Mrs Bethany nodded approvingly. "So, Charlotte is merely using Mr Collins. She believes she is acting from necessity; he believes that he is acting from love, or at least the proper regard for a potential wife. Mr Collins is honest. Charlotte is not." I thought about the lies I'd told Lucas, gripping the edges of my notebook so hard that the crisp paper edges seemed to slice into my fingertips. Mrs Bethany must've known what I was feeling, because she continued, "Doesn't the deceived man deserve our pity instead of our scorn?"

I wished I could sink into the floor.

Then Balthazar gave me an encouraging smile, the way he used to, and I knew that even if we weren't hanging out any longer, at least we were still friends. In fact, none of the Evernight types were looking down their noses at me like they used to. Even if I wasn't really a vampire yet, I'd proved something to them. Maybe I was "in the club."

In some ways, it felt like I'd gotten away with something—that I'd pulled off a trick of some kind—closed my eyes and said abracadabra and turned the whole world upside down. When I was holding hands with Lucas, laughing after class at one of his jokes, I could believe that everything was going to be better from now on.

That wasn't true, though. It couldn't be true as long as I was deceiving Lucas.

Before, I'd never thought of keeping my family's secret from Lucas as lying; I'd been taught to keep that secret since I was a tiny child, drinking blood from the butcher's shop out of my bottle. Now I knew how close I'd come to hurting him, and my secret didn't seem innocent any longer.

Lucas and I kissed constantly—all the time, before breakfast in the morning, as we went to our different dorm areas at night, and basically pretty much any other time we could be alone together for an instant. However, I always stopped us before we got carried away. Sometimes I wanted more, and I could tell Lucas did too from the way he watched me, paying attention to how I moved or the way my fingers wrapped around his wrist. He never pushed me, though. When I lay alone at night, my fantasies became even wilder and more desperate. Now I knew what Lucas's mouth felt like on mine, and I could imagine his touch against my bare skin with a clarity that startled me.

But when I had those fantasies now, the same image always bubbled up: my teeth sinking into Lucas's throat.

There were times I thought I would do anything to taste Lucas's blood again. That was when I was the most frightened.

"What do you think?" I modeled the old-fashioned velvet hat for Lucas, thinking that he would laugh; surely the deep purple of the fabric looked bizarre next to my red hair.

Instead he smiled at me in a way that made me feel warm all over. "You're beautiful."

We were in a secondhand clothing shop in Riverton, enjoying our second weekend in town together much more than the first. My parents had taken chaperone duty at the theater again, so we'd decided to skip our chance to see *The Maltese Falcon*. Instead we ran in and out of the shops that were still open, looking at posters and books, and dealing with some eye rolling from the clerks behind the counter, who were clearly sick of teenagers from "that school" running amok.

Too bad for them, because we were having a great time.

I took a white fur stole from a shelf and draped it around my shoulders. "What do you think?"

"Fur is dead." Lucas said it sort of wryly, but maybe he didn't think people should wear fur at all. I personally felt like vintage things ought to be okay; the animals had died decades and decades ago, so it wasn't like you were doing any more harm. All the same, I hastily took the stole off.

Lucas, meanwhile, tried on a gray tweed overcoat he'd dug out of an overstuffed rack in the back. Like the rest of the shop, it smelled sort of musty, but in a good way, and the coat looked amazing on him. "That's sort of Sherlock Holmesy," I said. "If Sherlock Holmes were sexy."

He laughed. "Some girls go for the intellectual type, you know."

"Aren't you lucky I'm not one of them?"

Fortunately, he liked it when I teased him. He grabbed me, arms around my arms so that I couldn't even hug him back, and kissed me soundly on the forehead. "You're impossible," he murmured. "But you're worth it."

The way he held me, my face was buried in the curve of his neck; all I could see were the faint pink lines on his throat, the scars of my own bite. "I'm glad you think so."

"I know so."

I wasn't going to argue with him. There was no reason my one terrible mistake couldn't remain just that—one mistake, never to be repeated.

Lucas's finger brushed along my cheek, a gentle touch like

the soft tip of a paintbrush. Klimt's *Kiss* flickered in my mind, gold and gauzy, and for a moment it was as though Lucas and I really had been drawn into the painting with all its beauty and its need. Hidden behind the racks as we were, lost in a maze of old, cracked leather and wrinkled satin and rhinestone buckles dulled with time, Lucas and I could've kissed for hours without being found. I imagined it for a moment— Lucas placing a black fur coat on the floor, laying me atop it, lowering himself over me—

I pressed my lips against his neck, right on the scars, the way my mother used to kiss a bruise or scrape to make it better. His pulse was strong. Lucas tensed, and I thought maybe I'd gone too far.

It can't be easy for him either, I told myself. *Sometimes I think I'm going to go crazy if I don't touch him, so how much worse must it be for Lucas? Especially since he can't know the reasons why.*

The jingling of bells jolted us out of our trance. We both peeked around the corner to see who had come in. "Vic!" Lucas shook his head. "I should've known you'd show up here."

Vic sauntered toward us, thumbs beneath the lapels of the striped blazer he wore beneath his winter coat. "This style doesn't put itself together, you know. It takes effort to look this good." He then groaned as he looked longingly at Lucas's tweed overcoat. "You tall guys get all the best stuff, man."

"I'm not buying this." Lucas shrugged it off, ready to leave. Probably he wanted to give us a few more moments of privacy; it was almost time to return to the bus. I knew how he felt. As much as I liked Vic, I didn't really want him tagging along.

"You're crazy, Lucas. Something like that fit me? I'd snap it up." Vic sighed. He looked dangerously close to accompanying us out to the bus.

I thought fast. "You know, in the back of the store, I think I saw some ties painted with hula girls."

"Seriously?" Just like that, Vic was gone, pushing his way through the clothes display in search of hula ties.

"Good work." Lucas pulled the hat from my head, then took my hand. "Let's go."

We were almost to the door when we walked past the jewelry rack, and a dark, glittering object caught my eye. A brooch, carved of something that was as black as the night sky but shone brilliantly: I realized that it was a pair of flowers, exotic and sharp petaled, just like the one in my dream. The brooch was small enough to fit in my palm and intricately carved, but what amazed me the most was how much it looked like a flower that I had started to think only existed in my imagination. I had stopped in my tracks to stare at it. "Look, Lucas. It's so beautiful."

"That's genuine Whitby jet. Victorian-era mourning jewelry." The saleslady peered at us over the lenses of her blue-rimmed reading glasses, trying to evaluate whether we were potential customers or kids who needed to be scared off. Probably she decided on the latter, because she added, "Very expensive."

Lucas didn't like being challenged. "How expensive?" he

said coolly, like his last name was Rockefeller instead of Ross.

"Two hundred dollars."

My eyes probably bugged out. When your parents are schoolteachers, you don't get the biggest allowance in the world. The only thing I'd ever bought that cost more than two hundred dollars was my telescope, and my parents had chipped in for that. I laughed a little, trying to disguise my embarrassment and the sadness I felt at having to leave the brooch behind. Each black petal was more beautiful than the last.

Lucas simply pulled out his wallet and offered the clerk a credit card. "We'll take it."

She raised an eyebrow but took the card and started ringing up the purchase. "Lucas!" I grabbed his arm and tried to speak under my breath. "You can't."

"Can, too."

"But it's two hundred dollars!"

"You love it," he said quietly. "I can tell by the look in your eyes. If you love it, you should have it."

The brooch still sat in the display case. I stared down at it, trying to imagine anything so beautiful belonging to me. "I do—love it, I mean, but—Lucas, I don't want you in debt because of me."

"Since when do poor people attend Evernight?"

Okay, he had a point there. For some reason, I'd never really thought about the fact that Lucas must be wealthy. Vic, too, probably. Raquel was a scholarship kid, but there were only a handful of those. Most of the human students were actually paying through the nose for the chance to be surrounded by vampires—though, of course, they didn't realize that last part. They didn't come across like snobs, probably because they didn't have a chance. The ones who *really* acted like entitled rich kids were the ones who'd been saving money for centuries or who bought IBM stock back when the typewriter was a newfangled invention. The hierarchy at Evernight was so strict—vampires on top, humans hardly worthy of notice—that I hadn't realized that most of the human kids came from money, too.

Then I remembered that Lucas had tried to tell me once about his mother and how controlling she could be. They'd traveled all around, even lived in Europe, and he'd said that his grandfather or great-grandfather or somebody had attended Evernight as well, at least until he got expelled for dueling. I should've realized he wasn't poor.

Not that this was a bad surprise. In my opinion, all boyfriends should turn out to be secretly wealthy. But it reminded me that, as much as I adored Lucas, we were still only beginning to learn about each other.

And that made me remember the secrets I kept.

The saleslady offered to wrap up the brooch, but Lucas took it and pinned it on my winter coat. I kept tracing the sharp-carved petals with one finger as we walked out into the town square, hand in hand. "Thank you. This is the best gift anyone's ever bought for me."

"Then it's the best money I ever spent."

I ducked my head, bashful and happy. We would've gone

on being mushy for a while if we hadn't walked into the town square and found the students milling around the bus, talking animatedly with each other with absolutely no teachers around. "Why is everybody standing around like that? How come they aren't boarding the bus yet?"

Lucas blinked, obviously thrown off by the sudden change in subject. "Uh, I don't know." Then, more focused, he continued, "You're right. They should've started calling us by now."

We walked down into the crowd of students. "What's going on?" I asked Rodney, a guy I knew from chemistry.

"It's Raquel. She's taken off."

That couldn't be right. I insisted, "She wouldn't leave by herself. She gets scared easily."

"Really? She always seemed kinda standoffish to me." Vic joined us in the crowd, holding a clear plastic bag stuffed with garish ties. Then Rodney paused, like he realized it might not be good manners to speak badly about the missing person. "I saw her earlier at the diner. Some townie kid was trying to talk to her and striking out. I didn't run into her after that."

I grabbed Lucas's hand. "Do you think that guy's done something to her?"

"She could just be running late." Lucas was trying to be reassuring, but he wasn't doing a very good job.

Vic shrugged. "Hey, maybe he finally said the right thing and she's making out with him right now."

Raquel wouldn't ever do that. She was too cautious and too distrustful to ever impulsively hook up with a guy she didn't know. Guiltily, I wished that I'd asked her to hang out with Lucas and me instead of leaving her on her own.

My father walked into the town square, his forehead furrowed. I realized that he was even more concerned than I was. Dad said only, "Everyone, get on the bus and head back. We'll find Raquel, so don't worry."

"I'll stay and look for her, too." I stepped toward my father and away from Lucas. "We're friends. I can think of a few places she might have gone."

"Okay." Dad nodded. "Everybody else, get going."

Lucas put one hand on my shoulder. This wasn't the romantic farewell I'd planned earlier. He wasn't selfishly disappointed, however. All I saw was concern for Raquel and for me. "I ought to stay behind, too, help you guys out."

"They won't let you. I'm sort of surprised they let me."

"It's dangerous," he said quietly.

My heart went out to him—desperate to protect me, completely unaware how well I could protect myself. I said the only thing that I thought might reassure him. "My father will look out for me." I went up on tiptoe to kiss Lucas's cheek, then brushed my fingers across the brooch again. "Thank you. So much."

Lucas didn't like leaving me behind, but mentioning my dad had done the trick. He kissed me quickly. "I'll see you tomorrow."

As the bus pulled away, my father and I began hurrying toward the outskirts of town. Dad said, "Do you really know where she might've gone?"

"Not a clue," I admitted. "But you need every searcher you can get. Besides, what if you need somebody to cross the river?" Vampires don't like running water. It didn't bother me at all—at least, not yet—but it drove my parents crazy to cross even a small stream or brook.

"My girl can take care of herself." Dad's pride caught me off guard, but in a good way. "You're really growing up here, Bianca. Your time at Evernight—it's changing you for the better."

I rolled my eyes, tired of the father-knows-best routine already. "That's what happens when you survive adversity."

"News flash: that's high school."

"You act like you actually went to high school."

"Trust me, adolescence was lousy in the eleventh century, too. Humanity changes all the time, but there are a few constants. People get stupid when they're in love; people want what they can't have; and the years between ages twelve and eighteen always, always suck." Dad became serious again as we left the main road. "We don't have anyone on the west side of the river. Stay close to the bank if you're worried about losing your way."

"I can't get lost." I pointed upward at the bright, starry sky, where all the constellations waited to guide me. "See you later."

Although we hadn't yet seen our first snowfall, winter had claimed the countryside. The earth beneath my feet was crisp with frost, and dead grasses and leafless shrubs scraped against my jeans legs as I made my way along the riverbank. Pale beech trunks stood out from the other trees like lightning bolts in a stormy sky. I ended up staying fairly close to the water, not because I was worried about getting lost but because Raquel might be—and if she'd wandered this way, she'd have wanted the river to give her some direction.

She wouldn't have wandered off. If Raquel came this way, it isn't as simple as her being lost.

My overactive imagination, always quick to supply worst-case scenarios, kept flashing terrible scenes in my mind: Raquel robbed by some townie who wanted to steal from one of the "rich kids" at that school. Raquel trying to run from the drunken construction workers I'd seen in the pizza place, transformed by my fear from protectors of women to predators. Raquel overcome by whatever sadness it was that haunted her, walking into the icy waters of the river and being sucked down by its powerful current.

A swift, rushing sound above me made me jump, but it was only a crow, flapping from branch to branch. I breathed out in relief—then realized that, further to the west, there was a spot of brightness in the bushes.

I hurried in that direction, running as quickly as I could. Once, I opened my mouth to call Raquel's name, then shut it again without calling. If it was Raquel ahead, I'd find out soon enough. If it wasn't, I might not want to draw attention.

As I got closer, my breathing now heavy from exertion, I heard Raquel's voice. Whatever gladness I might've felt was destroyed by her frightened words: "Leave me alone!"

"Hey, what's the problem?" I knew that voice—too confident, slyly mocking. "You keep acting like we'd never met before."

It was Erich. He hadn't come into town on the school trip. None of the "Evernight types" had. They seemed to consider it boring—or, more likely, they were simply eager for some time to hang out and be themselves without having to hide their true natures. At the moment, though, Erich looked like he was way too close to his true nature. Apparently he'd followed us into Riverton and waited to find somebody who walked off alone—and that was Raquel.

"I told you I didn't want to talk to you," Raquel insisted. She was terrified. Normally she came across as tough, but Erich's stalking had scared her past that. "So stop following me."

"You act like I'm a stranger." He smiled. His teeth were white in the darkness, and I remembered films I'd seen of sharks. "We sit next to each other in biology, Raquel. What's the problem? What's the worst thing I could do?"

Now I knew what had happened. Erich had found Raquel on her own in town and started following her. Instead of waiting in the square with everyone else, where she would've had to put up with his presence or maybe even ended up sitting with him on the shuttle bus, she'd tried to slip away. In the process, she'd gone farther and farther from the center of Riverton, then out of town altogether. By then she would've known she'd made a mistake, but by then he had her out here alone. She'd walked almost two miles toward school, despite the coldness of the night, and I felt a flare of pride in Raquel's courage and stubbornness.

Okay, it had also been stupid, but she had a right to expect that one of her classmates wouldn't try to kill her.

"You know what?" Erich said casually. "I'm hungry."

Raquel's face paled. She couldn't have known what Erich really meant by that, but she sensed what I sensed. What had been taunting was about to become something else. The energy between them was changing from potential to kinetic. She said, "I'm going."

"We'll see where you go," he replied.

I yelled, as loudly as I could, "Hey!"

Both Raquel and Erich whirled around to see me. Raquel's face instantly melted in relief. "Bianca!"

"This is none of your business," Erich snapped. "Back off."

That startled me. I'd assumed he would be the one backing off as soon as he'd been caught in the act. Apparently not. Normally this would be the moment when I started getting terrified, but I didn't. I felt adrenaline pumping through me, but I wasn't going cold or getting shaky. Instead, my muscles tensed with the same kind of anticipation you feel before a race. My sense of smell sharpened so that I could detect Raquel's sweat, Erich's cheap aftershave, even the fur of small mice in the underbrush. I swallowed hard, and my tongue brushed against my incisors, which were lengthening slowly in my excitement.

You'll start reacting like a vampire, my mother had said.

This was part of what she'd meant.

"I'm not leaving. You are." I stepped closer to them, and Raquel stumbled toward me, trembling too hard to really run.

Erich's irritation made him scowl. He looked like a petulant child denied an after-school snack. "What, are you the only one allowed to break the rules?"

"Break the rules?" Raquel's voice was confused, near hysteria. "Bianca, what is he talking about? Can we get out of here?"

I went pale. He smirked at me. I recognized the threat at last. Erich was on the verge of telling Raquel who and what we both were. If he revealed the secret of Evernight, and he convinced Raquel that we were really vampires—and Raquel's earlier suspicions made me believe that he could—then she'd run from us both. That would give him the perfect opportunity to bite her. He could even claim he'd done it to erase her memory. I could try to stop him with the fighting instincts I already felt sharpening within me, but I wasn't a full vampire yet. Erich was stronger and swifter than I was. He'd beat me. He'd get Raquel. All he had to do was say a few more words.

Quickly, I said, "I'm reporting this to Mrs Bethany."

Erich's smarmy grin slowly faded from his face. Even he had sense to be afraid of Mrs Bethany. And after all her big speeches about how everyone had to keep the human students safe to protect the school? Oh, no, Mrs Bethany wouldn't like Erich's attitude at *all*.

"Don't," Erich said. "Just drop it, okay?"

"You drop it. Get out of here. Go."

Erich glared at Raquel one more time, then stalked off into the woods alone.

"Bianca!" Raquel stumbled through the last few branches that separated us. Quickly I ran my tongue across my teeth, settling down so that I looked and acted human again. "Oh, my God, what's wrong with that guy?"

"He's a jerk." It was true, even if it wasn't the whole truth.

Raquel hugged herself tightly. "Who comes after—acts like he would— Oh, man. Okay. Okay."

I peered through the darkness to make sure that Erich was really retreating. His footsteps had faded, and I couldn't see his pale coat any longer. He was gone, at least for the moment, but I didn't trust him. "Come on," I said. "We're going to make a quick side trip."

Too numb to ask questions, Raquel followed me as we walked back toward the river. We only had to go another quarter mile before we found a small footbridge made of stone. It hadn't been used regularly in a long time, and some of the stones were loose, but she didn't complain or ask questions as I led her to the other side. Erich could cross the river if he really wanted to, but his natural aversion to running water, coupled with his fear of Mrs Bethany, would almost certainly be enough to keep us safe. Once we were on the far bank, I asked, "How are you?"

"Fine. I'm fine."

"Raquel, tell the truth. Erich came after you in the woods—you're still shaking!"

Her skin was clammy, but Raquel insisted, her voice

shrill, "I'm *fine*!" We stared at each other in silence for a second, and then she added in a whisper, "Bianca, please. He didn't touch me. So I'm fine."

Someday Raquel might be ready to talk about this, but not tonight. Tonight she needed to get out of here and fast. "Okay," I said. "Let's get back to school."

"Never thought I'd be glad to go back to Evernight." Her laugh sounded broken, somehow. We started to walk away, but then she paused. "Aren't you going to—to call the police or the teachers or somebody?"

"We'll tell Mrs Bethany as soon as we get back."

"I could try to call from here. I have my cell—it worked in town—"

"We're not in town any longer. You know we don't get reception out here."

"It's so stupid." She was shaking so hard that her teeth chattered. "Why don't those rich bitches make their mommies and daddies pay for a tower?"

Because most of them haven't even gotten used to landlines yet, I thought. "Come on. Let's go." She wouldn't let me put my arm around her shoulders as we made our way out of the frosty woods. Instead she just kept twisting her leather bracelet over and over.

That night, after Raquel went to bed, I went to see Mrs Bethany in her carriage house office. Given her disdainful attitude toward me, I'd assumed she would doubt my word, but she didn't. "We'll see to this," she said. "You are dismissed."

I hesitated. "That's it?"

"Do you think you should be allowed to discuss his punishment? To mete it out, perhaps?" She arched one eyebrow. "I know how to keep discipline at my own school, Miss Olivier. Or would you like to write another essay as a reminder?"

"I just meant, what are we going to tell everybody? They'll want to know what happened to Raquel." Already I could envision Lucas's handsome face, maybe questioning again if something strange was at work within Evernight. "She'll tell people it was Erich. We'll just have to say he was playing a practical joke or something, right?"

"That sounds reasonable." Why did she look so amused? I realized the reason when Mrs Bethany added, "You're becoming quite adept in deception, Miss Olivier. Progress at last."

I was afraid she might be right.

Chapter Ten

THE FIRST SNOWFALL OF WINTER DISAPPOINTED
us all—only an inch and a half, just enough to melt into ice
and slick the sidewalks. The countryside appeared patchy and
dull, yellow-brown hills spotted with watery clumps of snow.
Outside the bedroom window of my turret room, the gargoyle wore beads of frozen water over his scales and wings. It
wasn't enough snow to play in or even to enjoy looking at.

"Suits me," Patrice said, artfully draping an acid-green
muffler around her neck just so. "I'm glad we're getting more
sunshine."

"Now that you can go back out in it again, you mean." I
had been so frustrated with Patrice and the others with their
constant "dieting" before the Autumn Ball; like all vampires
denied blood, they'd become thinner—and more vampiric.
Courtney and her admiring clique had all been staying out of
the sunlight, something that didn't bother a well-fed vampire
but was painful to a starving one. I'd had to put up with

Patrice spending hours in front of the mirror trying to see her-self as her reflection faded more and more, approaching invis-ibility. I thought they'd seemed bitchier, too, but with that crew, it was hard to tell.

Patrice knew what I was referring to and shook her head, so exasperated with me. "I've been fine since the day after the ball. It was worth a few weeks of hunger pangs and staying in the shade! Eventually you'll learn the value of self-denial." Her round cheeks dimpled with amusement. "But not while Lucas's around, right?"

We laughed a long time at one of our few shared jokes. I was glad we were pretty much getting along, because between Raquel's trouble and exams approaching, I needed as little stress in my life as possible.

Finals were brutal. I'd expected as much, but that didn't make the papers for Mrs Bethany write themselves or the trig exam any easier. My mother revealed an unexpected sadistic streak by covering every single thing she'd ever mentioned in class—though the main essay on the Missouri Compromise had at least been signaled in advance by some bouncing on the balls of her feet. *Guess that means Balthazar is doing okay*, I thought as I wrote so fast that my hand cramped around my pen. I hoped I was doing half as well.

I threw myself into my studying during finals week, not only because of the intensity of the tests but also because work served as a distraction. Making Raquel quiz me nonstop took her mind off what had nearly happened in the woods. It helped that Mrs Bethany had Erich on penalty, which involved him spending virtually every free moment scrubbing down hallways and glowering at me furiously when he got the chance.

"I don't trust that guy," Lucas said once as we walked past him.

"You just hate his guts." That was true as far as it went, though I knew other, better reasons for not trusting Erich.

Despite my efforts to keep Raquel busy, she remained haunted. Whatever fears she'd always carried within her had been magnified by Erich's harassment. I knew that she wasn't sleeping at night because of the dark circles under her eyes, and one day she came to the library with her hair freshly hacked off—obviously something she'd done herself, and not very carefully either.

In an attempt to be tactful, I shifted my books to one side so she could sit next to me at the table and began, "You know, I used to cut hair for my friends in my hometown—"

"I know my hair looks crappy." Raquel didn't even look at me as her backpack thudded onto the floor. "And, no, I don't want you or anybody to fix it for me. I hope it looks crappy. Then maybe he won't keep looking at me."

"Who? Erich?" Lucas said, immediately tense.

Raquel sank into her seat. "Who do you think? Yeah, Erich."

Until then, I hadn't realized that I wasn't the only one Erich was staring at. I'd interrupted Erich in the middle of a hunt; he'd made up his mind to drink Raquel's blood, maybe—maybe even to hurt her. Most vampires never killed,

Mom and Dad said. Was Erich the exception to that rule?

Surely not, I thought. *Mrs Bethany wouldn't let anybody like that in Evernight.*

As Lucas quickly changed the subject, asking Raquel for a copy of the study sheets for my dad's biology class, I looked at him and felt, once again, the surge of longing—of possessiveness—that I always knew in his presence. *Mine*, I thought. *I always want you to be mine.*

I'd always thought that was emotion talking, but maybe it was something else. Maybe that need to claim someone else was part of being a vampire and therefore more powerful than any human longing.

Erich certainly didn't care about Raquel the way I did for Lucas, but if he felt one-tenth as much possessiveness toward her as I did toward Lucas—

—then there was no way Erich was done with Raquel yet.

That night, in the bathroom, I ran into Raquel again. She was shaking the sleeping pills I'd recommended into her palm— four or five of them. "Watch it," I said. "You don't want to take too many."

Raquel's face was bleak. "And never wake up again? Doesn't sound that awful to me." She sighed. "Trust me, Bianca, this isn't nearly enough to kill anybody."

"It's more than you need to sleep."

"Not with the sounds on the roof." She popped the pills into her mouth, then bent over to gulp a couple of swallows of water directly from the cold tap of the sink. After wiping her face with the back of her hand, Raquel continued, "They're still there. Louder now, I think. All the time. And I'm not imagining them."

I didn't like the sound of that. "I believe you."

It was just something to say, but Raquel's eyes got wide. "You do?" Her voice was no more than a whisper. "Really? You're not just saying it?"

"Really, I believe you."

To my shock, Raquel's eyes teared up. She quickly blinked them away, but I knew what I'd seen. "Nobody ever believed me, before."

I stepped a little closer. "Believed you about what?"

She shook her head, refusing to answer. But as she walked past me to go to her own room, she touched my arm—just for a moment. From Raquel, that was almost like a bear hug. I had no idea what troubled her in her past, but I knew that Erich had her spooked. Probably he had no intention of actually hurting her, but he seemed like the kind of guy who would enjoy making her afraid.

That, at least, I could do something about.

Later that evening, well after curfew, I got up and slipped into jeans, sneakers, and my warm black sweater. My black knit cap slipped over my head and hid my red hair. Briefly I considered painting black smudges across my cheeks and nose, like cat burglars do in the movies, but I decided that was overkill.

"Going out for a snack?" Patrice mumbled into her pillow.

"The squirrels are hibernating. Easy meal."

"I'm just looking around," I insisted, but Patrice was already asleep again.

The night air was cold when I lifted myself onto the windowsill, but my dark gloves and sweater kept me from shivering. Once I'd balanced myself on the tree branch, I began stretching my arms to catch the higher limbs, then bracing my feet against the bark of the trunk to find purchase. Some branches creaked from my weight, but nothing broke. Within a few minutes, I had made it to the roof.

The roof of the lower part of the building, I mean. A few feet away, the south tower reached up toward the night sky; if I craned my neck, I could even make out the darkened windows of my parents' apartment. Across the way was the vast north tower. Between was the shingled roof of the main building—not a single flat surface, but one that sloped at different angles, reflecting the fact that the school had been built slowly, over centuries, and not every new addition perfectly matched the rest. It looked a little like a stormy sea with waves that jutted up and down, all of them gleaming blue-black in the moonlight.

Gritting my teeth, I crawled up the slope nearest me and made sure to move as quietly as I could. If anybody was out for a snack, it wouldn't matter if they saw me or not. However, if anybody was up here for another reason, I wanted the advantage of surprise.

I was scared to death, even though I kept telling myself

that there was really no reason to be afraid. I knew that I was no good at confrontations; when challenged, I usually wanted to curl up into a ball. Still, somebody had to stand up for Raquel, and it looked like I was the only one who could. So I ignored the butterflies in my stomach and told myself to deal.

I tried to imagine the layout of the rooms below, doing my best to figure out where Raquel's room would be. She was well down the hall from me. The room I shared with Patrice was below the south tower, but Raquel wouldn't have that same luxury. No, somebody could stand right on top of her room, only a few feet above her sleeping head.

Once I had the location fixed in my head, I started walking. Fortunately there was no ice, so I didn't slip and slide too much as I climbed up one gable and down another, sometimes walking, sometimes crawling. The whole way, I listened carefully for any sound: a footstep, a word, even a breath. Even the thought of danger had awakened my darker instincts, and every sense was sharp. I was ready for anything—or so I thought.

When I got within a few feet of the area above Raquel's room, I heard a scrape along the roof: long, slow, and probably deliberate. Somebody was up there. Somebody wanted Raquel to hear.

Cautiously I pulled myself up the next high slope. There, crouching in the shadows, was Erich. He clutched a broken-off branch in one hand and was dragging it back and forth over one of the slates.

"You," I said quietly. Erich jerked upright, startled. Something about his reaction and the way he hurriedly drew his long coat around him made me wonder just what his other hand had been doing. Grossed out and nervous, I wanted to run, but I managed to stand my ground. "Get lost."

"We're both breaking the rules now," Erich muttered, glancing from side to side. "You can't turn me in without turning us both in."

I stepped closer to him, close enough to touch. His skinny face and sharp nose made him look more like a rat than ever. "Then—then I'll turn us both in."

"Big damn deal. Breaking curfew. So what? Everyone does it. They don't really care."

"You're not out to grab something to eat. You're harassing Raquel."

Erich gave me the most disgusted look I'd ever seen on someone's face, like I was something he would step over on the sidewalk. "You can't prove it."

Anger flared up inside me, submerging my fear. All my muscles tensed, and my incisors began pushing forward, lengthening into fangs. Reacting like a vampire meant never backing down. "Oh, really?"

Then I grabbed his hand and bit him hard.

Vampire blood doesn't taste at all like human blood or the blood of anything else living. It's not filling, not even food, really. It's *information*. The taste of a vampire's blood tells you how that vampire is feeling at that very instant—you feel it, too, a little bit, and images flash in your mind that were in the other vampire's mind just a moment before. My parents had taught me this and even let me try it out on them a couple of times, though the one time I asked them if they ever bit each other, they both got really embarrassed and asked whether I didn't have any homework I should be doing.

Tasting my parents' blood, I had felt only love and contentment and seen only images of myself as a child prettier than I really was, curious to learn about the world. Erich's blood was different. It was horror.

He tasted like resentment, like rage, and a bone-deep craving to take human life. The liquid was so hot it burned and so angry that it made my stomach turn over, rejecting it and rejecting him. An image flickered in my mind, bigger and brighter every second like a fire blazing quickly out of control: Raquel as Erich wanted her to be—sprawled on her bed, neck ripped open, gasping for her last breath.

"Ow!" Erich wrenched his hand back. "What the hell are you doing?"

"You want to hurt her." It was hard for me to keep my voice steady; I was shaking now, freaked-out by the violence I'd seen. "You want to kill her."

"Wanting isn't the same as doing," he retorted. "You think I'm the only guy here who wants to tear into some fresh meat once in a while? No way could you get me punished for that."

"Get the hell off her roof. You leave tonight and you don't ever, ever come back. If you do, I'll tell Mrs Bethany. She'll believe me, and you'll be out of here."

"Do it, then. I'm sick of this place. But I deserve a good meal before I go, don't you think?" Erich laughed at me, and for one horrifying moment, I thought he meant to fight me after all. Instead he leaped off the roof, not even bothering to catch a tree branch on the way down.

I'd never felt anything like that kind of sick rage before. I hoped I never would again. For all the pettiness and darkness of Evernight, I felt like I'd just seen true evil for the first time.

Do you believe in evil? Raquel had asked me. I'd said yes, but I hadn't known what it looked like before. Shaking, I breathed in and out a couple of times, trying to get my bearings. I'd have to think long and hard about what had just happened, but for tonight, I just wanted to get the hell out of here.

I took another couple steps and slid down the far slope of the roof, trying to get a look at where Erich had landed. I wanted to make sure he was leaving for real. But as I started down, I saw another shape in the darkness—like a shadow down in the deepest of the waves. Maybe Erich hadn't come alone.

"Stop!" I insisted. "Who is it?"

The shape stood up slowly, rising into the moonlight. It was Lucas.

"Lucas? What are you doing here?" As soon as I asked it, I felt stupid. He'd come up here for the same reason I had, to see if Erich was stalking Raquel. Lucas didn't answer. He was staring at me as if he didn't know me at all, and he took one step backward.

"Lucas?" At first I didn't understand, but then it hit me. My fangs were still sharp. My mouth was still wet with blood. If he'd crouched there for a couple of minutes, he would have heard me talking to Erich—he'd seen me bite him—

Lucas knows I'm a vampire.

Most people don't believe in vampires anymore and wouldn't believe no matter how hard you tried to convince them. But Lucas didn't have to be convinced, not while he was staring a fanged, bloody-lipped vampire in the face. He looked at me like I was a stranger—no, like a monster.

Every secret I'd fought my whole life to protect had just been revealed.

Chapter Eleven

"WAIT," I PLEADED. MY LIPS WERE STILL STICKY with blood. "Don't go. I can explain!"

"Don't come near me." Lucas's face was stark white.

"Lucas—please—"

"You're a *vampire*."

I couldn't say anything else. My new talent for lying couldn't help me now. Lucas knew the truth, and I couldn't hide any longer.

He kept backing away, stumbling over the slate shingles, his arms jerky as he tried to steady himself. Shock had made him clumsy—Lucas, who always moved with purpose and strength. It was like he'd been blinded. I wanted to go after him to keep him from losing his balance and falling, if for no other reason. More than that, I was desperate to explain. But he wouldn't let me help him, not anymore. If I followed, Lucas would panic and run away. Run away from *me*.

Shaking, I sat down on the rooftop and watched Lucas

make his way across the roof. He didn't dare turn his back on me until he was more than halfway to the north tower and the guys' rooms. By then, my arms were wrapped around my knees and tears trickled down my cheeks. I was more frightened and ashamed than I'd ever been in my life, even more than when I'd bitten him.

Had he already realized what had really happened the night of the Autumn Ball and that I had been the one to hurt him? If he hadn't, I knew he would soon.

What should I do? Tell my parents immediately? They'd be furious with me—and they'd also have to take action against Lucas. I didn't know what the vampires would do to a human who learned the secret of Evernight, but I suspected it wouldn't be good. Report this to Mrs Bethany? Out of the question. I could try waking Patrice for advice, but she would probably shrug, readjust her satin eye mask, and fall back to sleep.

Now that the secret was out, all of those people were in danger. Lucas probably wouldn't tell anyone, for fear of being called insane; even if he did, nobody was likely to believe him. But the risk—that one chance that we could all be exposed— was terrible. And it was all my fault.

There had to be some way I could fix it. Something I could do.

I'll talk to Lucas. First thing in the morning— No, he has an exam first thing. It was so strange, even having to think about something as mundane as an exam in the middle of this. *I can catch him after that. He won't want to talk to me, but he won't start yelling about vampires in the hall. So that gives me a chance, and if I can only figure out what to say—*

Then what? I'd lied to Lucas. I'd hurt him. Maybe he was right to get as far away from me as possible.

Still, I knew I had to try. If I was in danger of losing Lucas forever, there was nothing I wouldn't do—plead, cry, or reveal every secret I'd ever had. I only knew that I had to make Lucas understand.

After a long, sleepless night, I got up late, put on my black sweater and kilt, and went stiffly downstairs. I thought I'd timed it to the end of Lucas's exam, but apparently the students were being allowed to leave as they finished—and Lucas had finished early, according to some other guys in the class. That meant he was already back in his room, probably. Screwing up my courage, I sneaked into the guys' dorm area. Vic and Lucas had once pointed out their window from the grounds, so I could find the room if I just didn't get caught.

Would showing up in Lucas's room unannounced scare him to death? Maybe. I'd have to risk it. I couldn't take it any longer. The suspense was gnawing at me, turning me inside out. Even if Lucas told me never to come near him again, at least then I'd know. Not knowing was worse than anything.

I knew I'd reached my destination when I found a door decorated with two posters—one of Alfred Hitchcock's *Vertigo* and another from something called *Faster, Pussycat! Kill! Kill!*

Nobody answered my knock, so I hesitantly pushed the door open. No one was inside. Lucas's room smelled like him—spicy and woodsy, almost like being back in the forest. Half the room was covered in posters from action movies, guns and babes spilling out in every direction; this was the half with the bed that had a tie-dyed cover on it. In other words, Vic's half. Lucas's half of the room was almost bare. No pictures or posters hung on the walls, and on the small bulletin board that hung above everyone's bed, he had pinned up only his class schedule and a movie ticket—*Suspicion*, from our first date. An army surplus blanket covered his bed.

Apparently there was nothing for me to do but wait. Unsure what to do, I walked toward the window, which showed a stretch of the school's gravel driveway. A few cars were there, mostly parents picking up their kids on the last day of exams, taking them back home for Christmas. The human kids, of course. I watched people hugging, loading up luggage—and Lucas, striding out the front door with his duffel bag slung over one shoulder.

"Oh, no," I whispered. I pressed my hands against the window so hard that I thought it would shatter—or I would—but Lucas never hesitated. He went straight toward a long black sedan with tinted windows. The sedan's door opened, and I tried to get a look at who was inside, but I couldn't see anyone. His stripped-down half of the room made sense to me now. I knew immediately that Lucas had left Evernight for Christmas break without saying good-bye and that he probably would never return.

"Whoa, the rooms are going coed? That's made of awesome." Vic came in behind me. I gave him a wan smile before turning back to watch Lucas's car driving away. The car was speeding off as if they were in a hurry. "Good job sneaking in. You guys just said good-bye, huh?"

"Uh-huh." What else could I say?

"Don't get too depressed, all right?" Vic gave me a little punch on the shoulder. "Some guys know what to say to girls when they're upset, but man, I'm not one of them."

"I'm okay. Honestly." I studied Vic carefully. He was the only person at school that Lucas might have shared his suspicions with. "Has Lucas seemed . . . okay to you?"

"He turned down my invitation to Jamaica." Vic shrugged. "Something about getting together with family friends, but it didn't sound like they were doing anything special. Wouldn't you rather spend Christmas lying on the beach instead of hanging out with some old farts who know your mom?"

That wasn't at all what I meant. Still, if that was the strangest behavior Vic could mention, probably Lucas had kept his thoughts about vampires to himself. Vic wasn't the kind of guy who could bluff his way through something like that. With a sting, I realized that Vic was more honest than I was.

"Cheetos?" Vic offered me a half-empty, orange-powdery bag. I shook my head and tried very hard to pretend that I didn't feel a whole lot like being sick. "He's gonna regret it. Wait and see. Me and my family—we're going to be having the time of our lives. And what's he going to be doing? Minding his table manners somewhere." Through a mouthful of Cheetos, Vic predicted, "It's gonna be a long month."

"Yeah," I muttered. "It really is."

I suppose most people would assume that vampires don't really get into Christmas. Most people would be wrong.

The religious part was uncomfortable. Crosses didn't set us on fire or turn us to smoke, like in horror movies, but being in a chapel or church felt all wrong—sort of a strange creepy-crawly sensation as if someone unseen were watching. So no midnight mass, no crèche, nothing like that. However, vampires like getting presents as much as anybody. Add some time off from school, and you've got a holiday even the undead can enjoy.

Most of the undead, anyway. I was more miserable that Christmas than I'd ever been before in my life.

The stifling atmosphere eased up when the other kids left, so that only the vampires remained behind. People stopped putting on so much attitude; nobody remained for them to pick on or impress. A few departed, including Patrice, who insisted that the skiing in Switzerland this time of year was not to be missed. The rest of us, teachers and students alike, remained at Evernight because it was our home, or as close to a home as some people had.

"We're the exception, Bianca." My mother hung holly garlands over our doorway as I stood beneath her, steadying the ladder. She and Dad had picked up on my black mood and were trying extra hard to get me into the holiday spirit. "We're the only family at Evernight, do you realize that? None of the others here now have had a family since—well, since they were alive, I guess."

"It's just weird to me that they don't have homes to go to." I handed up a thumbtack for her to secure the garland in place. "We had a house. How do people get by without houses?"

"We had a house for sixteen years," Dad corrected me from his place on the couch, where he was busily going through his old records, trying to find *Ella Wishes You a Swinging Christmas*. "That's your whole life, but to your mother and me, it seems like—"

"The blink of an eye." Mom sighed.

Dad smiled at her, and something about his smile reminded me that he was about six hundred years older than her—that even the centuries they'd spent together might be, to him, the blink of an eye. "There's no such thing as permanence. People drift from place to place, getting lost in pleasure or luxury or anything else with the power to divert you from the occasional boredom of immortality. Life moves on, and those of us who aren't alive have trouble catching up."

"Which is why there's an Evernight," I said, thinking of Modern Technology and how confused people got when Mr Yee introduced the concept of e-mail. Many of them had heard of it, and several even knew how to use it—but I was the only one who understood how it actually worked before

Mr Yee explained. It was one thing to bluff your way through twenty-first-century life, another to really comprehend what was going on. "What about the ones who look too old to be in school?"

"Well, this isn't the only place we've got, you know." Mom reached down for another garland. "There are spas and hotels, places like that where people are expected to be somewhat isolated from the rest of the world, and where you can control who gets in. Back in the day, we used to have a lot of monasteries and convents, but it's difficult to establish new ones now. The Protestant Reformation took out quite a few— Huguenot mobs, fires, stuff like that. The residents couldn't exactly explain they weren't Catholics without making things a whole lot worse. These days we mostly stick to schools and clubs."

Dad added, "They're opening up a fake rehab center in Arizona next year."

I imagined all of us, scattered throughout the world, brought together only here and there, and only once every century or so. Was that the way I would lead my entire existence?

It sounded unbearably lonely. What was the point of having unending life if that life was without love? Mom and Dad had been lucky enough to find each other and be together for hundreds of years. I'd found Lucas and lost him within just a few months. I tried to tell myself that someday it would seem like nothing—that the time I'd spent with Lucas would be "the blink of an eye"—but I couldn't believe that.

So, for the first week of vacation, I mostly stayed in my room. A lot of the time, I just stayed in bed. Once in a while, I'd check my e-mail in the now-deserted computer lab, hoping against hope for a note from Lucas. Instead, all I got were various joke photos of Vic on the beach, wearing sunglasses and a Santa hat. I wondered if I should write Lucas instead of waiting for him to write to me, but what could I possibly say?

My parents drew me out for holiday activities whenever they could, and I tried to go along with them. Just my luck, to be born to the only vampires in the history of the world who baked fruitcake. Every once in a while, I'd catch them exchanging glances. Obviously they realized that I was miserable and were on the verge of asking me what was wrong.

In some ways, I wanted to tell them. At times I wanted nothing more than to blurt out the whole story and cry in their arms—and if that was immature of me, I didn't care. What I did care about was the fact that, if I told my parents the truth, they'd have to report it to Mrs Bethany, and I didn't trust Mrs Bethany not to go after Lucas and make his life miserable.

For Lucas's sake, I had to keep my unhappiness to myself.

I might have carried on that way for the whole holiday break if it hadn't been for the next snowfall, two days before Christmas. This was more generous than the first, blanketing the grounds with silence, softness, and blue-white glitter. I'd always loved snow, and the sight of it, shining and perfect across the landscape, nudged me out of my depression. I tugged on jeans and boots and my heaviest cable-knit green sweater. My brooch safely pinned to the lapel of my gray coat, I trudged downstairs for a walk. I knew I'd get chilled to the bone, but it would be worth it if mine were the first footprints on the grounds and in the woods. When I reached the door, I saw that I wasn't the only one who liked that idea.

Balthazar smiled at me sheepishly above his red muffler. "Hundreds of years in New England, and I still get excited about snow."

"I know how you feel." Things between us were still awkward, but it was only polite to say, "We should walk together."

"Yeah. Let's go."

We didn't say much at first. It wasn't strained, though. The snowfall and the pinkish-gold early morning light asked for silence, and neither of us wanted to hear anything louder than the muffled crunching of our boots in the snow. Our path took us across the grounds and into the woods—like the walk we'd taken the evening of the Autumn Ball. I breathed in and out, a soft gray puff of warmth in the winter sky.

Balthazar's eyes crinkled at the corners, like he was amused, or at least happy. I thought about all the centuries he must have known, and the fact that he still didn't have someone to share them with. "Can I ask you a personal question?"

He blinked, surprised but not offended. "Sure."

"When did you die?"

Instead of answering me immediately, Balthazar walked a

few more steps. The way he studied the horizon made me think that he was trying to picture how things had been for him, before. "1691."

"In New England?" I asked, remembering what he'd said.

"Yeah. Not far from here, actually. The same town where I grew up. I only left it a handful of times." Balthazar's gaze was distant. "One trip to Boston."

"If this is making you sad—"

"No, it's all right. I haven't talked about home in a long time."

A hungry crow perched on a branch of a nearby holly bush, black and shining amid its sharp-cornered leaves, plucking at berries. Balthazar watched the bird at its task, probably so he wouldn't have to look me in the eyes. Whatever it was he was preparing to say, I knew it was difficult for him. "My parents settled here early. They didn't come over on the *Mayflower*, but they weren't far behind. My sister Charity was born during the voyage. She was a month old before she ever saw dry land. They said it made her unsteady—that she wasn't rooted to the earth." He sighed.

"Charity. That was a Puritan name, wasn't it?" I thought I remembered reading that in a book once, but I couldn't imagine Balthazar dressed up like a Pilgrim in a Thanksgiving pageant.

"The elders wouldn't have said we were among the Godly. We were only admitted to membership in the church because—" My face must've betrayed my confusion, because he laughed. "Ancient history. By any modern standard, my family was deeply religious. My parents named my sister for one of the sacred virtues. They believed in those virtues as something real enough to touch, just far away—the way we believe in the sun or the stars."

"If they were so religious, why did they name you something edgy like Balthazar?"

He gave me a look. "Balthazar was one of the Three Wise Men who brought gifts to the Christ Child."

"Oh."

"I didn't mean to make you feel bad." One broad hand rested on my shoulder, for just a minute. "Very few people teach their children that any longer. Back then, it was common knowledge. The world changes a lot; it's hard to keep up."

"You must miss them all very much. Your family, I mean." It felt so inadequate. What must it have been like for Balthazar, to have not seen his parents or his sister for centuries? I couldn't begin to imagine how badly that must hurt.

(What will it be like when you haven't seen Lucas for two hundred years?)

I couldn't bear to think about that question again. I concentrated on Balthazar instead.

"Sometimes I think I've changed so much that my parents would hardly know me. And my sister—" Balthazar paused, then shook his head. "I realize that you're asking me how different things were then. How much things change. But we don't change, Bianca. That's the scariest part. And it's one reason a lot of people here act like teenagers, even when they're centuries old. They don't understand themselves or the world they have to join. It's sort of like perpetual adolescence. Not so much fun."

I hugged myself as I shivered from the cold and from the thought of all those years and decades and centuries stretching out before me, shifting and uncertain.

We walked on for a while after that, Balthazar lost in his thoughts, and me lost in mine. Our feet kicked up small plumes of fresh snow as we left the only footprints in a still sea of white. Finally I got up the courage to ask Balthazar what was really on my mind. "If you could go back, would you bring them with you? Your family?"

I thought he might say yes, that he would do anything to have them with him. I thought he might say no, that he couldn't have brought himself to kill them, no matter what. Either answer would tell me a lot about how long grief lasted, how long I would have to endure the misery of having lost Lucas. I didn't expect Balthazar to stop in his tracks and give me a hard stare.

"If I could go back," he said, "I'd die with my parents."

"What?" I was too stunned to come up with any other response.

Balthazar stepped closer and laid a leather-gloved hand on my cheek. His touch wasn't loving, like Lucas's. He was trying to wake me up to something, to make me see. "You're *alive*, Bianca. You still can't appreciate what it means, to be alive. It's better than being a vampire—better than anything else in the world. I remember a little of what being alive was like, and if I could touch that again, even for a day, it would be worth anything in the world. Even dying again, forever. All the centuries I've known and all the marvels I've seen don't compare to being alive. Why do you think the vampires here are so vicious to the human students?"

"Because—well, they're snobs, I guess—"

"That's not it. It's jealousy." We looked at each other in silence for a long moment before he added, "Enjoy life while you have it. Because it doesn't last—not for vampires, not for anyone."

Nobody had ever said anything like this to me. My parents didn't wish they were still alive—did they? They'd never spoken a word about it. And Courtney, Erich, Patrice, Ranulf: Were they all wishing to be human after all?

Perhaps recognizing my doubt, Balthazar said, "You don't believe me."

"It's not that. I know you're telling me the truth. You wouldn't lie to me about anything important. That's not the kind of person you are."

Balthazar nodded, a slow half smile playing across his lips, and I felt like I'd said more than I meant to say. The hopeful light in his eyes now was something I hadn't seen since the night of the Autumn Ball, before I'd let him down.

What bothered me more, though, was the fact that what I'd said was true. Balthazar really wouldn't lie to me about anything important, even when that truth was difficult for me to hear. He was a trustworthy person—a good person. I wished I could've been as good a person, someone who would have put other people's interests first, one who would have deserved Lucas's trust.

Then I thought, *Maybe it's not too late.*

After we returned to the school, our footprints winding a track all around the grounds, I waved good-bye to Balthazar and hurried upstairs to the computer lab. Luckily, the door was unlocked. As I waited for my computer to boot up, I remembered the print of Klimt's *Kiss* above my bed. Those two lovers held each other for eternity, two parts of the same whole, fused together in a mosaic of pink and gold.

If you loved someone, you couldn't let lies come between you. No matter what happened—even if you'd already lost each other forever—you owed each other the truth.

With trembling fingers, I typed in Lucas's e-mail address and put as the subject line "and nothing but the truth." Then I started typing, spilling out everything I'd held back from him all this time. As quickly and simply as I could, I told him that what he'd seen that night was real.

That I was a vampire, born to two other vampires and destined to become like them someday.

That Evernight was full of vampires, that the school existed to teach us about the changing world and to protect us from people who were frightened of us because they didn't understand.

That I'd bitten him the night of the Autumn Ball, not

meaning to hurt him but because I'd wanted to be near him so much.

The words gushed out of me. It was a mess, really; I'd never tried to tell these secrets before and I kept repeating myself, putting things badly, or asking questions I wasn't sure of the answer to. That didn't matter. What mattered was telling Lucas the truth at last.

Finally, I wrote:

> *I'm not telling you all of this because I expect to get you back. I know I don't deserve that, not after what I did, and even though you're not in danger at Evernight, I guess you don't want to come anywhere near the school ever again.*
>
> *Mostly I'm writing to ask you, please, if you haven't already told anyone what you saw here, don't. Don't show anyone this e-mail. Keep this secret for me. If the truth got out, my parents and Balthazar and a lot of the other students would be in danger, and it would be all my fault. I couldn't bear it if I were responsible for hurting anybody.*
>
> *I didn't tell any of them that you saw me and Erich up on the roof. I did that to keep you safe. You can do that much for me in return, right? That's all I ask. Maybe it's more than I deserve, but it's not about me. It's about the people who could get hurt.*

I also wanted you to know that I do care enough about you to tell you the truth. I'm sorry that I waited until too late. But I hope it means something to you when you understand how I really feel.

I'll never stop missing you.

Good-bye, Lucas.

Before I could talk myself out of it, I quickly hit Send. As soon as I'd done it, a chill swept through me. What if Lucas didn't listen to me? What if the e-mail I'd sent didn't convince him to remain silent—but instead just provided him with evidence?

Maybe I should have regretted it, but I didn't. Maybe Lucas couldn't trust me any longer, but I still trusted him.

I didn't really expect Lucas to answer. However, expectations are different from hopes. I kept rechecking my e-mail that whole next day, and the next, and then throughout Christmas Day, whenever I could slip away from the unwrapping of gifts.

No answer from Lucas.

New Year's Day. Nothing.

I'd told myself that the truth was worth telling for its own sake, and I believed it. But that didn't make it any easier to face the fact that my confession had meant nothing. Lucas was still gone for good.

Chapter Twelve

WHEN THE STUDENTS RETURNED TO THE school, I stood on the front steps, hoping to see a friendly face. I knew Lucas wouldn't return. Although I kept fantasizing that I saw him, it was just my imagination playing cruel tricks. In some ways, I told myself, today would be a turning point. When Lucas didn't show, I'd at least be certain. Instead of torturing myself with useless wishes for something that couldn't be, I could face the hard facts and force myself to keep going.

If I was going to do that, I'd need the few friends I still had at Evernight.

I glimpsed Raquel making her way through the crowd, huddled over and nervous. I realized why she was so nervous when I turned my head and saw Erich watching her intently from the top of the steps. Quickly I went to her side and shouldered one of her bags. "You came back," I said. "I wasn't sure you would."

"I didn't want to." Raquel kept staring down at her feet.

"No offense. I would've missed you. But I didn't want to see *him* again." There was no need to explain who she was talking about.

"Didn't you tell your parents?" I'd figured they would call Mrs Bethany, furious that Erich hadn't been expelled, and maybe withdraw Raquel from the academy altogether.

She shrugged. "They thought I was making a big deal out of nothing. They always do."

I remembered how moved Raquel had been when I'd said that I believed her; now I understood why. "I'm sorry."

"Whatever. I'm back. I have to deal. Besides, I lost my favorite bracelet here right before the break. Had to come back to find that, at least."

I glanced over my shoulder at Erich. His dark eyes remained locked on us. When he saw me watching him, one corner of his mouth lifted in a smirk. Disgusted, I turned my head back toward the crowd—

Lucas.

No. It couldn't be. It was just my imagination trying to fool me again, so that I'd get my hopes up. There was no way Lucas would ever come back to Evernight, not after what he'd seen and what I'd told him.

But then the crowds parted, and I saw him clearly, and I realized that I was right. Lucas had returned.

There he was, just a few steps away. He looked scruffier than he had before—his bronze hair unruly, his threadbare navy sweater more beat-up than his Evernight uniform was.

On him, it looked amazing.

I brightened when I saw him; I couldn't help it. As soon as our eyes met, Lucas turned away, like he didn't know what else to do. It felt like a slap in the face.

My first impulse was to drop Raquel's bag and flee to the restroom before I started bawling right there on the steps. But that second, a plaid blur raced by me and tackled Lucas from behind. "Lucas!" crowed Vic. "My man! You're back."

"Get off me." Lucas laughed as he pushed Vic away.

"Check it out." Vic fished in his backpack and pulled out an honest-to-God pith helmet, like they used to wear in old safari movies. He showed it to me and Lucas both; apparently Vic hadn't realized that we weren't standing together. "How great is that?"

"You're never going to get away with wearing that to class," I said, pretending that everything was okay. Maybe Lucas would pretend, too, and that would give me an opening to talk to him. "They let you wear the Chucks, but I think a pith helmet is pushing it."

"I intend to wear it around Casa del Lucas y Victor." Vic placed the hat on his head to demonstrate. "For casual relaxation and study time. Whattaya think, Lucas?"

Nobody answered. Lucas had already vanished into the crowd.

Vic turned back to me, clearly confused by his roommate's disappearing act. I was confused, too—but I couldn't imagine why Lucas had come back at all.

Obviously it was going to take Lucas a while before he could talk to me again. Given what he'd learned about me, Evernight, and vampires, I figured he probably deserved as much time as he needed. Until then, there was nothing for me to do but wait.

A couple of days later, as I got ready for class, I pretended to be really fascinated by Patrice's tales of her Swiss holiday.

"I'm always shocked that there are people who claim to prefer skiing in Colorado." Patrice wrinkled her nose. Did she honestly think every place in America was tacky? Or was she compensating for something, pretending to be more sophisticated than she really was? Now that I kept so many secrets myself, I was starting not to take everyone at face value. "Switzerland is so much more civilized, I think. And you meet a more interesting cross section of people."

"I don't like skiing," I said blithely as I brushed on my mascara. "Snowboarding's more exciting."

"What?" Patrice just stared at me. I'd never dared disagree with any of her opinions before. Even on a subject as unimportant as skiing versus snowboarding, apparently, she didn't like being contradicted.

Before I could state my case, the door burst open. It was Courtney, who actually looked rumpled—Courtney, who had perfectly polished hair and makeup even when you ran into her in the bathroom at two A.M. "Have you guys seen Erich?"

"Erich?" Patrice raised an eyebrow. "I don't remember

inviting him to my bedroom. Did you, Bianca?"

"Not last night, anyway."

"Cut the sarcasm, okay?" Courtney snapped. "I would think you'd care that one of your classmates is missing. Somebody runs away, and you act like it's a big joke. Genevieve's crying her eyes out over here."

"Wait, Erich's missing?" Raquel appeared in the doorway, along with a couple of the other students, all in various stages of readiness for class. The news was traveling fast.

"You know his roommate, David? He only just got back today." Courtney's concern, I noticed, wasn't too deep for her to enjoy being the center of attention. With relish, she continued, "David says that Erich's room looks like it's been ransacked. The place is completely trashed! And there's no sign of Erich at all. He and Genevieve were supposed to hang out this weekend, and now she's crushed."

"We'll only laugh silently from now on," Raquel promised, obviously not that worried about Erich. Who could blame her? Courtney scowled at us, then flounced out again.

Later that morning, on the way to our first class, Raquel muttered, "I just bet Genevieve hates missing out on that prime opportunity for date rape."

"I guess Erich got sick of school," I said. "I hear that every year, a lot of students leave before the term is up." Of course, I knew that Erich had been just one of the dozens of vampires who came to Evernight to learn the ropes of the modern day, got bored with being treated like a student, and took off to amuse himself elsewhere. Or maybe Mrs Bethany had seen the danger in him that I had seen, and she'd ordered him to leave the premises immediately.

"The students who escape are the smart ones. Which makes me surprised that Erich was the first to leave." Raquel paused. "They seem awfully sure that he ran away, given that he didn't talk to anybody about it. And you'd think he would've cut out over Christmas break, if he was going to go. Do you think the cops are coming? They ought to at least be asking us questions."

"Probably he just called his parents to come pick him up, ship him off to some other fancy boarding school. Mrs Bethany knows all about it, I'm sure. Courtney's just being a drama queen."

"Yeah, that wouldn't be a surprise. And he's just the kind of jerk who'd trash his room before he left to make a mess somebody else would have to clean up." But Raquel didn't appear to be convinced. "They should be asking questions, though. The teachers, and maybe even the cops."

"Everybody just found out." The whole subject made me uneasy. "Give it time."

"People at this school act like it's no big deal when a student disappears." Shaking her head, Raquel said, "What I said last semester goes double now. I am never coming back here next year."

I wondered if that was what Erich had said.

Everyone behaved strangely the rest of the day. Students

were distracted in class, placing bets about where Erich had gone. David pointed out that Erich had taken all his books and papers but left his clothes behind—pretty much the opposite of his usual priorities. I kept waiting for Mrs Bethany to call an assembly and offer some kind of explanation, but she never did.

That night, I found myself hanging out in the turret stairwell, the one with narrow windows one brick wide that provided the best view of the gravel pathway that led from the main road to the school. I didn't expect to see Erich down there, but all the same, I was waiting for something.

"So, I guess the police won't come."

I turned from the window to see Lucas standing a few steps behind me. He wore the black version of the uniform, and the light from the next story's hallway silhouetted him so sharply that I couldn't make out his face. Only his outline was clear—his broad shoulders, the way he leaned against the stone wall of the stairwell. All my fear melted away into longing.

When I answered him, the words came out slightly breathless. "No. Mrs Bethany wouldn't call the police. It would attract the wrong kind of attention."

"But there's no worry that one of the—one of the 'rich kids' got him."

"No, Erich was as much of a 'rich kid' as anyone else here."

Lucas took one step closer to me, and now I could see his

face despite the shadows. All the hours I'd spent missing him over Christmas seemed to well up inside me at once, and I wanted so badly to put my hand on his cheek or lay my head against his shoulder. But I didn't. There was a barrier between us now, one that might never go away.

"I'm sorry I didn't answer your e-mail before," Lucas said. "I was—in shock, I guess."

"I don't blame you." My heart beat faster.

Lucas said only, "We ought to talk. Alone."

If he trusted me enough to be alone with me, even knowing that I was the one who had bitten him, then there was a chance for us after all. I tried to sound calm as I said, "I know a place. Come there with me?"

"Lead the way," Lucas said, and I dared to let myself hope.

Chapter Thirteen

"WHERE ARE WE HEADED?" LUCAS ASKED AS I LED him up the back staircase.

"The north tower. Above and behind the guys' dorm. It's just storage up there—we can be alone."

"Isn't there someplace else we could go?"

My heart sank. He didn't trust me enough to be alone with me, maybe. "I think this is the only place we can be sure of having some privacy. If you'd rather—I don't know, wait until daylight or something—"

"No, it's all right." Lucas sounded wary, like it wasn't all right at all, but he kept walking behind me. I guessed that was as much as I could hope for.

Students usually left the back staircase alone, mostly because it was close to the faculty apartments. The rest of the faculty, of course, were other vampires—mostly very powerful vampires. Maybe students like Vic and Raquel didn't know that difference between the students and teachers, but they certainly felt it. At my old school, people snarked at the teachers all the time, but at Evernight, everyone—human and vampire alike—gave the teachers respect. Some of the teachers, like my parents, lived in the other tower, but most of them lived here. I suspected that Lucas and I were the first ones to make our way up past the faculty apartments all year.

Our footsteps clattered against the stone, but nobody seemed to hear us. I hoped not, anyway. This was the last conversation I'd ever want anybody to overhear.

"How do you know about this place? Do you come up here sometimes?" Lucas still seemed uncomfortable.

"Remember how I said I did some exploring before the school year started? This is one of the places I found then. I haven't been back since, but I bet nobody else has discovered it either."

When we got to the door at the very top of the stairs, I pushed it open carefully. Last autumn, I'd been rewarded with a shower of spiderwebs and dust. The spiders must have moved on, because now we were able to step inside easily. Inside were rooms laid out just like my parents' apartment, but instead of being cozily furnished, they were piled high with boxes upon boxes, a few yellowed corners of paper peeking out of the lids. These were Evernight's records—the histories of every student who had ever attended the school since it was founded in the late eighteenth century.

"It's cold up here." Lucas pulled the sleeves of his sweater down over his hands. "Are you sure we can't find someplace else?"

"We need to talk about this. And we need to be alone."

"The gazebo—"

"Is covered with ice, Mr-it's-cold-up-here. Besides, we could be seen outside, and they'd make us come in, and—and then we won't end up talking." I turned toward the window so that I could look out at the stars; even now, they comforted me. "We're both too good at avoiding the subject."

"Yeah, we are." Lucas gave in and sat down heavily on a nearby trunk. "Where do we start?"

"I don't know." I hugged myself and looked down at the gargoyle on the windowsill, the twin of the one outside my bedroom window. "Are you still scared of me?"

"No. I'm not. Not at all." Lucas shook his head slowly, his eyes disbelieving. "I ought to be— Hell, I don't know how I ought to feel. I keep telling myself to stay away. To forget about you, because everything's changed. But I can't do it."

"What?" I was too dumbfounded to hope.

Lucas's voice was hoarse. "When I first saw what you were, up on the roof—Bianca, it was like nothing I'd ever believed was true."

"I guess it's not easy, accepting that vampires are real."

"That wasn't the part that got to me, actually." I knew then that, no matter how freaked-out Lucas had been by the revelation about vampires, my lies had hurt him worse.

"Did you tell your mother? Did you tell anybody?"

Lucas laughed again. "Not hardly." When I gave him a weird look, he said, "Can you think of a better way for me to end up in an adolescent psychiatric unit?"

"No," I admitted. "It would probably get you a one-way ticket to the loony bin."

Gruffly, he added, "Besides, you asked me not to."

He had read that long letter full of revelations, learning that I had lied—that I was something he should consider a monster—but Lucas had still been able to hear my plea for secrecy and do what I asked. "Thank you."

"I wasn't going to come back here. I wasn't ever going to see you again. It hurt so bad, and I thought the only way it would ever stop hurting was if I made myself forget you." He dragged the back of his hand across his eyes, as if it tired him even to remember that struggle. "I tried hard to forget, Bianca. I couldn't. Then I convinced myself that it was my duty to come back to Evernight."

"Duty?" That confused me.

Lucas, apparently at a loss, shrugged. "To learn the truth? To see things through? I don't know." His expression changed as he looked up at me—and it was the same way he'd looked at me before, the way that made me weak in the knees. The way he looked when he said that the man in the Klimt painting had only one precious thing in the world. "But as soon as I saw you again, I knew that I still needed you. That I still trusted you. Even though you're a vampire—or almost a vampire—whatever you are." Lucas still said the word *vampire* like he couldn't believe it. "It doesn't matter to me. It should, but it doesn't. I can't help how I feel about you."

I couldn't hold back any longer. I went to Lucas and sank to the floor. He cradled my face in his hands, and his whole body shook. "You still want to be with me? Even though I lied to you?"

Lucas closed his eyes tightly. "I'd never hold that against you."

"Then you understand why I had to keep it secret." All the fear and dread I'd felt poured out of me in a great rush, and I wanted to put my arms around Lucas and melt against him. "You really understand. I never thought you would."

"I can't believe I want this," he whispered. "I can't believe how badly I want you."

Lucas brushed his mouth against mine, just once. Maybe he meant for us to stop there, but I didn't. I slipped my arms around his shoulders and kissed him again. I stopped worrying about everything else and just thought about Lucas and how close he was, the cedary scent of his skin, the way we breathed together when we kissed, like we were two parts of the same person. Little shivers of excitement made me tingle in my fingertips, my belly, everywhere.

"I ought to be running like hell." His breath was hot against my ear. His fingers slipped into the waistband of my skirt, using it to pull me nearer to him. "What have you done to me?"

When he clutched me against his chest, I wanted to draw

back. I was used to drawing back at this point because I was afraid of what my desire for Lucas could do. Now I would've expected Lucas to be the one who was afraid, but he wasn't. He trusted me enough to kiss me, to sink down on the floor so that we were kneeling opposite each other, to close his eyes when I ran my hands through his hair.

"This is when it's hard for me to stay in control," I whispered, warning him.

"Let's find out how much control we need."

He tugged at the neck of his sweater, exposing his throat to me. Daring me, basically, to prove that I could hold back. I simply pressed one hand against his bare skin, and I opened my mouth wider beneath his. Lucas made a low sound that did something strange to my whole body, like I'd stood up too quickly and made myself dizzy. His hands slowly edged up the hem of my uniform sweater, testing my reaction. I kissed him harder. So Lucas pushed the sweater up my back, all the way, and I lifted my arms to help him shrug it off. Now I only wore a thin undershirt and my bra, midnight-blue, clearly visible beneath the white sleeveless T.

Lucas's eyes were wide, and his breath was coming fast and shallow. Our kisses were more desperate now. He peeled off his own sweater and spread it out on the floor, like a blanket, then lowered me so that I lay on it, beneath him. He was still breathing fast but struggling for control. "Not here, not tonight—but maybe we could bring some stuff, find some other place to be alone one night—"

I silenced him with another kiss, deep and passionate enough to say yes. Lucas returned the kiss and held me tight—though not so tight that I couldn't roll him over so that he was the one with his back against the floor. Now Lucas lay beneath me, and I was hyperaware of everything: his thighs around mine, the cool square of his belt buckle against my abdomen, his fingers playing with my bra strap, edging it aside.

For one second—just one second—I wondered what it would be like if Lucas and I had come up here prepared, with blankets and pillows and music and protection, and we had all night to be together. "I wish we could," I gasped. "I wish we could be sure that I could stop."

"Maybe—maybe it doesn't matter."

"What?"

Lucas's eyes were bright, and his breath was fast and hot against my cheek. "You bit me once and you stopped in time. You didn't need to kill or to change me. Just to bite. If that's all it is—then maybe— Oh, God. Okay."

He wanted what I wanted. The hunger blazed inside me, and there was no reason to stop. I pushed Lucas down against the floor and bit deep.

"Bianca—" Lucas struggled for only the first second as the rapture caught up with us both: my pulse flowing into him as his blood flowed into me, more powerful than the most passionate kiss, weaving us both together. The taste of his blood was familiar to me now but even more irresistible. I swallowed it down, relishing the heat and life and the salt against my tongue. He shuddered beneath me, and I knew that the bite felt just as amazing for us both.

Lucas gasped, and I forced myself to stop. Slowly I pulled back from Lucas. He was dizzy and weak but still awake. He put his hands on both sides of my face, and suddenly I felt self-conscious. My lips were stained with his blood, and my fangs were still sharp. How could Lucas look at me as a vampire with anything but revulsion?

Instead he kissed me, blood and all.

When our mouths parted, I whispered, "That's all it is. I promise. Is that okay? Can you take that?"

"I want to be with you, Bianca," he said. "No matter what you are. No matter what."

Chapter Fourteen

"CAN YOU SIT UP?"

"Not yet." Lucas held his hands over his eyes, then let his arms sag back onto the floor. "I need another second."

"I tried not to take too much blood." I really, really did not want to have to go to Mrs Bethany for help again. "You gave me permission, right?"

"I did. I'm not sure I was thinking straight, but that's my fault, not yours." Something in me that had been strung too tight finally relaxed, and I could breathe deeply again. As long as Lucas felt that way, everything would be all right. "Did your parents or Mrs Bethany tell you to do this?"

"To bite you?"

"I know better than that. I meant, to tell me about the school?"

"The exact opposite. They wanted me to lie to you, which is why I did at first." This part still made me feel ashamed. "I'm sorry, Lucas. I thought it would be safest for both of us if I went along with the story Mrs Bethany made up to cover the hours you forgot."

"It's weird. I remember you biting me this time—but it's hazy. Like how sometimes you can't quite remember a dream five minutes after you wake up. If you hadn't been here with me the whole time and kept me awake, I probably would have forgotten that, too. You'd think being bitten by a vampire would be one of those things that would stick in your memory. You know, stand out from the usual?"

"The forgetting is part of the bite. I don't know why. Maybe nobody knows why. It's not like there are scientific explanations for vampires."

Lucas breathed in deeply, then slowly pushed himself up on his elbows until he was sitting. I braced his shoulder with my free hand, but he shook his head. "I'm okay, I think."

"Now you know why, when we kiss, sometimes I have to, well, hold back."

"I understand now." His smile looked a little funny. "That part is sort of a relief. I was starting to think I needed to switch to a new mouthwash or something."

I giggled and kissed him on the cheek. "Don't worry. I didn't turn you into a vampire."

"I know. I mean, my heart's beating. So no vampire." Lucas took the handkerchief from his pocket and held it to his neck. As he dabbed at the wound, he winced. "I still can't believe you were born a vampire. I've never heard of that."

"How could you have heard of it before you ever knew that vampires were real?"

"Good point."

"I'll never bite you again, unless you ask me to."

"I believe you." Lucas laughed, and it was a strange sound—like he was laughing at himself for some reason I didn't understand. "I believe you completely. Even now."

I hugged him tightly. For Lucas to say that after he'd learned how I lied to him, well, it was as much as I could ever have asked for.

We bandaged Lucas so neatly that nobody would notice while he wore his uniform shirt, went back downstairs, and just managed to avoid missing curfew. He kissed me easily at the entryway to the guys' dorm and then walked away, giving no hint that tonight was different from any other.

"You're acting weird," Raquel said that night as we brushed our teeth at the sinks. "I know things have been tense with you and Lucas. Is everything okay?"

"We're great. We kind of had a misunderstanding over the holiday, but everything's all right now." What she'd perceived as me "acting weird" had been me trying to angle myself so that Raquel couldn't see that the toothpaste I was spitting out was pink with Lucas's blood. "How are you?"

"Me? I'm awesome." She said it with real relish, which made me stare at her in surprise. Raquel laughed. "Sorry. Now that Erich's gone, Evernight seems halfway bearable."

"Really? Listen to you. By next year you'll be Evernight's one and only cheerleader."

"One, if you ever call me a cheerleader again, I will wipe the floor with you," Raquel said around her toothbrush. "Two, it wouldn't be very exciting to cheer for a school whose only sports are equestrian events and fencing. Seriously, talk about being stuck in the Dark Ages."

"More like the early eighteen-hundreds." I turned off the cold water tap and gave her a smug smile. "And I notice that you didn't say you wouldn't come back next year."

This earned me a wet washcloth thrown at my head, but I managed to duck.

That night, as I lay in bed and Patrice slipped out the window for a late snack, I tried to evaluate how I felt. Once again, I knew that almost mystical closeness to Lucas, but this time it was even better. He knew now; he understood everything. I didn't have to lie any longer, and that alone was a vast, soaring relief. Nothing else really mattered.

Or so I thought, until the next morning.

I awoke with the same heightened senses I'd felt before. My parents had said that I would get used to the sensations, but I certainly hadn't yet. I tugged my pillow over my head in a futile attempt to muffle the sound of Genevieve singing madrigals in the shower, the birds cawing outside, and someone downstairs who was already sharpening pencils. The pillowcase felt coarse against my skin, and the smell of Patrice's nail polish was almost overpowering.

"Do you have to give yourself a pedicure every single day?" I threw back the covers.

Patrice glanced down at my bare feet, which obviously hadn't been given much attention in a while. "Some of us place a higher priority on hygiene and grooming than others.

It's simply a matter of preference. I try not to look at it as a reflection on anyone's character."

"Some people have better things to do than paint their nails," I retorted. She ignored me and continued brushing burgundy polish onto her little toe.

By the time I got downstairs, I felt like I was getting a handle on my enhanced senses. What worried me more was the suspense about seeing Lucas. Even though he'd asked to be bitten, the wound had to hurt. What if that had scared him off?

He wasn't waiting for me when I came downstairs. Last term, when we'd been together, he'd usually waited at the entry to the girls' dorm, backpack over one shoulder, but today, nothing. I shrugged it off and told myself that Lucas had simply overslept again. Sometimes he did, and after the previous night, no doubt he needed his rest.

At lunchtime, I looked for him on the grounds. Lucas was nowhere to be seen. Still, I said nothing to my parents or anyone else. Lucas had said last night that he believed in me, and that meant I had to believe in him. Even when I got to chemistry class and saw that Lucas had skipped, I kept telling myself that I had to have faith.

It was just after class when Vic sidled up to me in the hallway, doing a very poor job of acting casual. "Heya. Remember that time you sneaked into our room?"

"Yeah, just before Christmas." I squinted at him. "Why?"

"You think you could do it again? Something weird is going on with Lucas, and he won't say what's up. I figure if anybody could talk him into going to the doctor, it's you."

The doctor? Oh, no. Stricken, I grabbed Vic's arm. "Get me up there. Now."

"Okay, already!" He started leading me toward the guys' dorm, glancing around furtively as if we were being followed. "Don't panic. It's not like appendicitis or something. Lucas's just acting strange. Stranger than usual, that is."

Everyone was on edge since Erich's disappearance, so it wasn't quite as easy for me to sneak up there this time. Vic had to scout each hallway, wait for the coast to be clear, and then motion frantically to me. Then I hurried into the next hallway and ducked into a corner while Vic checked the next hall. Finally we made it, and I stepped inside their room.

Lucas lay on his bed with his hands on his stomach, as if he felt sick. When he looked up at me, I saw surprise—and then relief. He was happy to see me, despite everything, and that made me so glad I had to smile. "Hey," I said, kneeling by the side of his bed. "Stomachache?"

"I don't think that's the problem." He closed his eyes as I brushed a few strands of hair away from his sweaty forehead. "Vic, could you give us a few seconds?"

"Sure thing. Just hang your necktie on the doorknob if you get busy in here. Usually I'm all about the free porn, but—"

"Vic!" we protested in unison.

He held up his hands and backed out, grinning. "Okay, okay."

The second the door shut, I turned back to Lucas. "What's wrong?"

"Ever since this morning, it's like— Bianca, I can hear

everything. Everything in this whole school. People talking, walking, even writing. The pens scraping on paper. It's all so loud." It was all so familiar that an eerie shiver swept through me. Lucas squinted, as if the light was too much for his eyes. "Smells are intense, too. Everything is just . . . exaggerated, I guess. It's unbearable."

"It happened to me, too, after I bit you."

Shaking his head, Lucas insisted, "It can't be the bite. I didn't feel this last time. I woke up at Mrs Bethany's sort of light-headed, but that was all."

"More than once," I whispered, remembering what my mother had told me. "You can't become a vampire until you've been bitten more than once."

Lucas jerked upright, so that his back was wedged against the metal headboard. "Whoa, whoa. I'm not a vampire. I'm alive."

"No, you're not a vampire. But you *could* become a vampire now. It's possible for you. And maybe—maybe once it's possible—your body starts to change."

He grimaced. "You're kidding me, right?"

"I wouldn't joke about something like this!"

"Well, can we, like, reverse it? Fix it so I couldn't become a vampire?"

"I don't know! I don't know how any of this works."

"How can you not know this? Don't you get some kind of vampire facts-of-life speech?"

Lucas was hinting again that my parents had kept important facts from me; I still found it irritating, but now I had the sinking realization that he might be right. "They told me how I would become a vampire. They prepared me for my own change. Not for you."

"I know, I know." His hand on my arm was reassuring, and I hated that he had to comfort me while he was so scared and uncomfortable himself. "I'm having a hard time wrapping my mind around this."

"That makes two of us."

Why hadn't I realized until now how little I understood about the hard facts of being a vampire? It never seemed like anything I had to question, before. Maybe my parents weren't willfully hiding the truth from me; maybe they were simply waiting until I was ready. It hit me that this might've been the real reason they'd insisted I attend Evernight Academy. They could have been trying to prepare me to learn the entire truth.

If that were the case, they'd get their wish. "I'll try and find something out. There must be books in the library. Or I could ask someone who wouldn't get suspicious—Patrice, maybe. Balthazar would tell me, I know, but he'd figure out that I bit you again. He might not tell my parents, but he might, if he thought it was for our own good."

"Don't take any risks," Lucas said. "We'll figure this out somehow."

Learning that truth proved harder than I thought.

"See how easy it is?" Patrice was so happy that I'd asked her to teach me the art of the pedicure, you would've thought I was paying her for private tutoring. "Tomorrow we'll switch to a color more suitable to your skin tone. That coral looks a bit sickly."

"Oh, great. I mean, that would be great." I hadn't counted on having to repaint my toenails for the rest of the school year, but if I could learn something useful, it would be worth it. I began, "It must have been difficult keeping things up in the old days, before, like, nail polish remover and stuff like that."

"Well, we didn't have nail polish to remove. But grooming was a challenge. Talcum powder helped a lot." Patrice sighed, a soft smile on her lips. "Florida water. Scented sachets, too, and perfume on little handkerchiefs that you could tuck in the bosom of your dress."

"And that drew the guys in?" When she nodded, I pushed it a little further. "So you could, well, bite them?"

"Sometimes." Her face changed then, shifting into an expression I'd hardly ever seen on Patrice's face: anger. "The men I met weren't beaus, you know. They were bidders. Buyers. The balls I went to before the War Between the States were octoroon balls— You don't even know what those are, do you?"

I shook my head.

"Girls like me—who were part white and part black, pale enough for plantation owners to consider pleasing—a lot of us were sent to live in New Orleans, and we were brought up as proper young ladies. You could almost forget you were a slave." Patrice stared down at her half-painted toenails, three of which gleamed wetly. "Then, when you got old enough, you could go to octoroon balls so that white men could look you over and buy you from your owner, as a kind of concubine."

"Patrice, that's horrible." I'd never even heard of anything so disgusting.

She simply tossed her head and said airily, "I was changed the night before my first ball. So I went through the entire social season, drinking from man after man. They thought they would use me, but I used them instead. Then I ran away."

This was the first time Patrice had ever shared anything with me—at least, anything real. I would've liked to let her keep talking, so that she could reveal more about her past, but I had to change the subject for Lucas's sake. "Did you ever drink from the same guy more than once?"

"Hmmm?" Patrice seemed to be coming back from a great distance. "Oh, yes. Beauregard. Fat. Self-satisfied. He could lose two pints and not even feel it, which came in handy."

"Did anything happen to Beauregard?"

"On the last night of the social season, he fell from his horse and broke his neck. Maybe it's because he was light-headed from blood loss, but probably he was just drunk. Do you think plum works with my skin tone?"

"Plum looks great on you."

And just like that, it was over. The open door between us

was shut again, and Patrice was again cocooned in her silks and perfumes, safe from having to look at the harshness of her past. I knew I couldn't ask again without making her suspicious, so the entire conversation had been useless.

And the library? Worse than useless. You would think a library in a vampire school would have some books about vampires, right? But no. The only volumes they had were horror novels (shelved in the Humor section) and serious studies of folklore, more fiction than fact, like the ones we'd read in Mrs Bethany's class. Apparently there weren't any books written by vampires for vampires. As I leaned my head back against a row of encyclopedias, sighing in frustration, I wondered if maybe I ought to break into the market someday. That helped with my potential career choices but not so much with Lucas's situation.

Fortunately, Lucas felt better in a couple of days. His enhanced senses dulled slower than mine had, but they did eventually get back to normal, so that wasn't a problem any longer. But there were other changes, too—ones that were harder to understand that felt even more familiar to me.

"Look at this," Lucas said, as we walked out on the edge of the grounds the weekend after. As I watched, he jumped for the lowest branch of a nearby pine and grabbed it, hanging easily from the branches. Then, slowly, he pushed his legs upward, changing his grip on the branch as he pulled himself up and up, curling around the branch and finally stretching into a handstand, his feet up straight above his head.

"I don't guess you're actually an Olympic gymnast," I joked, uneasily.

"Aw, damn, my secret life is out."

"Thought I saw you on a Wheaties box one time."

"Seriously, I'm in shape, but there is no way in hell I ought to be able to do this. And coming back down should hurt, but"—Lucas curled downward, dropped, and landed solidly on his feet—"it's not a problem."

"I can do that, too," I confided, "but only right after I've eaten. My parents could do stuff like that anytime."

"So you're saying this is vampire power." Lucas didn't like the sound of that, I could tell. "That I'm stronger than a human—maybe even stronger than you now—even though I'm not a vampire."

"It doesn't make sense to me either, but—maybe."

As January turned into February, we made other discoveries about the changes in Lucas. We would run together through the countryside, and I didn't hold back. We ran faster than any human could, sometimes for hours. It tired us both out, but we could do it. At nighttime, we slipped out onto the grounds or onto the roof, and I quizzed Lucas on what he could hear. He could pick up the hooting of an owl half a mile away or the snapping of a twig. His hearing wasn't quite as acute as mine, and neither of us felt anything as vividly as we had right after I'd drunk his blood, but it was still superhuman.

We didn't make another trip up to the room at the top of the north tower. Although I wanted to be with Lucas as badly as ever, and I knew he felt the same way, we were both cautious. We had enough trouble controlling my hunger for blood as it was; if something had changed deep within Lucas, there might be other dangers if we started kissing and got too carried away. So you can guess how much I wanted to finally get some answers.

One evening, I decided we ought to try the ultimate test.

I met Lucas at the gazebo with a thermos in my hands. "What's that?" he asked, obviously unsuspecting.

"Blood."

"Oh." His expression was strange. "If you're hungry, just—you know, don't mind me." As he shifted from foot to foot, Lucas avoided meeting my eyes. Apparently Lucas still wasn't comfortable with the idea that I drank blood, which didn't bode well for the experiment I was about to try.

"It's not for me," I began. "It's for you."

Appalled, he retorted, "No way."

"Lucas, let's face it. When I bit you the second time, something changed, down deep, maybe forever. If I've made you part vampire, or a vampire-to-be like me, then we have to know."

He looked pale and drew his long coat more snugly about him. "You really think that's what happened? Because— Bianca, I can't face turning into a vampire. Not ever."

His blunt rejection of the idea hurt; I'd already begun to

dream about us going through the centuries together, vampires forever young and beautiful and head over heels for each other, just like my mother and father. Lucas obviously hadn't gotten that far yet. It was disappointing, but I remained focused on the test. I wore fingerless gray gloves, so I was able to unscrew the lid on the thermos easily. "We have to find out how you react to blood. You know it's true. Just take a drink and get it over with."

"This isn't, like, from a person, right?"

"No! It's cow blood. Superfresh."

Lucas looked like he would rather have stripped naked in the freezing night air. But he took a deep breath, accepted the cup, and managed not to make too much of a face as I poured a rivulet of blood. I only gave him a sip; that would be enough to tell. With a grimace, Lucas lifted the cup to his mouth, slowly tilted it back, and drank—

—and then spat blood all over the ground. "Ugh! Jesus Christ, that's *disgusting*!"

"That answers that." Grimly I screwed the thermos cap back on. I'd heated the blood and sampled it myself, so I knew it was delicious. If Lucas didn't like that, then he still had no appetite for blood at all. "You're not what I am. You're something else."

"How are we supposed to figure that out?" Lucas was busily wiping his mouth with the back of his hand, trying to remove every last trace of the blood. "We don't have reference works; and it's not something either of us has ever run into before.

And before you ask, no, they don't have anything on this on Wikipedia. I got so desperate, I checked. Nothing. There's just . . . nothing."

I wished Lucas would stop talking like he knew something about vampires; it was sort of annoying. Still, he'd just tasted something really gross, so I figured I'd let him off this time. "I have a suggestion. You won't like it, but I think that if you consider it, you'll realize it's the best thing to do."

"Okay, tell me this suggestion I won't like."

"Let's ask my parents."

"You were right about my not liking it." Lucas ran his hands through his hair, like he wanted to rip it from its roots in frustration. "Just . . . tell them? Tell the vampires what's wrong with me?"

"Stop thinking of them as 'vampires' and think of them as my parents." I knew it would take Lucas a while to make this transition, but that didn't mean I wasn't going to push. He'd learned to see me for myself, given time. Eventually he could do the same for Mom and Dad. "They'll hear you out, and if they can help, they will." Lucas shook his head. "If they're going to be mad at someone, that's going to be me. I'm the one who bit you again and started all this."

"Then we shouldn't get you into trouble."

"If you need help, then that's what's important. Nothing else." I faced him squarely. "Think about it, Lucas. Once they know, we can talk openly. Get answers to all your questions and mine, too. If you're destined to be a vampire—"

He shuddered. "We don't know that."

"*If*, I said. You need to know all about us, don't you? Even the history and powers that I don't know about yet. We could learn all about it together." And perhaps Lucas would like what he heard and decide to join me as a vampire forever. I could hope, couldn't I? "Once you're one of us—in whatever way—then they can talk to you openly. You can ask whatever you want. And maybe this will make my parents realize that I'm old enough to hear the whole truth now. We won't be confused or lost anymore. We'll learn what we need to learn; we'll learn everything. Don't you see?"

Lucas froze. For the first time, he seemed to understand what I'd been saying—that whatever had happened to him would, in some way, let him become a part of Evernight. Despite his dislike of the school, I sensed that he wanted to know more about it, so much so that it surprised us both. Maybe Lucas needed to belong to something after all.

Or maybe he was starting to think about becoming a vampire and staying with me forever.

"Don't ask me to do this," Lucas said quietly. "Don't give me that chance."

"Are you afraid you'll like what you hear?" I challenged him.

Lucas didn't answer. Finally, slowly, he nodded. "Let's talk to them now."

I'd predicted that Mom and Dad would be upset with me, but I hadn't guessed the half of it. First Mom read me the riot act about ignoring all their warnings. Then Dad wanted to know just what Lucas was thinking taking a young girl to the top of the north tower alone.

"I'm almost seventeen!" I shouted at one point. "You keep telling me to make mature decisions, and when I make one, you yell at me!"

"Mature decisions!" My father was so outraged that I half expected him to grow fangs any second. "You reveal all our secrets because you *like a boy* and you want to talk about mature decisions? You are on thin ice, young lady."

"Adrian, calm down." Mom put both her hands on his shoulders. I thought she was sticking up for me until she added, "If Bianca wants to spend the next thousand years looking too young to get a job or rent a car or do any of the basic things that make life manageable, then we can't really stop her."

"That's not what I want!" I couldn't even imagine getting carded for all eternity. "I didn't kill him. I didn't change. Okay?"

Dad retorted, "You came damn close to it, and you know it."

"I don't know that at all! You never explained to me what would happen if I bit a human and didn't kill him! You never explained to me what humans would or wouldn't know the next day! There's a whole lot you never explained to me, and now I finally realize how stupid you've kept me all these years!"

"Excuse us for not knowing exactly how to handle this! There's only a handful of vampire babies born a century. It's not like we had anybody to turn to for advice, you know." Mom looked mad enough to pull her hair out. "But, yeah, Bianca, at this point, I agree with you. Clearly, somewhere, we screwed up. If we hadn't, you'd be behaving sensibly now instead of carrying on like this!"

From his place on my parents' couch, where he had been forcefully told to remain, Lucas attempted to defend me. "This is mostly my fault—"

"You keep quiet." Dad's glare could have melted metal. "I intend to have a long talk with you later."

Just when I thought it couldn't get worse, Mom said, "We'll have to tell Mrs Bethany."

"What?" I couldn't believe what I was hearing. Lucas's eyes opened wide. "Mom, no!"

"Your mother is right." Dad stalked toward the doorway. "You've told a human the secret of Evernight. We have to explain that to Mrs Bethany, which you should have realized from the start."

As the door slammed shut behind him, Mom added, more quietly, "Our secrets protect us, Bianca. Someday you'll understand that."

It felt like I would never understand any of this. I sank down beside Lucas on the sofa, so that at least we'd be together when the boom fell. All three of us sat in sullen silence for several minutes, until footsteps began to echo on the stone staircase outside. The sound made me shiver. Mrs Bethany was near.

She swept in as if she owned the place and the rest of us

were merely intruders. My father, behind her, might as well have been her shadow. Lavender fragrance followed her, changing the space subtly from ours to hers. Her dark eyes focused instantly on Lucas, who faced her steadily but said nothing.

"So much for your promised self-control, Miss Olivier." Her long skirts brushed along the floor as she stepped closer. Tonight she wore a silver bar pin at the collar of her blouse, so bright that the light glinted off it. Her long fingernails were painted the darkest imaginable purple, but it didn't hide the deep grooves in each nail. "I suspected it would come to this sooner or later. Sooner it is."

"This isn't Bianca's fault," Lucas said. "It's mine."

"How very gallant of you, Mr Ross. But I think it's rather obvious who was the active party here." She tugged his collar open, a weirdly intimate gesture from a teacher toward a student. Lucas tensed, and I thought that if she actually put her hand on his neck, he might snap. His temper had frayed from less. Instead, she merely glanced at the pink scars left after two weeks. "You've been bitten twice by a vampire. Do you know what that means?"

"How could he?" I asked. "He didn't even know vampires were real until a couple of months ago."

Mrs Bethany sighed. "Remind me to go over the concept of the 'rhetorical question' in class. As I was saying, Mr Ross, you are now marked as one of our own."

"Marked," Lucas repeated. "You mean, as Bianca's?"

"The change is subtle at first." She paced slowly around

Lucas, studying him from head to toe. "I sense it now, but only because you called my attention to it. As time goes on, however, the change will become more pronounced. The other vampires around you will notice. Eventually they will be unable to ignore it. You have surrendered to a vampire, and more than once. That has brought you to the very brink of being changed into one of us."

Lucas interjected, "Does that mean I have to become a vampire no matter what?" I fidgeted, unable to wholly conceal my hope. My mother shot me a look that made me go still.

Mrs Bethany shook her head. "Not necessarily. You might yet live a long life and die of other causes, if that's the sort of thing you consider cause for celebration. However, soon you'll find yourself more and more drawn to Miss Olivier, whose lack of discipline has already been made very clear." Dad took a step forward, like he was going to defend me, but Mom put one hand on his shoulder to keep him back. "Other vampires will find you equally appealing, although the taboo against hunting another vampire's chosen prey should protect you—for a time. Eventually, Mr Ross, you'll find the prospect entices you as much as it does her. You will desire it more powerfully than you can possibly guess. It is a craving no pure human can ever understand. When that time comes, you will probably choose to join us."

If Lucas was going to lose it, I thought this would be the moment. But he remained calm. "Does that mean I'm sort of . . . in between? Like Bianca?"

"Not exactly like her, but close enough." Mrs Bethany's prim mouth relaxed slightly, and I realized that she was almost smiling. "You are a quick study, Mr Ross."

"I'd like to know more," he said, seizing upon her approval. "I want to understand these . . . senses. Abilities. Powers."

"And limitations, too. Those take root in humans more slowly than our powers, but they will arrive. You cannot afford to forget that." Mrs Bethany considered it for a few more seconds, then nodded. "This was not what I intended when I opened the school to human students, but I ought to have anticipated it. I'll send over some papers that might help you. Old letters, studies, things like that regarding those who have been in your situation and who have chosen to follow our path. Just remember this, Mr Ross: Our secret is now your secret. The more you learn, the more you belong to us. You can no longer betray the truth about Evernight without also betraying yourself. I will be watching you very closely from now on."

"I believe you. I'm not going to say a word about vampires to anybody." He gave me a sidelong glance. "Well, at least not to anybody who doesn't already know."

I squeezed his hand, happy and relieved. It didn't matter what my parents said to us now or how long I was going to be grounded. All that mattered was that the truth was out at last, and Lucas would be okay. And he might—just maybe—be mine forever.

Not until much later that night did I realize that Mrs

Bethany had never told Lucas what would happen if he didn't choose to become a vampire. She didn't offer it as an option. I wondered if that was because it was impossible for him to choose anything else—or because he wouldn't be allowed to choose.

Chapter Fifteen

WITH MARCH CAME RAIN, TORRENTS OF IT, blurring the windowpanes and turning the earth to mud. For the first time, the grounds weren't available to us as an escape. But for the first time, we didn't need it. Lucas and I were learning about Evernight now. We were becoming a part of it.

"Look at this." Lucas pushed one of Mrs Bethany's heavy, black, leather-bound books toward me as we sat together in a private corner of the library. The only other sound was raindrops pattering against the window. The book's pages were brownish with age and the ink had faded, so I had to squint to make out the words. I read as Lucas explained, "They keep talking about 'the Tribe.' Some older group of vampires. Is anybody here from this Tribe?"

"I never heard of the Tribe before." I'd never imagined how complicated vampire lore was; my parents had never hinted at any of this. "But what do they mean by older? My dad is nearly a thousand years old. Surely that's about as old as it gets."

"Not if everyone is immortal. There ought to be vampires two, three, ten times older than him. Ancient Romans. Ancient Egyptians. Whoever came before those guys. Where are they? Not here, I don't think."

He was right. The oldest vampire at Evernight was probably Ranulf, who had died in the seventh century. Of course, some vampires did die, like, *finally* die; if you didn't get any blood for months and months, or even if you didn't drink blood for a shorter time and then were exposed to the sun—that could get you. My parents had made that clear when I was a little kid who didn't want to finish her glass of goat's blood. Everyone's worst nightmare was fire, which killed vampires even more quickly than it did humans. Despite all those dangers, a lot of vampires should have survived even longer than Ranulf.

"Mom and Dad say some people get lost," I murmured. "That they lose track of time and humanity altogether. Evernight Academy was built so that vampires wouldn't fall into that trap. Do you suppose that's what my parents meant? Maybe the Tribe is all the vampires who get lost. They're hermits and recluses, with no connection to humanity." The thought made me shiver.

"Is this creeping you out?"

"Yeah, a little."

Lucas brushed his thumb across my cheek. "You want us to take a break?"

I realized that I did, kind of. "I ought to study history. It's hard enough to get As when you're being graded on a curve alongside people who actually witnessed about half the events in the book. Now Mom's being tougher on me than ever."

"Go ahead." Already he had turned his attention back to the book of vampire lore. "I'll be right here." Lucas didn't lift his head from the book for the next hour, and when I bundled up my things to go downstairs, he let me leave without him so that he could keep working until the moment the library closed. (There was no taking the book back to his room; we agreed that Vic might be oblivious, but he wasn't stupid, and leaving the real vampire information out where Vic could see it would be crazy.)

Every once in a while I asked myself if Lucas could have any other reason for immersing himself in Mrs Bethany's books. But I always pushed the thought away almost instantly. Mostly I encouraged him, thinking that he was getting closer to becoming a vampire—and staying with me—forever.

Not that everybody liked that idea, of course. Courtney had kind of chilled out after I bit Lucas for the first time, apparently figuring that I was now "in the club." However, she didn't want Lucas in the club with us, which meant that after news of the second bite spread around the school, she was in high bitch mode.

"Can you imagine hanging around with that guy for a hundred years?" she complained loudly to Genevieve in Modern Technology one day, while Mr Yee was in the corner patiently explaining something to the perpetually bewildered Ranulf. "I mean, eww. One school year of Lucas Ross's attitude is too much. If he thinks I'm going to acknowledge his sorry existence in a couple of decades, when he's trying to suck up to all the people he put down here, he can think again."

Balthazar, who had been attempting to program the microwave that provided the lesson for the day, casually called, "Hey, Courtney, refresh my memory. The other day, I was thinking that I'd seen you in French Indochina, but then I realized that wasn't quite right. You were changed—what—fifty years ago?"

"Um." Courtney suddenly became really interested in the tip of her ponytail. "About that."

"Wait, no. Not fifty." Balthazar's forehead furrowed, as if the microwave had deeply confused him, although I could see he'd already figured out the controls. "It was—no, not the seventies either—1987, right?"

"No!" Her cheeks were pink now. Genevieve stared at her friend; she hadn't heard this before and looked appalled. Courtney retorted, "It was 1984."

"Ohhh. 1984. Three years earlier. Way after the French left Indochina. My mistake." Balthazar shrugged. "Forgive me, Courtney. The decades sort of run together for those of us who've been around awhile."

I pretended not to overhear, but I couldn't help smirking as Balthazar triumphantly hit Start and the microwave started nuking a cup of blood. Age meant status: Anybody who hadn't even lasted half a century yet was a newbie, so all Courtney's posturing was completely blown. Lucas and I belonged at the school every bit as much as she did—

—which felt weird, but was true. Perhaps we would return here in forty years, or four hundred. Maybe we would come back to learn about how human life had changed and revisit the place we'd first met. It still spooked me to think about the vastness of the years that stretched out in front of us both. I got a little scared every time I thought about how much I might have to adapt to a world that could change as much as it had changed for my father since the Norman Conquest. The feeling that came over me was a lot like the fear of heights—so far to fall.

But when I thought about facing those years with Lucas by my side, I wasn't afraid.

The worst storm of all blew through about the middle of March, a Saturday night so windy that even the thick antique glass of the school's windows rattled in the frames. Lightning lit up the sky so often that sometimes, for a minute or more, it looked like daylight outside. With absolutely everyone trapped inside, every single common room was packed. Fortunately, a few friends and I had a way to escape.

"Okay, how can you have this much Duke Ellington and no Dizzy Gillespie?" Balthazar demanded of my father. He sat on the floor cross-legged, going through the albums to find music for us to listen to. I could've grabbed a few CDs and the player from my room, but that would've meant leaving my place beside Lucas on the sofa. Lucas had his arm around my shoulder, so I wasn't budging.

"I used to have some Dizzy," Dad said. "Lost that in a fire in sixty-five."

Patrice, who sat primly in a nearby chair, sighed. "I had a terrible fire in 1892. It's horrifying."

"I would've thought you wouldn't mind the chance to shop for a whole new wardrobe," Lucas teased. Everyone sort of looked at him. "What did I say?"

"Fire is one of the few things that can kill us," Mom explained, arms folded in front of her chest. She and Dad were still wary of Lucas, but they were trying to make the best of things. Like Mrs Bethany, they had rationalized that the more Lucas knew, the less likely he was to make another terrible mistake. "That makes fire scary stuff."

Lucas's expression clouded, and for a moment I had no idea what he was thinking or feeling. Mostly I was pleased because Mom had said "us," like Lucas already belonged.

Then Lucas said abruptly, "We were wondering about this the other day, actually. What are the other ways? That vampires can die, I mean?"

"Well, let's see." Dad clapped his hands together, like he had to work to remember this after a millennium. "Pretty short list, actually."

"Stakes," Lucas said firmly. "That's what they show on TV, anyway."

"Idiot box." Patrice obviously thought television was too

newfangled to merit her attention. But she was willing to talk to Lucas about being a vampire. I hoped she might open up a little, the way she had to me about her life in New Orleans, but so far she had mostly stuck to hard facts. "Stakes 'kill' us, but only temporarily. Once the stake is pulled out, you'll be fine again in no time."

Balthazar put a Billie Holiday album on as he added, "You just have to make sure you have a friend who can dig you up and take care of that."

"It's pretty much fire and beheading." Mom ticked these two options off on her fingers.

"And holy water?" Lucas asked.

"Hardly." My father didn't bother to hide his contempt for Lucas's suggestion. "I've had holy water thrown at me a few times. If there's any difference between that and rainwater, I never felt it."

Lucas looked skeptical, but he simply nodded. "Okay. Sorry, I know these are stupid questions."

"It's a lot to absorb," Patrice said. From her, this was extremely charitable, so I gave her a smile as I leaned my head against Lucas's shoulder. Sheets of rain washed against the windows, a constant whisper of noise beneath Billie's croaky singing.

Mom must have noticed my snuggling a bit with Lucas, because she quickly tapped my father on the shoulder. "Okay, Adrian. We've hung out long enough. I'm sure the kids would rather talk without us."

"Kids? Save that for the classroom. We're almost exactly the same age!" Balthazar laughed. He was right, which was incredibly weird to think about. "You should stick around."

"I don't mind." Patrice shrugged.

Lucas and I shared a look. We kind of did mind, but in an ideal world, Mom and Dad would've taken Balthazar and Patrice away with them so we could make out on the couch. That wasn't going to happen.

Doing her eerie maternal-telepathy thing, Mom sighed sympathetically. "I guess there are times when no amount of privacy from the parents is enough, huh?"

"Evernight is definitely a challenging place to date," Lucas agreed. Balthazar acted really interested in the Billie Holliday album cover all of a sudden.

Remembering how I'd shot Balthazar down, I cast about for any way to lighten the moment for him, then remembered a funny story I could tell. "Hey, at least it isn't as bad for us as it was for your great-grandfather-whatever. Right, Lucas?" Lucas gave me a blank look. His face went pale, like I'd said something scary. Surely he was thinking about the wrong thing.

"Is this a family anecdote?" Mom asked. "Those are usually the best kind." Everyone was listening now.

"One of Lucas's ancestors came to Evernight, a great-grandfather or something around a hundred and fifty years ago. Come on, you tell it better!" I elbowed Lucas, but now his body was totally tense, as rigid as a board. He had said the story was a secret, but that had to be a joke, didn't it? A story more than a hundred years old couldn't be a secret. Maybe Lucas thought it was embarrassing, but I couldn't see why he'd be ashamed of something that didn't really have anything to do with him. "Anyway, he came here to study. He got into a duel with one of the other students, maybe over a girl, and they fought right in the great hall. That's how that one stained-glass window was broken—did you know that? Neither of them died, but they expelled him, and . . ."

My voice trailed off as I saw that my parents and Balthazar had all gone completely still. They were staring at Lucas. His fingers were digging into my shoulder.

The only other person in the room who looked as confused as I felt was Patrice. "They let humans in before?"

"No," Balthazar said sharply. "Never."

"You had an ancestor who was a vampire?" I was astonished. "Lucas, you never knew this? Is that even possible?"

"I don't think that's what we're dealing with." My father stood up slowly. He wasn't a very tall man, yet something about the way he loomed over us on the sofa was incredibly intimidating. "I don't think that at all."

"A hundred and fifty years ago." Mom's voice shook. "That was when . . . the one time that they . . ."

Dad never took his eyes off Lucas. "Yes."

Then he grabbed Lucas by the throat.

I screamed. Had Dad gone crazy? Suddenly Lucas pushed his arms through my father's, prying him off, and then Lucas's fist smashed into Dad's nose. Blood sprayed out, wet drops hitting me across the face.

"Stop! What are you doing? Stop!" I cried.

Everything after that happened so fast. Balthazar pulled me away from the fight, hard, so that I stumbled and fell onto the floor. He threw a punch at Lucas, too, but Lucas ducked it. Patrice wrapped her arms around me, screaming loudly, and because of that unable to move. My mother slammed one of the wooden dinner chairs onto the floor so forcefully that it broke. I thought at first that she was trying to get the guys' attention, to figure out what the hell was going on, but instead she took one of the chair legs in her hand as a club and swung it into the small of Lucas's back.

He shouted in pain, but instantly he spun, broke Mom's grip, and left her clutching her hand. Dad and Balthazar were both on Lucas, trying to fight him as one, but he was as fast as they were, blocking every blow. I remembered the pizza parlor and the fight there. As formidable as Lucas had come across then, that had been nothing. *This* was how he could really fight—powerful enough to fend off two vampires at once.

I was strong enough to fight with them, but I didn't want to fight my parents for Lucas, or Lucas for my parents, not until I understood what the hell had just happened.

"What are you doing?" I shrieked. "Stop it, everyone, stop it!"

They didn't stop. My father swung at Lucas's gut, and when Lucas dodged it, he seemed to fall backward—but he was faking, crouching to grab the chair leg my mother had dropped. Immediately Dad and Balthazar edged backward, and I realized Lucas now possessed a stake. Maybe he couldn't kill either of them forever with that alone, but he could take them out of commission.

Patrice screamed in my ear as Lucas plunged the stake toward Balthazar's chest. Balthazar leaped backward, only barely avoiding the blow. I could see a cut along his cheekbone, crescent shaped from Lucas's fist. Then, to my horror, Lucas focused on my father. He was actually trying to stake Dad.

"Lucas, don't!" I pleaded. "Mom, tell him to— Where's Mom?" She seemed to have vanished while I was distracted by the fight.

"She's run downstairs for help." My father's words came out in a growl. "Mrs Bethany will be here soon, and then we'll get this taken care of."

Lucas only hesitated for a second. "Bianca, I'm sorry. I'm so sorry."

"Lucas?"

His eyes met mine. "I love you."

And then he ran, out the door, down the steps. At first all of us were too stunned to do anything, but then Dad and Balthazar took off after him. I turned to Patrice, who still huddled next to me on the floor. "Do you understand any of this?"

"No." She ran her hands over her smooth, plaited hair, as if she could erase her earlier panic by fixing her own appearance. Nothing else mattered to her.

Though my legs shook, I got up and rushed after them, stumbling down the steps. I could hear Balthazar's shouts echoing against the stone: "Stop him! Stop him now!"

Then there was a terrible crash, the silvery sound of splinters of glass ricocheting against floors and walls, and my father swore. My heart pounded so hard that I felt almost like I'd die if I didn't stop running, but I'd die if I did stop, because Lucas was in danger and I had to be with him.

I half ran, half fell the last spiral of the steps to see Balthazar, Dad, and a few students standing around, staring at the one clear glass window of the great hall. The window was shattered, and I realized that Lucas had used the chair leg to break it and escape. He hadn't even had the minute it would've taken to run halfway down the hall to the door. My parents had probably stopped chasing him only because plenty of human kids were in the room, freaked-out and about to start asking difficult questions.

My mother walked into the great hall, clutching her wrist. A few steps behind her was Mrs Bethany, whose dark eyes flashed with barely suppressed rage.

"What the hell is going on?" Raquel came down the steps behind me. "Was there—was there a fight or something?"

Mrs Bethany drew herself upright. "This is none of your concern. Everyone, back to your rooms."

Raquel shot me a look as she started edging back up to our floor. Obviously she wanted me to explain, but how could I? My entire body flushed hot, then cold with every heartbeat, and I couldn't really breathe. It hadn't been five minutes since

I'd sat next to Lucas while we laughed at my parents' jokes.

Mom, Dad, and Balthazar didn't move when the others did, so I remained still, too. As soon as everyone else had left, I wanted to ask Dad what this meant, but I didn't get the chance. Mrs Bethany demanded, "What happened?"

"Lucas is part of Black Cross," my father said. Mrs Bethany's eyes went wide—not like she was scared but definitely surprised, the first time I'd ever seen her show any vulnerability at all. "We found out only now."

"Black Cross." She balled her hands into fists and stared at the broken window. The rain blew through the jagged opening with the gusts of wind, and thunder boomed out again. "What can they mean by this?"

"We have to go after him immediately." Dad looked ready to run outside that second. Mom laid her good hand on his arm.

Very quietly, she said, "There will always be hunters. Nothing has really changed."

Mrs Bethany turned toward her, head cocked, eyes narrow. "Your pity is useless to us, Celia. I understand your desire to spare your daughter pain, but if you and your husband had been more vigilant, she would not be in this situation now."

"This kid came here for a reason. He hurt our daughter to accomplish it. I intend to find out what it is." Dad peered through the darkness. "He can't move as fast in the storm as we can. We should go now."

"We have time to assemble a team," Mrs Bethany insisted. "Mr Ross will summon help as soon as he can, which means we cannot be sure of finding him alone. Mr and Mrs Olivier, both of you, come with me to fetch and arm the others."

"I'm on the team, too." Balthazar's jaw was set.

Her eyes swept up and down as though taking his measure. "Very well, Mr More. For the moment, I suggest you see to Miss Olivier. Explain her folly and keep her quiet."

Mom held out a hand toward me. "I should talk to her."

"Given your willingness to ignore the hard facts, I think the task is better left to a more neutral party." Mrs Bethany pointed toward the staircase.

I half expected Mom to tell Mrs Bethany where she could shove her attitude, but Dad grabbed her good arm and pulled her upstairs with him. Long skirts in her hands, Mrs Bethany followed.

The moment we were alone, I turned to Balthazar. "What just happened?"

"Shh, Bianca, calm down." He put his hands on my shoulders, but I wasn't having any of it.

"Calm down? You guys just attacked my boyfriend, who attacked back. I don't understand this, none of it! Please, Balthazar, just tell me—tell me, oh, God, what? I don't even know what to ask!" So many questions welled up inside me that they seemed to stick in my throat, choking me.

Balthazar said evenly, "You've been lied to. We've all been lied to."

One question rose to blot out all the others. "What is Black Cross?"

"Vampire hunters."

"*What?*"

"Black Cross is a group of vampire hunters who have plagued us ever since the Middle Ages. They track us down. They separate us from others of our kind. And they kill us." Balthazar wiped the drops of my father's blood from my face as tenderly as though they were tears. "They tried to infiltrate Evernight Academy once before. Every so often, a human talks or bribes his way in here, and they tolerate it as a way of avoiding attention. One of those humans turned out to be a member of Black Cross."

"Around a hundred and fifty years ago." The story I'd told upstairs, the one Lucas had revealed when we first met, suddenly made sense. "The fight in the story—it wasn't a duel, was it?"

Balthazar shook his head. "No. The Black Cross operative was discovered and fought his way out. The same thing happened tonight."

Black Cross. Vampire hunters. Lucas hadn't mentioned finding them in the books Mrs Bethany gave him; I realized he had kept them from me.

Lucas had come here to hunt down and kill creatures like me. He'd even coaxed me into biting him again—and giving him the strength and power to truly fight back. He'd used me to become a more efficient killer, and then he'd tried to murder my parents, and he'd lied about everything, all along.

In the beginning, before Lucas knew I was a vampire, he kept trying to protect me. I thought he was taking care of me because I was lonely, but it wasn't that at all. He thought I was a human surrounded by vampires, and that's why he kept looking out for me.

But ever since he found out what I really am, he's been using me to get deeper inside Evernight. To gain our powers. To get whatever he wanted. He made me feel guilty about lying to him when he was telling an even bigger lie.

What had seemed like love was betrayal.

Chapter Sixteen

I SAT NUMBLY ON THE BOTTOM STEP OF THE staircase, listening to the preparations taking place all around me.

Mrs Bethany's team contained only five vampires: her, my parents, Balthazar, and Professor Iwerebon. All of them wore heavy slickers and knives strapped to their calves and forearms.

"We should have guns." That was Balthazar. "To deal with situations like this."

"We have only been forced to confront 'situations like this' twice in more than two hundred years." Mrs Bethany, icier than ever. "Our abilities are usually more than sufficient to deal with humans. Or do you not feel up to the task, Mr More?"

Lucas is a vampire hunter. Lucas came here to kill people like my parents. He told me to distrust them; he probably thought they stole me as a baby. He tried to drive a wedge between us. I thought he was just being rude, but maybe he was really going to kill them after all.

"I can handle myself," Balthazar said. "But it's possible that Lucas has armed himself as well. He's Black Cross. There's no way he came here unprepared. Somewhere on campus, he's got a stash of supplies. You can bet that includes weapons."

We went up the stairs of the north tower together, and he protested the entire way. I thought it was because Lucas was scared of me, scared of vampires, but that wasn't it at all. Even when we were making out on the floor, he asked for us to be together again somewhere else.

"The room at the top of the north tower." My voice sounded so strange, hardly like mine at all. "That's where it is."

Mrs Bethany drew herself up. "You knew about this?"

"No. It's just a hunch."

"Let's check it out." Balthazar held out his hand to help me up. "Come on."

The room didn't look any different to me than it had when Lucas and I were up there together. Mrs Bethany closed her eyes for a moment in dismay. "The records room. If he's been up here, he's read almost all of our history. The hiding places of so many of us—now, Black Cross knows."

"A lot of these records are decades out of date," Dad reasoned. "The more recent years are in the computer."

"He broke into that, too, I think," I said, remembering the day I'd found Lucas sneaking out of Mrs Bethany's carriage house office.

Mrs Bethany whirled on me, her temper clearly at the

breaking point. "You saw that Lucas Ross was breaking rules, yet you never warned anyone in authority. You let a member of Black Cross run rampant at Evernight for months on end, Miss Olivier. Don't think I'll forget this."

Whenever she spoke to me like that, I usually cringed. This time, I shot back, "You're the one who admitted him in the first place!"

After that, nobody said anything for a second. I'd spoken only to defend myself, but I realized that Mrs Bethany had screwed up—really, seriously screwed up—and her attempt to pin the blame on me had just failed.

Instead of strangling me, Mrs Bethany stiffly turned back to searching the room. "Open every box. Look in every closet and in the rafters. I want to know everything Mr Ross kept up here."

Memories of Lucas and I together nearly overwhelmed me, but I concentrated on one moment in particular. When we'd first come into this room, Lucas had immediately taken a seat atop the long trunk against the nearby wall. I'd thought he just wanted to sit down, but maybe he'd done that for a different reason: to keep me from opening it.

Balthazar followed my eyes. He didn't say anything out loud, but he raised one eyebrow, questioning. I nodded, and he went to the trunk and opened its lid. I couldn't see what was inside, but my mother gasped and Professor Iwerebon swore beneath his breath. "What is it?" I asked.

Mrs Bethany stepped closer and peered down into the trunk. Her face remained imperiously cool as she bent her knees and picked up a skull.

I screamed, then immediately felt stupid for doing so. "That's got to be really old. I mean, look at it."

"When we die, our bodies decompose rather rapidly, Miss Olivier." Mrs Bethany kept turning the skull that way and this. "To be precise, they decompose to the stage they should have reached since the time of human death. Though the flesh is gone, a few scraps of skin remain—which suggests this skull belonged to a vampire who died decades ago, perhaps even a century."

"Erich," Balthazar said suddenly. "He said once that he died in World War I. Lucas and Erich always had it in for each other. If Lucas lured him up here, and Erich had no idea that he was dealing with a Black Cross hunter, then it would've been no contest."

"Not if Lucas had one of these." My father had opened another box nearby, from which he lifted a huge knife—no, a machete. "This thing could make quick work of any of us."

Balthazar gave a low whistle as he looked at the blade. "Those two used to fight, but Erich always got the better of Lucas. Either Lucas threw the fights on purpose, or he knew if he showed what he could really do, we might have caught on."

I protested, "I thought Erich ran away." Surely that had to be the truth. Lucas and Erich had fought, but Lucas couldn't have *killed* him.

"We all thought that, but we were all wrong." Mrs Bethany

let Erich's skull drop unceremoniously back into the trunk. "Keep searching."

The others did as she said. Trembling, I stepped closer to the trunk to look inside. There lay a jumble of bones, a dusty Evernight uniform, and, in the corner, a tan hoop. With a jolt I realized it was Raquel's leather bracelet, the one that had been missing. Lucas wouldn't have stolen it. No, Erich had taken it, and he'd had it on him when he died.

When Lucas killed him.

"Bianca? Honey?" My mother came to my side. She wore jeans and boots; normally she refused to dress in what she still thought of as men's clothes, but to catch Lucas, she'd made an exception. "You should go to our apartment. You don't need to see any more of this."

"Go to the apartment and do what? Read a nice book? Listen to records? I don't think so."

"We should be able to track him despite the rain. You will never tell anyone else at this school what transpires here tonight." Mrs Bethany glared at me over Iwerebon's shoulder.

Slowly I shut the lid of the trunk. "I'm coming, too."

"Bianca?" Mom shook her head. "You don't have to do this."

"Yes, I do."

"Don't." Balthazar stepped closer to me. "You've never done anything like this, and Black Cross—they're good. Deadly. Lucas might be young, but he knows what he's doing. That much is obvious."

"What Balthazar is too polite to say is that it's dangerous."
Dad looked furious. His nose was red and swollen—probably
broken. Even vampire injuries take a while to heal. "Lucas
Ross could hurt you, even kill you."

I shivered, but I stood my ground. "He could kill any of
you. You're still going."

"We're going to take care of everything," Balthazar insisted.
"The worst part of all of this is what he did to you, Bianca.
Your parents won't let Lucas get away with it, and neither
will I."

Mrs Bethany raised one eyebrow. Obviously she didn't
consider my broken heart the "worst part of all this," and I
expected her to shoot me down as usual. Instead she said,
"She may join us."

My mother stared at her. "She's only a child!"

"She was old enough to bite a human. Old enough to give
him powers. That makes her old enough to face the consequences." Her gaze bored into me. "Will you require a weapon,
Miss Olivier?"

"No." I couldn't imagine plunging a knife into Lucas's
body.

Mrs Bethany misunderstood me—on purpose, maybe.
"You might as well complete your transformation tonight, I
suppose."

"Tonight?" My parents said as one.

"All children must grow up eventually."

She wants me to bite Lucas again. This time, she wants me

to kill him. They'd set fire to the body before he could rise again
as a vampire. Lucas would be gone forever.

Mrs Bethany went to the door and pushed it open. Balthazar draped one of the slickers across my shoulders, and I struggled to slip my arms into the overlong sleeves. "Let's go."

We began our trip downstairs into the dark.

My parents had told me they were vampires as soon as I was old enough to understand about keeping secrets, so that was as ordinary to me as the fact that Mom's hair was the color of caramel or that Dad liked to snap his fingers to jazz from the 1950s. They drank blood at the dinner table instead of eating food, and they liked to reminisce about sailing ships and spinning wheels and, in Dad's case, the time he saw William Shakespeare acting in one of his own plays. But those were little things, more funny and endearing than frightening. I'd never thought of them as unnatural.

As soon as we began our pursuit, I realized how little I truly knew them.

They moved faster than I could, faster than most humans could. Lucas and I had thought we were stretching our powers when we'd run across these grounds a few weeks ago, but that was nothing compared to this. Mom, Dad, Balthazar, every one of them—they were sure-footed despite the mud and able to see their way in the dark. I had to rely on the flashes of lightning and their voices to guide me.

"Here!" Professor Iwerebon's Nigerian accent was thicker

when he was agitated. "The boy came this way."

How could they know that? I realized that Iwerebon's hand rested upon the branches of a bush. When I touched it as well, I could feel the soft buds of new leaves fuzzy against my chilled palms. One of the branches was broken. Lucas had snapped it when he'd run by.

He's running for his life. He must be so scared.

He said he loved me.

Lightning flashed once more, making it bright as day for a split second. I could see Mrs Bethany's profile against the dark forest, and I recognized the landscape enough to know that we were very near the river. It was the first time in a while I'd had any idea where we were, because the rain clouds shrouded the stars. "This isn't one of the usual paths the students take," Mrs Bethany said. "Black Cross would've trained him well enough to have an escape plan. That means he'd marked this route in advance."

Thunder rolled over us, blotting out whatever Professor Iwerebon said in response. Wearily I pulled my feet out of the mud they were sinking into; Balthazar took my elbow, balancing me as I got to more solid ground.

All this time I thought Lucas was protecting me, but instead he put me in danger. How can that be true?

Then Balthazar's fingers tightened upon my arm. "This way. Over here."

When lightning forked through the sky again, I saw what Balthazar had glimpsed: mucky, foot-sized holes in the mud, leading toward the river. Lucas had been forced to pull his feet out just like me. Despite the new powers we shared, he wasn't as quick or as unearthly graceful as the older vampires all around me. Lucas was just a guy, running as fast as he could through a terrible storm and knowing that, if he was captured, he might die.

It was raining too hard for footprints like that to last long without being washed away. We'd already nearly caught up to him.

He lied to me from the beginning. From the very first day. All those fears I had about keeping secrets from him, and Lucas was playing me for a fool every single time we kissed.

"Hurry!" Mrs Bethany urged us forward. Despite her long skirts, she could move faster than anyone else. I straggled behind, breathing hard and cold to the bone, but I was able to keep close enough to hear the rain pattering against their coats. "He will have crossed the river. We'll lose time there."

The river.

All my life, my parents had joked about how terrible running water was. When we took road trips, they would always try to arrange it so that we never crossed any rivers on our way. If we had to, they could do it, but usually it took a while— Dad pulling the car over once we were in sight of the bridge, Mom biting her fingernails anxiously, me laughing at them for the entire half hour or so it took them to get up the nerve. They both described their shipboard voyage to the New World as the absolute worst experience they'd ever endured.

Vampires have trouble crossing running water. Some of the human students had wondered why the teacher chaperones traveled into Riverton ahead of us, but I'd always known it was because they wanted to cross the bridge in their own time, without revealing how badly the experience unsettled them. Now I realized that Lucas had understood, too, and he was counting on that fact to keep himself alive.

We kept going, until the others stopped in front of me. I didn't need the lightning to show me the path anymore. Breathing hard, I caught up and kept walking past Professor Iwerebon, past Balthazar, past my parents, and finally up to Mrs Bethany, who stood only a few feet from the bridge.

"Wait here for us," she commanded. "We will proceed shortly." She pressed her lips together, perhaps willing herself to conquer her one weakness.

"He'll get away." I walked past her.

"Miss Olivier! Stop this instant!"

My feet touched the bridge. Old wooden planks, water-logged with rain, were easier to cross than thick mud.

"Bianca!" That was my dad. "Bianca, wait for us. You can't do this alone."

"Yes, I can." I started to run, drops of water pelting my face, my side aching from exertion and the raincoat heavy across my shoulders. All I wanted to do was fall down upon the bridge and cry. My body didn't have the strength for this.

And yet I ran. I ran even though my legs were as heavy as lead, and my throat was tight with unshed tears, and my parents and my teachers and my friend were all shouting for me to come back. I ran anyway, and with every step I went faster.

Ever since I'd come to Evernight—no, really, throughout my whole life—I'd counted on other people to take care of my problems. Nobody could take care of this for me. I had to face it myself, alone.

I didn't know if I was chasing Lucas or running with him. I only knew I had to run.

After I'd made it over the river, I didn't have much trouble tracking Lucas on my own. It was dark, and I didn't have the extrasensitive sight or hearing of true vampires. However, it was obvious that he was going into Riverton, and at this point, there were only so many routes he could take that weren't far out of his way. Lucas would know that he didn't have much time to waste, and he'd want to get away as fast as possible.

I'd spent a while at the bus station with Raquel before she left for Christmas, after Lucas was already gone. Although she'd been eager to get out of Evernight, her family wouldn't be home until late, so we'd waited for a later bus—one that left for the Boston area at 8:08. It was almost 8 now. I felt certain that Lucas was going to try to be on that next bus. The one after that one probably wasn't for another couple of hours, and that was too much leeway. Mrs Bethany and the others would have him for sure by then. The Boston bus was

Lucas's only real chance at escape.

The downtown area was almost entirely deserted. No cars sped down the streets, and the few businesses that had bothered staying open appeared to be empty. Nobody wanted to be out on a night like this. With my hair plastered to my scalp with rain, I couldn't blame them. I looked in a couple of the open businesses, including the shop where we'd found the brooch. Lucas wasn't there.

No, I realized. *He knows that's where they'd look first.*

I knew then that I had an advantage over Mrs Bethany and my parents, something that even their centuries of experience and supernatural senses couldn't give them. I knew Lucas; that meant I knew what he'd do.

They, too, would probably guess that Lucas wouldn't try to hide in public. They might even make the next inference I made, which was that Lucas would hide as close to the bus station as possible, so he wouldn't be exposed in town for long before he could jump on the bus and make his getaway. However, the bus station was in the dead center of town. A dozen shops surrounded it, and as far as they knew, Lucas might be in any one of them.

Lucas had gone with me to see an old movie and bought me the brooch at the vintage clothing shop. And he had said that he loved me.

Which meant that maybe, just maybe, he would have chosen the same place to hide that I would have.

I walked toward the antiques store on the southeastern

corner of the square, jumping over puddles as I went. Any doubts I might've had about my hunch vanished as soon as I reached the store's back door and saw that it had been left slightly ajar.

Slowly I pushed it open. The hinges didn't squeak, and I trod carefully upon the wooden floorboards. With the lights out, the darkness was nearly complete inside. I could barely discern the shapes of the strange items that surrounded me. At first I didn't trust my eyes: a suit of armor, a stuffed fox, a cricket bat. I realized that the jumble wasn't meaningless. These objects were the antique store's spare inventory, the things fewer people would want to buy. It felt completely surreal, as if I'd somehow fallen into a bad dream while wide awake.

At first I tried to keep quiet, but as I stepped farther inside, I realized that could be dangerous. Lucas might hurt anyone else who was coming after him, but I still believed that he wouldn't hurt me.

"Lucas?"

No answer.

"Lucas, I know that you're here." Still no reply, but I could tell now that I was being watched. "I'm alone. They aren't far behind. If you have anything to say to me, you'd better say it now."

"Bianca."

Lucas said it as a sigh, like he was too tired to hold it back any longer. I peered through the darkness but couldn't see him; I knew only that his voice came from someplace ahead.

"Is it true? What they're saying about you?"

"Depends on what they're saying." I heard footsteps now, coming slowly toward me.

I laid one shaking hand on the nearest thing I could use to steady myself, a chair slipcovered in threadbare velvet. "They said that you're a member of some group called Black Cross. Vampire hunters. That you've been lying to m— lying to us all along."

"All true." Lucas sounded wearier than I'd ever heard him. "Were you telling the truth when you said you were alone? Won't blame you if you weren't."

"I only ever lied to you once. I'm not doing that again now."

"Once? I can think of a lot of times you just 'neglected' to mention you were a vampire."

"Like you didn't say you were a vampire hunter!" I could've slapped him.

My fury didn't seem to move him at all. "I guess so. I guess it's the same kind of thing, in the end."

"I told you the whole truth in that e-mail! I didn't hold anything back!"

"Because you got caught. Doesn't count, and you know it."

Why did he keep pretending we were the same? "I didn't choose to be what I am. You—you people plot to hunt down my family, my friends—"

"I didn't choose this either, Bianca." His voice was rough, as if he were choking up, and my anger dissolved into another emotion, one I couldn't name. Lucas took another couple of steps forward. When I squinted into the dark, I glimpsed his outline several feet away. "Not who or what I am, not even coming to Evernight."

"You chose to be with me." Though he'd tried to talk me out of it, hadn't he? Only now did I understand why.

"Yeah, I did. And I know I've hurt you. I'm sorry for that. You're the last person in the world I ever wanted to hurt."

He sounded completely sincere. I wanted to believe him as badly as I'd ever wanted anything in my life. After the night's revelations, though, I was done taking anything on faith. "Can you just tell me why?"

"It would take a long time to explain, and we don't have much time left."

The 8:08 bus to Boston. I glanced down at my watch; the hands, phosphorescent, told me we had no more than five minutes left.

I walked toward Lucas, my hands in front of me to feel my way. My fingers brushed against ostrich feathers, dusty with age, and something slender, hard and cool, perhaps a brass bed frame. Lucas dodged to the left, behind a panel— but no, I could see through that a little. As I got closer to him, I realized that the panel was a stained glass window.

This was the front room of the antiques store, and it was both less crowded and slightly brighter. Greenish watery light from the streetlamps trickled through to us. Lucas remained behind the stained glass window. Was he afraid of me? Ashamed to face me? Instead of circling around the panel, I walked to the opposite side of it, so that we saw each other through the tinted panes of glass. Lucas's face was cut into four squares of color, and his eyes were dark and haunted.

For a moment, neither of us knew what to say. Then Lucas gave me a sad smile. "Hey."

"Hey." I smiled, too, then nearly started to cry.

"Please, don't."

"I won't." One sob escaped me, but then I swallowed hard and bit down on the side of my tongue. As always, the taste of blood gave me strength. "Am I in danger?"

Lucas shook his head. Through the glass his face was the color of jewels—topaz, sapphire, and amethyst. "Not from me. Never from me."

"Tell it to Erich."

"So you found him." Lucas didn't sound even slightly sorry. "Erich was stalking Raquel. Remember? When I heard her talking about her lost bracelet, I knew she'd run out of time. Stealing possessions is a classic sign of a vampire stalker getting ready to strike. Erich wanted to kill her, and, given a chance, he would have done it. Deep down, I think you realize that."

It scared me that I believed him. If I hadn't tasted Erich's blood and felt his malevolence for myself, maybe I wouldn't have. But I had seen the evil in Erich's mind, and I suspected that Lucas was telling the truth, at least about this. "It's still hard to think about."

"I realize that. I know it's got to be tough for you to understand."

"Tell me what I need to know."

Lucas was quiet for a while, and I wasn't sure that he would answer me. At the moment when I was ready to give up, though, he began to speak. "At the start I lied to you for the same reason you lied to me. Black Cross is a secret I've kept all my life, something my mother signed me up for when I was born." Lucas's voice was distant now, lost in his own memories. "They taught me to fight. Taught me discipline. Sent me on missions as soon as I was old enough to hold a stake."

I remembered what Lucas had told me in the past about his mother being hard core, and about how he sometimes felt he didn't get to make decisions for himself. At long last, I understood what he'd really meant. Even when he was five years old, running away from home, he had brought a weapon.

"At first I thought you were one of the other human students at the school. When you told me about your parents, I thought that they'd killed your real parents and adopted you. I figured you didn't know what they really were." His eyes met mine through the stained glass, and his smile was sad. "I told myself to stay away for your sake, but I couldn't. It was like you were a part of me almost from the second we met. Black Cross would've told me to push you away, but I was tired of pushing everyone away. Once in my life I wanted to be with someone without worrying about what it meant for Black Cross. To live like a regular person for a little while. After that first conversation we had—would you believe I thought you were such a nice, normal girl?"

That was both the funniest and the saddest thing I'd ever

heard. "You know better now."

"What you are—it doesn't matter to me. I told you that already, and I was telling the truth when I said it." He turned toward the window, so that I could see his profile and the worry deeply etched there. "There's more to say, but the bus is about to go— Dammit, maybe I can catch a later one—"

"No!" I pressed one of my hands against the stained glass. Although I still didn't know if I could ever trust Lucas again, I knew now that I could never hurt him, much less stand by while Mrs Bethany and my parents tried to kill him. "Lucas, the others aren't far behind me. Don't wait. Go quickly."

Lucas should've run out of there that instant. Instead he stared at me through the glass and slowly unfolded his hand opposite mine so that our hands were pressed against the same pane of glass, finger to finger, palm to palm. We each moved closer, so that our faces were only a few inches apart. Even with the stained glass window between us, it felt as intimate as any kiss we'd shared.

Quietly he said, "Come with me."

"What?" I blinked, unable to grasp what he was asking me to do. "You mean—run away from home? For real? Like you told me to do on that first day?"

"Just so I can talk to you about everything that's happened and—and so we can say good-bye like we should instead of—" Lucas swallowed, and I realized for the first time that he was just as upset and scared as I was. "I've got enough money to buy us both tickets out of town. Later I can get more money to send you home again if you want. We can go right this second. Run across the street, hop on the bus. We'll get out of here together."

"Are you going to turn me over to Black Cross?"

"What? No!" Lucas honestly sounded like he'd never considered that. "As far as any human can tell, you're human. I'll take care of you if you'll just come with me."

Slowly I said, "Tell me one thing before I answer."

Lucas looked wary. "Okay. Ask."

"You said you loved me. Were you telling the truth?"

If he'd lied about everything else, even his name, I thought I could handle it, as long as I knew this.

He breathed out, not quite a laugh or a sob. "God, yes. Bianca, I love you so much. Even if I never see you again, even if we walk out of here into an ambush you set up with your parents, I am always going to love you."

In the midst of all the lies, at last I had one thing that was true.

"I love you, too," I said. "We have to run."

Chapter Seventeen

AS I SANK ONTO THE SEAT OF THE BUS, TREM-bling with exhaustion, I said, "We made it."

Lucas shook his head. "Not yet."

The bus jerked into motion, rolling slowly onto the road. We had been the last passengers to board; another three minutes, and we would have lost our chance to escape. "I know my parents are fast, but I don't think they can catch a bus on the highway."

An older lady a few rows ahead of us glanced backward, obviously wondering what the hell we were talking about. Lucas gave her his most charming smile, which made her dimple up and turn back to her novel. Then he took my hand and led me to the very back of the near-empty bus, where we could speak freely without any of the other passengers overhearing talk about vampires.

Lucas slid into the seat next to the window. I thought he might take me in his arms, but he remained tense, staring at the water-blurred glass. "We haven't made it out of here until we make it past that overpass. The one three miles out of town."

I didn't know what he was talking about. Obviously Lucas had made a more thorough tactical survey of the area than I had. "What do you think they would do? Stand in the middle of the road and make the bus stop?"

"Mrs Bethany's not stupid." He never took his eyes from the window. Passing streetlights illuminated him in soft blue, then dimmed as we passed them, casting us back into shadow. "Yeah, they might've followed me into town. But she might've figured out that I was going to take the bus. If she did, her hunting party is going be to waiting on that overpass. They'll jump down on the bus, snatch me out, let the cops try to explain it to the passengers later."

"They wouldn't!"

"To stop a Black Cross hunter? You bet your ass they would."

"If you're with this Black Cross, why did you come to Evernight Academy?"

"I was sent to infiltrate the school. It was my assignment. You don't refuse Black Cross assignments. You get them done or die trying."

The dull certainty with which Lucas said this frightened me as much as anything about vampires ever had. "Did you guys just now learn about the school?"

"Black Cross has known what Evernight was almost since it was founded. Those places, where the vampires stay—"

"Where *we* stay."

"Whatever. That's where vampires do the least damage. Nobody wants to create a scene or make people nearby suspicious; vampires always control themselves in those areas. They don't hunt, don't cause trouble. If vampires acted like that all the time, there would be no need for Black Cross."

"Most vampires don't hunt," I insisted.

The bus hit a pothole, jarring us all, and fear made me gasp out loud. Lucas put one hand on my knee to steady me, but he turned his eyes back toward the window. We were almost out of Riverton at this point, getting closer to the overpass every second. "Remember what you said to me at the antique shop?" he muttered. "Tell it to Erich. He was damn sure hunting Raquel."

How could I make him understand? I cast around for an example I could use. "You like hamburgers, right?"

"We have seriously got to go over the right and wrong times for small talk. Dinner party, yes. Five minutes from a vampire ambush, no."

"Hear me out. Would you eat a hamburger if there was any chance it could punch you in the face?"

"How is a hamburger supposed to punch me in the face?"

"Just say that it can." This was no time to bicker about metaphors. "Would you bother? Or would you eat something else?"

Lucas considered this for a couple of seconds. "Leaving aside the weirdness of a hamburger that can attack—which is a lot of weirdness to leave aside—no, I guess I wouldn't."

"And this is why most vampires don't attack humans. Humans hit back. They scream. They throw up. They call nine-one-one on their cell phones. One way or another, humans cause more trouble than they're worth. It's a lot easier to buy blood from butcher shops or eat small animals. Most people always take the easy way, Lucas. I know you're cynical enough to understand that much at least."

"Nice and practical. I bet you told me just the way your parents told you. But you never said that killing people is wrong."

I hated that he'd recognized the explanation as my parents' and not my own. I hated that I only had their word to go on. "That goes without saying."

"Not for a lot of vampires, no, it doesn't. What you say makes sense, but it's not as reassuring as you think. One of us is wrong about how many vampires kill people, but I *know* that a lot of people get killed. I've seen it happen. Have you?"

"No, never. My parents—they're not like that. They'd never hurt anyone."

"Just because you haven't seen it doesn't mean it's not real."

"Have you seen it?" I challenged him.

My stomach sank as he nodded. Then he said the worst thing he could've said. "They got my father."

"Oh, my God."

Lucas stared at the window, even more tense than he had been before. We had to be very close to the overpass now. "I wasn't there for that. I was just a little kid. Hardly even remember him. But I've seen vampires attack other people, and I've seen the bodies they've left behind. It's horrible, Bianca. More horrible than I think you realize, maybe even more than you can imagine. Your parents only ever showed you the pretty side. There's an ugly side, too."

"Maybe you've only seen the ugly side. Maybe you're the one who doesn't understand the real balance." My stomach was churning, and my fingers tightened on the back of the empty bus seat in front of me. Were we about to have to fight for our lives? "If my parents hid the full truth from me, maybe your mother hid the full truth from you."

"Mom doesn't pretty things up. Trust me on this." Lucas breathed out. "Get ready."

The bus took a sharp turn, shaking the few passengers from side to side. Through the blur of rain, I could see the overpass lights coming up. I squinted at the darkness, trying to make out shapes or movement, some hint that Mrs Bethany might be waiting there for us.

Lucas took a deep breath. "Love you."

"Love you, too."

Two more seconds, and the bus rumbled beneath the overpass. Nothing happened. Mrs Bethany had led the group into town after all.

"We made it," I whispered.

He folded me in his embrace. As Lucas sagged against my shoulder, I realized for the first time how exhausted he was and how frightened he had really been. I combed through his wet hair with my fingers to soothe him. There was time to have arguments later, to talk about Evernight and Black Cross and everything else that divided us. For now, all that mattered was that we were safe.

I hadn't been to Boston since I was very small. Dimly I remembered what it was like to be in a city rather than the countryside—noise and trash, asphalt and traffic signs instead of earth and trees, and lights everywhere, bright enough to hide the stars forever. Though I braced myself for a seemingly inevitable panic attack, by the time we got to our destination— an area on the outskirts of town, and so far as I could tell one of the seedy neighborhoods—it was late, and we were exhausted. I wasn't scared; I was only numb.

"We should figure out what we're going to do tonight." Those were the first words Lucas had spoken to me since we got off the bus. Our hands still tightly clasped, we wove our way through the shifty-looking characters. They wore clothes that were too large, laughed too loud, and stared sharply at every car that rounded the street corners. "It's going to be morning before anybody picks us up."

"Picks us up? Who's picking us up?"

"Somebody from Black Cross will come. When I broke in the antique store, I used their phone, left a message that I was headed here. I'll call back and tell them where to pick us up, once we know ourselves."

"I don't want to walk around this neighborhood for too long." I cast a suspicious glance at a broken window.

"Bianca, think." Lucas stopped in his tracks and, for the first time all night, looked like his old snarky self. "Who should be afraid here? Us or them?"

Why would these people be scared of me? Then it hit me, the punch line to the joke of my life: *I'm a vampire.*

I started to giggle, and Lucas joined in. When I lost control, tears welling in my eyes, he wrapped his arms around me and hugged me tight.

I'm a vampire. Everybody's scared of me. ME. And Lucas? He's the only guy who can scare vampires. All these rough-looking people—if they knew—they'd run for their lives.

When I could breathe again, I stepped back from Lucas and tried to examine our situation calmly. It was hard to think about anything besides him, though, and how lost we were. The fluorescent streetlights drained all the brightness from Lucas's bronze hair, so that it looked simply brown. Maybe it was exhaustion that made his face so pale and drawn; I could only imagine how tired I looked.

"It's nearly midnight. Where are we going to stay?" My cheeks flushed with heat as I realized what I'd said—which sounded a lot like an invitation for Lucas and me to spend the night together. Then again, hadn't we run off together? Maybe it was natural for him to assume that we'd go to bed. Maybe it would've been natural for *me* to assume that, and there had been times I'd wanted to be with him too desperately to sleep.

Tonight, though, on top of everything that had just happened, the prospect only made me feel awkward and nervous.

Lucas seemed to have realized our predicament at the same moment I had. "I haven't got my credit cards with me. Kinda left in a hurry. We just spent the only cash I had in my pocket."

"The only thing I brought was a flashlight." Too-bright signs from the few open stores made me squint. "We'd have been better off with a slingshot and Oreos."

The rainstorm that had been raging in Riverton hadn't made it here, so we didn't have to worry about getting soaked as we walked around, trying to think of what to do. We were damp and exhausted and unsure of each other, and we did a poor job of acting casual as we passed bail bondsmen and liquor stores. Spending the night curled on different benches in some run-down park wasn't an appealing prospect.

For reassurance, I lifted my hand to my sweater, the place just beneath my collarbone where I'd pinned my brooch this morning. It seemed like a thousand years ago. But the brooch was still there, the carved jet edges of each petal cool against my fingertips.

At that moment, we walked past a pawnshop, three golden spheres outlined in neon above its door, and I realized what I had to do.

"Bianca, don't," Lucas protested as I pulled him inside the seedy little store. Shelves were piled with randomly stacked junk, all the things people had to get rid of, like brightly colored leather coats, sunglasses with metallic frames, and high-end electronics that were probably stolen. "We can go back to the bus station."

"No, we can't." I unfastened the brooch from my sweater, trying hard not to look at it. If I caught sight of the perfect black flowers, I'd lose my nerve. "This isn't about being comfortable, Lucas. It's about being safe and having a place to talk. And—" *And to say good-bye*, I thought but could not say.

Lucas thought that over for a second before he nodded.

We probably both looked completely dejected as we walked to the pawnbroker, but he didn't seem to care. A skinny man in a polyester shirt, he hardly paid any attention to us. "What's this? Plastic or something?"

I quickly said, "It's genuine Whitby jet."

"I don't know from Whitby." The pawnbroker tapped his fingernails against the carved leaves. "This thing is pretty old-fashioned."

"That's because it's antique," Lucas said.

"I hear that a lot," the pawnbroker sighed. "Hundred dollars. Take it or leave it."

"A hundred dollars! That's only half what it cost!" I protested. And it was worth so much more than money. I'd worn it virtually every day for months, the visible symbol of the love I felt for Lucas. How could this man look at it so coldly?

"People don't come here for the best return on their investment, sweetie. They come here to get some cash in their hands. You want the cash? You've got my offer. Otherwise, get outta here and stop wasting my time."

Lucas wanted to take the brooch back rather than let it go for so much less than it was worth. I could tell that much by the stubborn set of his jaw. I was learning that Lucas would often do something he felt strongly about, even if it wasn't the right move—and for us, keeping the brooch wasn't the right move. Resolutely, I held out my hand, palm up. "A hundred dollars, then."

For our sacrifice, we received five twenty-dollar bills and a paper ticket that promised us we could reclaim the brooch later, if we somehow came into a fortune in the next couple of days. "I'll get the money," Lucas insisted as we walked outside and turned toward the one motel we could see. "I'll get it back for you."

"You said you were rich, when you bought the brooch for me. Was that true?"

"Uh—"

I raised an eyebrow. "Not exactly?"

"I have access to Black Cross money, and there's a decent amount of that. But I'm supposed to spend it on supplies. Necessary stuff." He shrugged. "Not jewelry."

"You got into trouble, for buying that for me."

Lucas shoved his fists into his pockets, his mood black. "I told them that I work for them, basically. But I don't get a salary or hazard pay, so as far as I'm concerned, they owe me. That's exactly what I'm going to tell them when I explain that I'm buying the brooch back. Because it's yours, Bianca. It belongs to you, period."

"I believe you." I put my hands on either side of his face. "But it's not the most important thing, okay? The most important thing is that we're safe, we're together, and we get a chance to figure this all out."

"Yeah." Lucas's damp, rumpled hair was warm against my fingers, and he closed his eyes as I brushed it backward. "Now let's find a place to stay."

We had to walk only a couple more blocks before we found a cheap hotel. At the front office, a small room that smelled like beer and cigarettes, Lucas made sure to get us a room with two beds, which made the clerk look at us funny from behind her wall of bulletproof glass. I tried not to think about the precious brooch being sold to pay for one night in a small room with rickety twin beds and dark blue woolen covers, with only the light from one small porcelain lamp to see by. We didn't touch each other as we walked in, not even to hold hands, but I was incredibly aware of the fact that we were alone together in a bedroom. He turned on the lamp between our beds, but that didn't put me at ease. Instead, I found myself noticing how Lucas's white shirt was slightly stuck to his body because of the rain. The near-transparent cotton outlined the muscles of his back.

"You want to get undressed in the bathroom?" Lucas asked gently. "I'll slide under the covers. Turn off the lamp. By the time you come out, I won't be able to see a thing."

I laughed, both relieved and nervous. "You have some of our powers now. And some of us can see in the dark."

"Not me. I swear." He gave me a lopsided grin.

So I went into the tiny bathroom and peeled off my waterlogged clothes, piece by piece. At least my T-shirt and underwear were fairly dry. I washed my face and braided back my damp, curling hair; on the other side of the door, I could hear Lucas speaking briefly, then hanging up the phone. No doubt he had just left the message that would tell Black Cross where to find us.

Then I stared at myself in the mirror. It wasn't as if I'd never paid attention to my body before, but I'd never looked at myself and wondered how somebody else would see me. Lucas would see me, any second. Would he think I was beautiful? I realized that I felt beautiful, that I wanted him to see me. I brushed my hands over my stomach, then down the sides of my hips, newly sensitive to my own touch. The whole time, Lucas was just on the other side of the door. Getting undressed. Waiting for me.

The sliver of light beneath the bathroom door went dark. I took a deep breath, snapped off the light, and opened the door. Only the dim glow of city lights, filtered by the curtain, illuminated our room. Peering into the dark, I could see Lucas in the shadows; he'd taken the bed farther from the bathroom. He was already beneath the covers, one bare arm and shoulder visible.

I took a couple of breaths, then walked to Lucas's bed. He looked up at me, disbelieving, but lifted up the cover to invite me in.

"Just to sleep." My words came out as a whisper. My pulse pounded in my veins, and my voice sounded thin and strange even to me. I felt warm all over, even between my fingers and my toes.

"Just to sleep," he promised. I wasn't sure I believed either of us.

So I slipped into the bed, and Lucas drew the blanket over us both. I lay my head upon the pillow, only inches away from his. The twin bed was so narrow that we couldn't help but touch each other—my bare legs brushing against his, his boxer shorts rough against my thighs, my breasts close enough to feel the body heat of his bare chest.

Lucas's eyes never left mine. "I need to know that you believe I'm doing the right thing."

I considered that. "I believe that you're doing what you think is right."

"Close enough," he said wearily.

"I love you."

"And I love you."

At that moment, I wanted to pull him against me so we could get lost in each other and forget about everything else. I didn't care if we were safe, if we would ever see each other again, even that it would have been my first time. But before I could make a move, Lucas simply folded my hands between his, as reverently as someone about to pray. "We can't get carried away," he murmured. His eyes burned into mine, as if there was nothing in the world he wanted more than to get carried away.

My voice shaky, I ventured, "Maybe we could."

His hands tightened around mine, and something inside me leaped in response. Still, Lucas didn't move to kiss me. "We can't." He said it like he was trying to convince himself as well as me. "We're both too close to changing into vampires as it is. If either of us lost control—if we both did— You know it could happen, Bianca."

"Would that be the worst thing?"

"Yeah, I think it would." Before we could start arguing again about what vampires were and weren't, who was good and who was bad, Lucas added, "Besides, we're meeting up with a group of vampire hunters tomorrow. Maybe it's a bad time to be a vampire."

Okay, that made sense. It didn't mean I had to like it. "All right," I murmured. "But, Lucas—"

"Yeah?"

"Someday."

His voice rough, Lucas repeated, "Someday."

I closed my eyes and lowered my face so that his fingertips touched my cheek. I could sleep now. I could believe that everything would be all right. Maybe it was only another dream, but we were in the place for dreaming.

"Lucas?"

I heard the woman's voice through a haze. At first I wondered why Patrice was talking about Lucas, then realized it wasn't Patrice speaking.

Startled, I sat upright. The events of the night before

✤ 299 ✤

flooded my memory, dazing me, even as I blinked in the sudden light. Instead of waking up in my dorm room, I was lying in bed next to Lucas, who was pushing himself up and running one hand through his rumpled hair—and a woman in her forties was standing in the doorway of our motel room, staring at us.

Lucas swallowed hard, then grinned. "Hi, Mom."

Chapter Eighteen

"OKAY, IT'S THE TWENTY-FIRST CENTURY, SO I never thought you'd wait until you were married." Lucas's mother leaned against the doorjamb and folded her arms across her chest. "But honestly, Lucas. You knew I was coming. Do you really have to throw it in my face?"

"It's not what it looks like," Lucas said. How could he be so calm? Instead of stammering out apologies and explanations like I would've done, he simply put one hand on my shoulder and smiled. "Bianca and I shared a room because we're broke. We had to hock something even to get this. And nobody made you pick that lock either. So take it easy, all right?"

She shrugged. "You're almost twenty. You make your own choices."

"You're twenty?" I muttered.

"Nineteen and change. Is it important?"

"I guess not." Compared to everything else I'd learned

about Lucas in the past day, what did it matter that he was three years older than me?

Lucas smoothly pushed himself out of bed. Just my luck: The first time I saw him wearing only boxer shorts, and I couldn't even relax to enjoy the view. "Bianca, this is my mother, Kate Ross. Mom, this is the girl I've told you about, Bianca."

She gave me a friendly nod. "Call me Kate."

Now that I was awake enough to focus, I could see how strongly she resembled Lucas. She was tall—even taller than Lucas, maybe—with chin-length golden-brown hair only a shade lighter than his and the same dark green eyes. Like Lucas, her face was angular: square jawed and sharp chinned. She wore faded blue jeans and a maroon Henley shirt tight enough to outline the sculpted muscles in her arms. I didn't think I'd ever met anyone who seemed less like a mom. I mean, what kind of mother found her son in bed with his teenage girlfriend and just smiled?

Then again, it beat having her flip out. I held up one hand in an awkward wave. "Hi there."

"Hey yourself. You guys must've had a rough night. Let's pour some coffee into you and figure out how to help Bianca." Kate nodded toward the street. Lucas was already running his hands through his hair and grabbing his jeans, unembarrassed in front of his mother. I wanted to wrap myself in the bedspread or something, but that would have been even more humiliating; instead I bounded out of bed and into the bathroom in about two steps.

Once inside, I recovered a little of my dignity by getting dressed again. My clothes were now dry, if rumpled. I loosened the braid I'd slept in, and my hair fell down around my face in soft waves. Not much of a hairstyling trick, but that was what they'd relied on in the seventeenth century. With a pang, I remembered my mom showing me. "Let's go."

Lucas shot me a look as we went out the door, perhaps trying to evaluate how I was holding up. Kate might be fooled by my false bravado, but he knew me better than that. I lifted my chin proudly, so that he'd know I was determined to make the best of our increasingly odd situation.

Kate led us to a battered old pickup truck from the 1950s, with faded aqua paint and headlights shaped like the engines of the starship *Enterprise*. The whole time we got in, she kept looking around us, scanning every single passer-by. "Do you guys think you were followed? The teachers can't look kindly on runaways."

"They didn't get as far as Riverton, not before we left," I said hastily as I scooted into the center and Lucas got in beside me. "The running water stopped them."

She froze that second, with one hand on the keys in the ignition. She stared at Lucas, not the usual upset-mom stare, the one that clearly says you're two seconds from being grounded. This was harder—the way I imagined army leaders looked when they sent traitors to firing squads. "You told her?"

"Mom, you need to listen for a sec." Lucas took a deep,

steadying breath and held his hands out, as if he could actually hold her back. "Bianca knew the truth about Evernight already. I only explained Black Cross because I had to. It's not like she didn't realize vampires existed before. Okay?"

"No, it's not okay. Your mistake might be understandable, but it's still a mistake. You should know that by now." She shoved her bangs back and studied me more intently than she had at first. Kate's casual attitude had dissolved. "How did you find out about them?"

I thought she meant Black Cross at first. It took a second for me to understand that "them" meant "vampires" to her. Lucas hadn't told her what I truly was—and I realized, as he shifted in his seat next to me, that he was hiding the truth for my protection. Undoubtedly he also hadn't mentioned the fact that he now had some measure of vampiric power himself.

So I did what Lucas and I were apparently best at: I lied. "There were all kinds of clues. The fact that the school never served food for its students, so everyone ate in private—the dead squirrels all around—the way that so many people had attitudes and ideas that came from other centuries. It wasn't that hard to figure it out."

"Doesn't sound like much evidence." Kate, unconvinced, gunned the motor and sped down a frontage road that led us out of the city area. "You never ran into the supernatural before, and you put it together from no more than that?"

"Bianca's hiding part of the truth because she's trying not

to scare you," Lucas said. "She was the one who helped me after this happened." He then carefully pulled open the neck of his shirt. There, still dark pink against his skin, were the scars left from my second bite.

"Oh, my God." Immediately Kate reached across me to touch Lucas's arm. So she really was a mom after all, even if she didn't always show it. "We knew this could happen—we knew it—but I told myself it wouldn't."

Lucas ducked away, abashed. "Mom. I'm fine."

"You got away. How did you manage it?"

"I killed one of them—a vampire called Erich, one who had been threatening other human students. We got into an altercation. He had the worst of it. That's really all there is to say."

Lucas's talent at lying was easier to admire when I wasn't the one he was lying to. Of course, the genius of it was that Lucas wasn't actually making any of it up. Every word he'd said to his mother was factually true. He'd simply unfolded those facts in a way that led his mother to believe in an alternate sequence of events, one in which Erich had bitten him and I was the sweet, savvy, totally normal girl who had helped him recover afterward.

"You've seen what we're up against." Kate spoke to me more respectfully than before. Anybody who had helped her son was apparently okay in her eyes. She never looked away from the road as she sped over the badly paved streets, steering us into a smaller suburb, one that looked older and fairly run-down. "This is dangerous work, and you're not ready for it, but I realize that we have a responsibility to keep you safe. If that demon Mrs Bethany realizes that you're helping a member of Black Cross, your life won't be worth a dime."

I'd always known that Mrs Bethany would do a lot to protect her secrets, but I still couldn't quite believe that she would be willing to kill, much less kill *me*.

"All that time, all that risk, and what was it for? Because I don't guess you managed to figure out the big secret after all," Kate said to Lucas. "Seems like the kind of thing you would've mentioned in one of your reports, if you had."

Wearily, Lucas shook his head. "I didn't get it. So cut me some slack, okay?"

"Secret?" I wondered if maybe it was something my parents might have mentioned. If I could help Lucas, if there was information I could reveal that wouldn't hurt my parents or Balthazar, I would do it. "What were you trying to find out at Evernight?"

"This is the first year they ever let humans in like regular students. The Black Cross fighter who got in before, the handful of other humans over the years—those were special cases, exceptions the Evernight vampires made to get their hands on a lot of money and avoid attention. Whatever they're up to now is different. They let in at least thirty humans. Why did it change?"

Mrs Bethany had said that "new students" were allowed into Evernight so that we could get a broader perspective upon the world. In reality, that was the last thing she really wanted. Yes, the students were there to learn more about the world, but Mrs Bethany had another agenda—and for that agenda, having human students at Evernight was a risk. Raquel understood that something was wrong, if not exactly what, and Lucas's example spoke for itself. The vampires were also forced to hide what they were in one of the few places on earth where they could've expected to relax and be themselves. Only a powerful motive could lead Mrs Bethany to permit such a thing—but what? "I don't know," I admitted.

"How could you?" Kate shrugged as she took us down a shady lane. The houses on this street all looked shabby, and one or two of them looked abandoned. She pulled into what appeared to be the rear driveway of one of the empty buildings, though I realized quickly it wasn't a home. It was an old-fashioned meetinghouse, the kind nearly every town in New England possessed, though nobody had held a meeting here for decades at least. The white paint was chipped and water-stained, and at least half the windows were broken. "Just the fact that you kept your head after you learned about the bloodsuckers is more than most people could manage. Lucas is a pro. If he couldn't figure it out, they buried that secret deep."

"A pro, huh?" Lucas grinned as we got out of the truck. I got the sense that his mother didn't praise him much, but he ate it up when she did.

She nodded, and I saw for the first time that her smile and

Lucas's looked a lot alike. "A pro who's already back on the clock, I'm afraid. We've got work to do."

I wondered what she meant by that. "On the clock?"

Kate caught herself. "I don't mean you. Bianca. You've done enough, and I'm always in your debt. Always. Helping Lucas in that slime pit—maybe saving his life—" She smiled at me as we walked to the back door of the meetinghouse. "I'm not going to repay that by sending you into danger. You'll stay here. Stay safe. We'll take care of everything else."

"By 'we' you mean—"

"Black Cross."

With that, Kate turned the key in the lock and tugged the door open. We stepped into darkness, and I felt a queasy shiver of unease, but my eyes adjusted quickly, allowing me to glimpse the scene inside. Almost a dozen people were gathered together in a long, narrow rectangular room with a wooden floor so old the boards had shrunk enough to separate. A few old benches still lined the walls, the wood so soft and old it peeled. Weapons were laid out upon each bench, as if for an inventory: knives, stakes, and even hatchets. The people inside were a motley crew, each as different from the other as they could be: tall and short; fat, skinny, and muscular; dressed in a dozen different kinds of everyday clothes. A tall black girl who looked no older than Lucas wore an oversized hoodie, and she stood next to an old man with short silvery hair who wore a baggy gray cardigan and reading glasses that dangled from a brown cord. The only thing they all had in common was the way each sighed in relief when they recognized Lucas.

Lucas took my hand in his as he said, "Hey, guys."

"You made it." This was the girl in the hoodie, who turned out to have a big smile with one crooked tooth that somehow made her look a little bit sweet. "Not quite finals time, though, unless they're having them in March now."

"I get it, Dana. I didn't make it a whole year, which means you win the bet." Lucas shrugged. "The vampires got my wallet, though, so I'm afraid you'll have to be content with a moral victory."

"Looks like you brought the most important thing." Dana held one of her hands out to me. I wasn't willing to let go of Lucas, but I shook with my left hand. "I'm Dana. Me and Lucas go way back. You must be Bianca."

"How did you hear about me?"

"Like he could talk about anything else all Christmas." Dana laughed. I glanced sideways at Lucas, whose bashful smile made me feel proud and—even in the midst of strangers—sure of myself.

"Oh, is this your young lady?" The gray-haired man beamed at us. "I'm Mr Watanabe. I've known Lucas since he was—"

"Long enough to embarrass him," interrupted someone else, a tall man with dark hair and a mustache. He unnerved me in some way I found hard to pinpoint, and the twin scars on his right cheek made him look scary even when he smiled.

Kate put one arm around him as he stood before us. "I'm Eduardo, Lucas's stepfather."

"Right. Hi. Pleasure to meet you." Lucas had never mentioned a stepfather. Apparently Lucas wasn't eager to admit him as part of the family.

Lucas's smile was thin. "I had to get Bianca out. I know I broke protocol by telling her about Black Cross, but I trust her."

"I hope Lucas's right about you, Bianca." His eyes narrowed, focusing hard on me before darting over to Lucas. Clearly he meant that *I* better hope Lucas was right. Giving away secrets wasn't something this group took lightly—especially not Eduardo and Kate, who seemed to be the leaders. "We don't have much time for explanations, not if we're about to move."

The others all started talking to Lucas about his narrow escape. I knew I ought to talk to them, too, to help Lucas with the cover story if for no other reason. Yet I remained distracted. My entire life was changing every second, pulling me away so quickly from the world I'd known that I felt a kind of psychological whiplash. And there was even more to it than that. I felt a sort of buzzing so low I couldn't quite find the sound, like a subtle vibration in the earth. Despite the fact that I hadn't eaten in almost a day, my stomach churned. Something was wrong with this place, deeply wrong.

Then I glanced at the wall and saw a shape on the wall where the plaster was brighter than everywhere else, where something had hung for years and blocked the light. It was the shape of a cross.

Too late I realized that this wasn't just an abandoned meetinghouse. Back in earlier centuries, a lot of meeting houses had served another function as well. During the week, they were halls for debate or community functions or sometimes even trials. Then, on Sundays, the meetinghouses became churches.

A church—ugh. Vampires don't burst into flames upon touching a cross, the way horror movies like to suggest, but that doesn't make churches a fun place to be. I felt slightly dizzy and turned my head away from the shape of the cross.

"Bianca?" Lucas's fingers brushed my cheek. "Are you okay?"

"I can't stay here. Is there someplace else I can go?"

"It's not safe for you to be out right now." To my surprise, it was Dana who spoke. "Forget those Evernight bastards. We've got bad news in town, and she's enough to worry about."

I should've asked who that "bad news" was, or pretended that I had a safe place to go, or something. But the buzzing in my brain was getting stronger—consecrated earth telling me to leave. My reaction was only a pale shadow of what my parents experienced in churches, but it was enough to confuse me and make me weak. "Can't I go back to the hotel? We didn't check out."

"A hotel? Oh, my." Mr Watanabe looked flustered. "These days, they grow up fast."

"We need to get Bianca to safety." Kate's sharp voice turned even a simple suggestion into a command. "We have to concentrate, and I suspect Lucas can't do that with her here."

"I'm *fine*." To Lucas, clearly, Kate's comment sounded like criticism. "Bianca helps me think straight. I'm better when I'm with her."

Mr Watanabe beamed at him. I would have, too, if I hadn't wanted to leave the church so badly. "It's okay," I swore. "You can find me later. I should go back to the hotel."

Eduardo shook his head. "The vampires might have traced you there. We should get you to a safe place. What about your home?"

The simple question knocked the breath out of me. My home—Mom and Dad, my telescope and my Klimt print, old phonograph records and even the gargoyle—seemed like the safest place in the world and the farthest away. I'd rarely felt so lost. "I can't go there."

"If you're worried about a cover story, we can help you with that," Kate said briskly, unwilling to be dissuaded. "We just have to get you to your family. Where are your parents?"

The back door slammed open, venting light and cold air into the room. I jumped, but I was the only one—all the Black Cross fighters, including Lucas, were instantly on guard, weapons in their hands, to face the enemies at the door. The vampires.

Standing in front of them all were Mom and Dad.

Chapter Nineteen

"BIANCA!"

My father's voice and Lucas's rang out at the same time, each of them trying to warn me about the other, and I felt as though I were being torn in two. Other people started shouting, words overlapping, and the buzzing in my brain mingled with panic so that I couldn't tell any of the speakers apart.

"*Let her go!*"

"*Get out of here!*"

"*Step back or you die. That's all there is to it.*"

"*If you try to hurt her—*"

"*Bianca? Bianca!*"

That was Mom. I focused on her and only her. She stood in the doorway, holding out one hand. The sunlight dappled her caramel-colored hair so that she was outlined with a sort of halo. "Come here, sweetheart." She opened her hand so wide that every tendon and muscle tensed, so wide it had to hurt. "Just come here."

"She's not going anywhere." Kate stepped forward so that she stood between us with her hands on her hips. One of her fingers rested on the hilt of the knife in her belt. "You're finished lying to this girl. In fact, I'd say you're finished, period."

"You have ten seconds," my father growled.

"Ten seconds until what? Until you storm inside to finish us all off?" Kate held out her arms, a gesture that took in the entire room—including the faded outline of the cross upon the wall. "You're weaker in a house of God. You know it as well as I do. So go ahead. Run inside. Make it easy for us to finish you off."

All around me, the members of Black Cross were armed. Eduardo wielded a huge knife, and Dana handled an ax like she knew how to use it. Even little Mr Watanabe held a stake. How could people who seemed so friendly be so instantly ready to kill people I loved? In the doorway, behind my parents, I could see Balthazar's profile. He had accepted his rejection, become my friend, and even risked his life to protect me. He deserved better than this. So did Lucas. It was so clear to me but invisible to everyone else.

"We're not coming in." My father's smile was crooked and strange—the broken nose changed his face somehow. "You're coming out."

"Look out." Lucas put one hand on my arm, but he obviously wasn't talking to me. What had he seen?

Instantly Balthazar shouldered a crossbow, moving swiftly, giving my mom just time enough to flick a silver lighter next to the arrow. Then a bolt of fire zoomed through the room, shimmering with light and heat, before striking the wall—which instantly burst into flame.

Fire. One of the only things that can kill us—one of the only things we all fear. And yet Balthazar kept going, shooting arrow after arrow into the church, not aiming at any of the ducking and dodging members of Black Cross or anywhere in particular, just setting the place ablaze. My mother stayed by his side, creating every fireburst with her lighter and never flinching. An arrow shattered the light fixture above us, sending thin shards of glass spraying out in every direction and the burning point thudding deep into the ceiling. All around us, the old, dry tinder of the meetinghouse flared immediately into a conflagration. Already dark smoke had begun to obscure everything.

"Run!" Kate shouted, turning toward the wide front doors, which Mr Watanabe was opening even then. But when the doors swung open, others were waiting: Mrs Bethany, Professor Iwerebon, Mr Yee, and some of the other teachers stood in a dark, forbidding line. None of them brandished weapons; they didn't have to in order to make the threat clear.

"Hang on!" Dana threw down her ax and grabbed what looked like a Super Soaker. "We're gonna give these bastards a shower!"

"Holy water?" Mrs Bethany called over the crackling of the flames. I couldn't see her very well, not with my eyes stinging from acrid smoke, but I could imagine the sneer on her face. "Useless. You could soak us in every fountain in every church in Christendom and it would do no good."

"Most priests can't make holy water," Eduardo agreed. Disturbingly, he sounded like he was enjoying this. "Most preachers of any faith aren't true servants of God. But those servants do exist—as you're about to find out."

Dana squeezed the trigger and sent a jet of water toward the teachers. Mr Yee and Professor Iwerebon immediately yelled and fell back, as if they had been sprayed with acid.

"That's it!" Kate cried. But even as Dana fired again, the next jet of water failed to make its mark. The air was growing so hot that the water was evaporating right away.

The timbers overhead creaked ominously. I could hear Professor Iwerebon shouting in pain and Mr Watanabe coughing hard from the smoke. The floorboards beneath my feet were beginning to feel hot. I no longer wondered which side would die; I wondered if we all would.

"I'll go!" I cried. "I'm going out!"

"Bianca, don't!" Lucas's face was painted in firelight, red and gold. "You can't go!"

"If I don't go, you'll die. All of you. I won't do that."

Our eyes met. I had never imagined saying good-bye to Lucas before; it had seemed like there couldn't be a good-bye, not for us. He wasn't just part of my life—he was part of me. Leaving him was like cutting off my own hand, sawing through sinew and bone, bloody and horrible and terrifying.

But for Lucas, I could do anything that had to be done.

That meant I could even do this.

"No," Lucas whispered, his voice almost inaudible above the crackling of the flames. The Black Cross group were edging toward the center of the room, creating a circle of defense. "There's got to be another way."

I shook my head. "There's not. You know it as well as I do. Lucas, I'm sorry, I'm so sorry."

He took one step toward me, and I wanted to fling myself into his arms and hold him at least once more. If I did that, though, I knew I'd never be able to let go. For both our sakes, I had to be strong.

"I love you," I said, and then I turned and ran toward my parents.

My father's hand closed around my arm as he and my mother pulled me outside. The door swung shut behind us. "Bianca!" Mom embraced me tightly, and I realized that she was crying. Her body shook with each sob. "My baby, oh, my baby, we didn't think we'd ever see you again."

"I'm sorry." I hugged her back while grabbing my father's hand in one of mine. I could see his bruised, black-eyed face over her shoulder. Instead of the anger or hurt I'd imagined, there was only relief in his eyes. "I love you both so much."

"Honey, are you okay?" Dad said.

"I'm fine, I promise. Just let them go. Please. For me. Let them go."

My parents both nodded, and if Balthazar disagreed, he didn't say so out loud. We all made our way toward the front of the meetinghouse. Thick smoke from the ceiling billowed upward in a dark, coiling pillar. A driver in her car on the nearby street was already shouting into her cell phone. The fire engines would be here soon.

As we stepped onto the sidewalk, the three of us still huddled together with Balthazar following closely, Mrs Bethany hurried toward us, her long black skirt flapping behind her. "What are you doing?" she demanded. "Guard the back! Don't let them out!"

"No!" I cried. "You can't do that. You can't just kill them!"

"It's what they'd do to us," Mrs Bethany rasped, her dark lips twisting in an unnatural smile.

Mom took a deep breath. "No. Let them go." Dad shot her a look, but he didn't object; he just kept holding my hand.

"You heard me." Stepping closer, Mrs Bethany fixed her black eyes on me, the way a hawk does before swooping down upon its prey. "Do you question my authority? I am the headmistress of Evernight!"

It was Balthazar who answered her by casually slinging his crossbow back upon his shoulder so that it just happened to be aimed straight at Mrs Bethany. He wasn't threatening her, exactly, but it was very clear that he wasn't going to back down. As she jerked upright in shock, Balthazar drawled, "School's out."

Mrs Bethany scowled, but she said nothing and didn't make another move, not even as we heard the ruckus in the back driveway that could only have been the members of

Black Cross making their escape. I closed my eyes tightly and wished for the sirens of the fire trucks, so that I wouldn't have to hear Lucas's footsteps as he ran away from me forever.

"Your parents say you were abducted."

Mrs Bethany stood behind the desk in her office, the one in the carriage house at Evernight. I sat in front of her in an uncomfortable wooden chair. My clothes were rumpled and filthy with soot. I was chilled to the bone, exhausted, and hungry for both food and blood. The day's last rays of sunlight filtered orange through the windowpane. It hadn't even been twenty-four hours since my world fell apart and the truth about Lucas came out. It felt like a thousand years.

"That's right," I said hollowly. "Lucas demanded that I come with him."

She pulled the gold locket around her neck back and forth, back and forth on its chain, so that I could hear the faint metallic clicking. Unlike me, Mrs Bethany was completely poised and collected, and the frilly lace at her throat remained crisp with starch. But she smelled like smoke, not lavender. "Curious, that you couldn't defend yourself. You are, after all, a vampire."

Am I? I wasn't even sure of that anymore. I said only, "He's in Black Cross. He has some of our powers. He outfought my father and Balthazar at once. What chance did I have?"

"Now you know how to answer difficult questions with more questions." Mrs Bethany sighed heavily, and for the first time, I saw a glint of dark humor in her gaze. "No longer the shrinking violet, I see. At least you've learned something this year."

I remembered what Lucas had told me the night before: Mrs Bethany had changed centuries-old rules in order to invite human students to Evernight. He hadn't been able to learn why, and I couldn't guess. As I looked at her, I knew only that she was older, stronger, and more devious than I'd ever imagined. Yet I wasn't afraid of her anymore, because I knew even Mrs Bethany was vulnerable.

If she had allowed human students at Evernight, there was something she needed, badly. That meant she had a weakness, and that made her no different from the rest of us. I could face her now, knowing that.

Without asking permission to leave, I rose from my chair. "Good night, Mrs Bethany."

Her dark eyes glittered dangerously, but she simply waved me off with a flick of her fingers. "Good night."

That night, my parents fussed over me like they hadn't since I was a little girl—finding me snuggly socks and soft pillows and microwaving a glass of blood to body temperature for me. I didn't have to ask if they really thought I'd been abducted by Lucas; they were smarter than that. I knew they didn't really understand, because any sympathy they might have had for Lucas was clearly obliterated by their hatred of Black Cross. But even if they didn't agree with my choices, they could forgive me for them. That was more than enough to remind me how much I was loved. They even piled up in bed on either side of me, with Rosemary Clooney on the record player in the other room, and told me old stories about the way the wheat fields in England used to look—sweet, pretty stories that held no danger or change, only beauty. They talked for a long time before exhaustion won out over misery and I finally, finally fell asleep.

That night I dreamed once more of the storm, the creeping hedge that grew up like a wildfire of brambles around Evernight, and the mysterious flowers that bloomed black beneath my hands. Even in my dream, I knew I'd seen it all before. I had been warned even before I met Lucas that the flowers weren't for me, but I reached for them anyway, despite the thorns and the storm.

"You're daydreaming again."

Raquel's words brought me back to reality. We were out in the fringe of woods closest to the grounds, beneath new, pale-green leaves so soft they curled at the edges. I'd been standing still, my hand on one branch for no telling how many minutes. She was a good enough friend to allow me space when I needed it and smart enough to know when it was time to bring me down to earth once more.

"Sorry." We started walking again, lazy steps that didn't really take us in any particular direction. "I wasn't thinking."

"You were thinking about Lucas." Obviously Raquel wasn't easily fooled. "It's been almost six weeks, Bianca. You have to forget him. You know that."

Raquel knew only what the other students like her knew: that Lucas had broken a slew of rules and run away, assaulting my father on his way out. That probably fit perfectly into her sad view of the world, in which every secret was only a cloak for violence. She'd warned me about Lucas a dozen times. Why shouldn't she believe he'd snapped? Never did she say anything remotely resembling "I told you so"—Raquel was too good for that.

Vic took it hard. Lucas had really been his best friend at Evernight, and there was a gap in Vic's life now that was beyond my power to fill. I'd assured him, as best I could without revealing secrets that would only endanger him, that Lucas was a good guy and that he'd had his reasons for running. I thought Vic believed me, but he didn't smile as often anymore. I could've used some of his smiles.

The other vampires, both students and teachers, knew more of the truth. They knew that Lucas was a member of Black Cross—one who now had some of the strength and power of a vampire, thanks to me. Before, Courtney and her friends had merely held me in contempt; now they hated me, pure and simple.

To my surprise, however, Courtney's group was in the minority. My parents forgave me, of course, and Balthazar blamed Lucas for everything, treating me more gently to make up for Lucas's supposed cruelty. But comfort and support came from others, as well—Professor Iwerebon, who had offered several off-topic lectures about the treachery of Black Cross while gesturing with bandaged hands, or Patrice, who insisted that no girl could be held responsible for her first love. For them, I suspected, a battle with Black Cross meant that I was more surely on their side. More purely a vampire than I had been before.

I was the only one who knew the whole truth about Lucas—who he really was, and what we felt for each other. That truth was all I had left of him, and I would have to carry it alone.

"We should go inside." Raquel nudged me with her elbow, which was as close as she ever came to showing affection. The tawny leather bracelet dangled upon her wrist once more; I'd told her it turned up in the lost and found. "Mail call soon."

"Expecting a care package?" Raquel's parents had let her down a lot, but at least they knew how to bake. "If there are going to be more oatmeal cookies—"

Raquel shrugged. "Gotta be there when I open the box, or else I'll end up inhaling them all before you know it."

"Exercise some self-control, would you?" I felt a rare smile creep across my face as we started back across the grounds. For the first time, I was able to walk past the gazebo without hoping that I'd see Lucas there waiting for me.

"Self-knowledge is better than self-control any day," Raquel said firmly. "And I know myself well enough to know how I act around cookies."

We got back to the great hall just as the first brown-wrapped packages and FedEx envelopes began making their way among the crowd. As she'd hinted, Raquel got a big box, and the two of us started up the stairs to her room to wolf the cookies down. But just as my foot hit the first step, a hand tugged at my elbow.

"Bianca?" Vic brushed his sandy bangs back from his face and smiled uncertainly. "Hey, can we talk for a sec?"

"Sure, what's up?"

He shifted from foot to foot. "Um, like, alone?"

I hoped Vic wasn't about to ask me out in some cracked attempt to get me on the rebound. "Well, okay." With a shrug, I turned back to Raquel and said, "There had better be cookies left when I get there."

"I'm not making any promises." She jogged up the stairs without me, and I resolved to make this quick.

Vic guided me to the far end of the great hall, near the one window that wasn't stained glass—the one broken by Lucas and also, so long ago, by a member of Black Cross. Instead of his ordinary casual slouch, Vic was tense and a little bit strange. I mean, stranger than usual. I asked him, "Hey, are you all right?"

"Me, I'm fine." He looked around, decided we were definitely alone, and then grinned. "And you're about to be a whole lot better, thanks to something I found in my care package."

"What do you mean by . . ." My voice trailed off as Vic slipped something into the pocket of my blazer.

Mail call. Lucas would've known that they'd double-check any letters for me, but not letters to Vic. If Lucas wanted to reach me, this is how he'd do it.

I put one hand over that pocket, which now bulged with a thick, padded envelope. Vic nodded quickly. "So, right, that's good, then. Glad we got that settled. See ya!"

As he loped away, I took a deep breath. My heart pounded inside my chest, but I walked calmly up the stairs until I reached my parents' apartment. They weren't home—probably Mom and Dad were downstairs grading papers and getting ready for finals. I went into my bedroom, shut the door, and, after a moment's hesitation, pulled the shade down so that even the gargoyle wasn't looking inside. Then, with trembling fingers, I unsealed the envelope.

Inside was a small white box. When I opened that, a cool dark shape tumbled into my waiting palm—my brooch. The black flowers gleamed in my hand again, as perfect and as beautiful as they had ever been.

He promised. Lucas promised he would get it back for me, and he did. He kept his word.

For a moment I couldn't think about anything but the brooch. I wanted to pin it to my shirt that second, just where I'd always worn it before, but I couldn't do that any longer. Too many people knew that I'd worn it as a gift from him, and if anybody realized that Lucas and I were still in contact, Mrs Bethany and those loyal to her would use that to go after him. No, for Lucas's own good, I had to hide it, keep it safe.

Maybe I would never have anything else of his, but I had this to remind me of the truth nobody else would ever understand. Lucas and I truly loved each other, and we always would.

Carefully I folded one of my winter scarves around the brooch and nestled it in the back of a dresser drawer. Then I very nearly tossed the envelope away to hide the evidence, but I realized that there was something else inside—a card. One of the expensive kinds that they sell in museums, on thick, shining white paper, with a work of art emblazoned on the front: Klimt's *Kiss*. I glanced up to see the identical print hanging beside my bed—the same print he'd seen when we were in here, laughing and talking and making out, during those few brief months we had together.

Reverently I opened the card and read what was written.

> *Bianca, this has to be short. You need to destroy*
> *this card as soon as you're done reading, because*
> *it would be dangerous for you if Mrs Bethany*
> *discovered it. And I know you—if I write too*
> *much, you'll hang on to this forever, no matter*
> *how dangerous it would be.*

I had to smile. Lucas really did understand me.

> *I'm okay, and so are my mom and my friends,*
> *thanks to you. You were stronger than I could*

*have been that day. I wouldn't have had the
courage to tell you good-bye.*

And I'm not telling you good-bye now.

*We'll be together again, Bianca. I don't know
where or when or how, but I know it beyond any
doubt. It couldn't happen any other way.*

*I need you to believe that. Because I believe
in you.*

"I believe it, Lucas," I whispered. We'd find each other
once more, and all I had to do was endure until that day
came. Someday Lucas and I would find a way to be together
again.

I folded the card against my chest. I'd burn it in a few
minutes—but not yet, not just yet.

Acknowledgments

THANKS ARE FIRST DUE TO MY EDITOR, Clare Hutton, who took a big chance on a new author, which this new author truly appreciates. I also want to acknowledge the wise advice offered by those who read the manuscript first, including Calista Brill, Michele De France, and Naomi Novik. Edy Moulton and Ruth Hanna not only participated in those early reads but also have tirelessly worked with me on my writing for a long time now, cultivating my better instincts as an author while ruthlessly pointing out the worst. The cultivation was helpful, the ruthlessness invaluable. Other friends such as Lara Bradley, Mandy Collums, Francesca Coppa, Rodney Crouther, Amy Fritsch, Jen Heddle, Jesse Holland, Eli Nelson, Stephanie Nelson, Tara O'Shea, Jessica Ross, Whitney Raju, and Michele Tepper have provided unfailing encouragement. Ashelee Gahagan traveled to Massachusetts with me for research and tried to view the countryside through a vampire's eyes—no mean feat. Robin Rue has proved to be a generous guide to the world of publishing, and I've benefited greatly from her insight. I also have been lucky enough to receive incredible support from my family: Mom, Dad, Matthew, Melissa, and Elijah. Above all, I want to thank my agent, Diana Fox, who first suggested that I might think about writing something with vampires. She believed in my writing before I did, and for that I will be forever grateful.

Finally, I've had the good fortune to be read, critiqued, questioned, and debated by many smart and opinionated readers over the years, a learning experience that has helped me immensely. So to anyone who's ever taken the time to comment upon something I've written, I offer my heartfelt thanks.

THE ROMANCE AND DANGER CONTINUES WITH

THE SECOND BOOK IN THE EVERNIGHT SERIES

COMING SOON IN MAY 2010